# The Discovered Sanctuary

## The Allies of Theo, Book 1

David E Dresner

Published by Clink Street Publishing 2021

Copyright © 2021

First edition.

ISBN:
978-1-913962-83-8 - paperback
978-1-913962-84-5- ebook

# About the author

Dave likens his adult life to rings on his personal Yggdrasil, the tree of life. The first ring followed graduate business school when he became a consulting mathematician, an actuary. The second ring happened when he had responsibilities for a consulting office, then a consulting region and finally as CEO/COO of a national consulting firm. The third ring was personal, he retired to raise his children. He home schooled them while living in rural France and rural Switzerland. Next came another professional ring as a licensed math teacher tutoring algebra in a rural middle school. The newest ring is being a story teller.

# Dedication

To my children, Margo, Joann, Morgan, Frank, and Blake
who grew up listening to my stories.

# PROLOGUE

Most events in people's lives have no consequence beyond their immediate, casual impact. A new haircut is a momentary change in appearance, which is noticed, commented on, and then forgotten. However, other common events start without fanfare but ultimately change the world.

The act of gifting is one such common event. The consequence of gifting is typically a short-term burst of pleasure for the receiver. Once presented, the gift rapidly disappears into the receiver's day-to-day life.

In a very few circumstances, however, gifting has altered the world. In the early 1970s China gifted America a pair of adorable giant Panda bears, named Ling-Ling and Hsing-Hsing. The pair became instant celebrities; TV brought them into American homes on a regular basis. Panda dolls became the rage for gifting. This gift from China set a tone of peace between the two countries.

Other gifts send a different message. The famous Trojan Horse gift of the Greeks to the besieged city of Troy was a gift with evil intentions. Troy accepted the gift and brought it inside their walled city. Subsequently the gift destroyed their city.

A few gifts have within them unseen but unbelievably powerful forces. The ability to unlock and direct these forces is often called Science. Others call it Magic.

The unlocking of these forces by magic can only occur in the rarest of situations. It requires a perfect alignment of people, events, and gods.

Daniel's simple act of searching for special gifts for his family will start a chain of events leading to such an alignment. This alignment will result in a world for his son, Edward, beyond anything Daniel's scientific training could imagine or accept.

# 1
# The Boston Gift Search

Daniel was an inspired gift giver. Virginia, his wife, saw Daniel as having a wizard's skill with gifting. Virginia thought that Daniel's gifting skills were the result of his being a modern alchemist in his professional life. He successfully blended creative elements of engineering, medicine, and business. Edward, his five-year-old son, simply saw his dad as a magic man. His dad would pull a surprise out of his briefcase and Edward would be fascinated with the gift.

It was late November and Daniel was sitting in a Boston hotel room preparing for a gift search. He'd been away on business for five days and knew his son, Eddie, would expect an exciting homecoming gift. Fortunately, any wrapped gift was exciting for a five-year-old. Still, Daniel held himself to a high standard of finding just the right gift for his son and, of course, his wife.

Looking out the window, he saw the late fall weather invited a walking search. Daniel changed from his business suit into casual jeans and put on his new running shoes. He double layered his T-shirts and wrapped an all-weather jacket around his waist.

Now that he was dressed for a walkabout search, he decided to change his normal Boston gift buying routine. Rather than leave out the front doors toward the major downtown shopping, he went out the back entrance of the hotel. The back exit opened to a side street that led directly down to the waterfront.

As he approached the waterfront promenade, the air off the ocean was brisk and clean. Gulls were soaring overhead and diving to feast on tourist leftovers. Bobbing in the water were hundreds of boats of all descriptions from simple nineteen-foot lightning class sailboats to yachts of all sizes. Tourists, boaters, and fishermen were all in abundance. He took deep breaths and could taste the salt in the air; he felt amazingly alive and energized.

As he was ambling along the harbor's main street, it suddenly branched. The main street continued to follow along the waterfront while the branch moved in an inland direction. He decided to take the branch and quickly found himself alone.

As he told his wife and son later, "I was clearly on the street less traveled." Daniel had looked at his son, "Eddie, that's a paraphrase line from a famous poem, by Robert Frost." Edward nodded politely, "Sure, Dad. What's a paraphrase?" Daniel had wisely pressed on with the storytelling.

As he walked along the deserted street, it seemed out of place with modern Boston. It was more of a memory lane than a working street. After half a mile, the surface turned from asphalt into old cobblestones. Daniel could still smell the ocean and feel the salty breezes, but he was now a fair distance from the waterfront.

As he continued walking, the diameter of the surrounding trees increased until he was looking at trees that had to be well over a hundred years old. While the trees had lost their leaves, the combination of the surface street and the surrounding thick trees formed a protective U-shaped tunnel. The tunnel was warm from the overhead November sun while offering shelter from the gusts of chilly breezes off the ocean.

He discovered how much he enjoyed this casual search. There was no pressing goal except to live in the moment, enjoy nature, and trust that the right gifts would be found.

Walking on old cobblestones may sound charming and look nostalgic in pictures and movies, but Daniel knew they are no walk in the park. Daniel's footing on the curved stone surfaces grew increasingly tricky. From his medical practice, he knew the risk of twisted ankles. Prudence demanded he look downward and control his balance. There were no cabs around to get him back to the hotel.

As the street headed further inland, it began a steep uphill climb. There were a series of twist backs as it ascended. As he climbed higher, he would stop and look back. He could still see the blue-green waves in the harbor being chopped by an ocean wind. He thought, *As long as I can see the ocean I'll never get lost.*

The increasing angle of ascent required him to lean further into the incline. As he climbed, he felt his heart speedup. He was pleased that his body was getting a solid workout after the last five days of travel, business meetings, and hotel food.

As his uphill hike continued, Daniel considered what the original purpose of this road could have been. In the middle of his musing, he noticed his breathing had gotten easier; the street had stopped ascending and had leveled out. He looked up from the cobblestones and saw that he was heading toward an old stone bridge.

The structure was large and impressive; it had a distinctive curved arch in the center anchored at each end by stone bastions. It reminded Daniel of ancient Roman stone bridges across rivers and creeks in rural Italy and France. Monet would have painted it, while man-made it presented as a work of nature.

As he got closer, he saw the bridge's underpass had a fairly low height; however, the arch's center was still tall enough that Daniel could bend down and pass through. As he stooped to enter, he noticed a name and date etched on the inside of the left support column. Both the name and date were worn down by the elements; however, he could still make out the dedication legend. The inscription read "John Winthrop 1640".

Daniel's immediate reaction was *Wow! John Winthrop, the first Governor of the Massachusetts Bay Colony, commissioned this bridge. This stone bridge is over 370 years old and still standing.* He knew the Pilgrims believed in building solid structures in all aspects of their lives, from their religion to their family life and apparently their bridges.

Daniel was surprised when he exited the bridge. Straight ahead was commercial Boston, or at least a downsized version. He could see colonial era New England style shops and homes lining a modern street.

When he reached the beginning of the shopping street, he turned around and read the sign behind him: End of State Maintenance. *So, this sign marks an elephant graveyard for one old, forgotten road. Sorry, we don't need you anymore.*

The single main shopping street had attractive walkways for pedestrians. There was the usual assortment of tourists of all ages cruising from shop to shop. Cars lined the metered street.

Many of the merchants lived here in houses dating back to colonial times. Daniel could see that these colonial homes were upgraded to include modern conveniences such as plumbing, heating, and air-conditioning.

Daniel walked past all the shops on the right side of the street, looking through their windows for special presents. Nothing jumped out at him. He noticed there were no side streets and that struck him as strange, even in a small village. When he got to the last shop at the top of the street, he crossed over to the other side and started back.

As he walked back on the opposite side, he noticed the sidewalk was gradually narrowing. *This must be the last side to be developed. Probably there was not enough demand to support any more commercial establishments. Commercial supply and demand, that's what still makes the world go round.*

His sightseeing and musings were abruptly interrupted; out of nowhere, a side street appeared to his right. The street was narrow and felt like more of an alley than a street. Daniel noticed that its surface had the same cobblestones that he had walked on before reaching the modern commercial street. *This is one old street.*

While standing at the alley's entrance and looking down, he saw a flickering gas light lantern; the lantern indicated a possible store. He noticed that other shoppers and tourists passed by without looking down the alley; *Maybe the locals know this is a dead end and the store is closed,* he thought. Then his imagination suggested, *Do they know something I don't? Maybe this alley had an earlier reputation for evil and is still avoided out of habit.*

Daniel continued to look down the alley and reflected, *I would never enter a deserted side street in a city, but this is a tourist village not a city. Fear begone! Today I'm a Viking explorer and something about this alley is calling out to me. I think this is the place to find my homecoming gifts.* When Daniel turned into the alley, the hair on his neck suddenly rose up. The scientist in him scoffed, *Normal male reaction to an unknown place. It's the old fight-or-flight instinct built into our survival DNA.*

When Daniel reached the entry door, he paused; the gas lantern's light illuminated an impressive entry structure. The door was constructed with heavy oak planks crossed with thick iron bars and was set into a stone arch. The effect of the entrance reminded him of a stout castle keep designed to protect those inside and keep out marauding Vikings.

In the door's center was a large iron knocker. The knocker was in the shape of a large cat-like creature's head. Its green quartz eyes seemed to study Daniel as the gas light reflected off their beveled edges. Daniel lifted the heavy head and knocked twice. Having announced himself, he pushed down on the iron entry bar and the heavy door opened.

# 2
# The Discovered Sanctuary

Once he was inside, the door automatically closed behind him with a solid thump. *Modern electronics,* he thought. He stood in a ten-foot wide entryway passage, looked forward and was stunned.

Both sides of the entry hall were lined with bookcases from floor to ceiling. The display cases were built from old oak, similar to the door. There were various figures carved into their sides and top and Daniel paused to study them. They were a mix of mythical creatures from dragons to unicorns to griffins. Each was a miniature work of carving art. Leather bound volumes filled the shelves.

The entryway opened up to reveal a wonderful place. His first impression was of an Arabian bazaar. Twisting aisles of shelves and peeking nooks promised exotic findings. Thick overhead wooden beams created the effect of a forest canopy with openings that hinted at the heavens above.

The welcoming message was "Enter friend, find a gift, sit down, and relax. Buying is optional." It was a compelling contrast to modern, sterile bookstores with their profit-messages of "Look, Buy, and Leave."

Daniel stood by the checkout counter and studied the room. Twenty-five feet from the entrance was a magnificent bronze fountain; it was a work of art. The fountain went up at least fifteen feet. Water cascaded down from a top figure onto a series of descending catch basins, each basin was larger than the one above. The top figure was clearly a figure from mythology but was hard to identify; it was shrouded by the darkness caused by the heavy overhead beams. To Daniel's squinting eyes it seemed that it could be a giant holding a spear.

Each catch basin permitted the water to flow downward through sculptured figures from mythology. As the water tumbled downward, it changed color at each plateau. The cascading water gave a soft lyrical sound reminding Daniel of wind chimes.

An ornate marble-topped iron table was located beside the fountain. The table would comfortably seat three people on deep leather armchairs. Daniel noted that the cascading water never hit the table or the chairs. *The engineer who developed this fountain is the Michelangelo of fountain builders.*

Daniel's eyes progressed from the fountain to the opposite sidewall. On the far side, across from the fountain, was an elaborately carved marble fireplace. Figures from history and mythology lived in the carved marble. The fireplace could be featured in *Architectural Digest*.

There was a cheery wood-burning fire in progress. The fireplace was close enough to the fountain to throw a bit of heat as well as a scent of cedar logs burning. It was also far enough away to avoid overheating the table space.

Daniel's eyes were drawn from the fireplace carvings down to a giant sleeping cat by the hearth. The cat's size was difficult to determine. It seemed far bigger than any domestic cat; panther in size, possibly even tiger size. It curled upon itself in a way that defied an accurate assessment. Even the tail's length was hard to determine given the curled-up body.

For a brief moment, the young boy in Daniel wanted to walk over and pull out the tail. The adult man thought, *Better I go and pet a hungry crocodile than pull that cat's tail. Best to leave sleeping dogs and large cats lie.*

Daniel noticed that his mouth had started to water; there were delightful bakery odors drifting on the air. They came from an arched doorway to the left of the fireplace. *Likely, the owner is preparing baked goods for sale. He'll put them by the checkout counter where people impulsively buy what catches their eye. Easy profits,* the businessman in Daniel reflected.

He called out "Hello" several times. Receiving no response, he decided to continue a Viking's exploratory search for special gifts. His instincts said, *Absolutely this is the right place to be and I'll know the gifts when I see them.*

Daniel left the entry area and moved into the rows of shelves. It felt like entering a bookshelf maze. As he entered the first grouping of tall cases, his spider senses tingled again on the back of his neck. *Get a grip, Daniel. Vikings have no fear.* Relaxed, he moved forward into the maze.

He was intrigued as he moved through the aisles. To the sides were frequent display nooks. The layout reminded Daniel of his visit to Notre Dame in Paris. The most interesting areas of the Paris church to him were the many alcove areas that presented stories and artifacts from distant centuries.

The aisles zigged then zagged then curved around. It was hard to say exactly how large the place was. He thought of *Dr. Who* and his TARDIS police box; the place seemed far bigger on the inside than was apparent on the outside.

As he wound around the curving shelves, he imagined he was Theseus exploring the fabled Cretan maze. *Will the minotaur suddenly appear to challenge me or hit me with a book?* He smiled at the image of a bull, wearing glasses, carrying a large book and walking on two legs.

The rational part of Daniel's mind knew he was just in a store, yet he was bothered by constantly changing direction. As a doctor and engineer he instinctively wanted to know where he was at all times. He also found it disconcerting not to know a quick way out.

His Boy Scout training came back to him. *When you are in the woods without a compass, and are concerned about getting lost, establish visual frames of reference. Go from one reference point to another, remember them, and you can always backtrack.*

Suddenly inspired he looked up and secured his navigation points. One huge beam seemed to run in a straight line and became his North Star. The crossed tie beams were the constellations. *Like all Vikings, I'll follow the stars to find my way home. Problem solved.*

Eventually his aisle opened and presented a hidden oasis. The oasis offered both a resting area as well as an entertainment center. The oasis seemed to be toward the back of the store, but after so many twists and turns, Daniel was not sure where "back" was.

The focal point of the entertainment area was an antique billiard table. The billiard table and legs were carved from the same rich dark wood that appeared everywhere. The wood appeared so old that it could have come from first cut trees.

Each of the table's legs was a masterpiece of sculptured art. Each leg presented a famous conqueror from antiquity. As a student of ancient history, Daniel was captivated by the carvings. He recognized renderings of Cyrus the Great from the year 550 BC, Alexander the Great from 340 BC, and Caesar from 50 BC. The last leg was loveable Attila the Hun, the Scourge of God as well as the scourge of Europe, from 440 AD.

He noted that their lives covered almost a thousand years and thought, *Was somebody keeping a celestial calendar using this billiard table?*

He remembered that each of the four great conquerors had died an unexpected and untimely death. At the peak of their power and glory, they were suddenly gone. Looking at the four generals he said aloud to the table, "Sic transit gloria mundi." Later he would tell his son, "That's Latin, Eddie, for, 'So passes the glory of the world'."

His eyes moved from the table legs to another stunning piece. It was about fifteen feet away and safe from any misdirected pool stick movement. It rested behind a remarkable bar. It was an ornate, ancient mirror that ran the length of the bar.

As he was looking at himself in the ancient mirror, childhood fairy tales came to mind. In the Walt Disney stories, magic mirrors were never a good thing for the beholder. As he stared at himself, he felt his reflection seemingly shift. He instinctively looked away, and then felt silly.

As he studied the mirror's frame, he found it to be another work of complex carved art. The frame had various mythical creatures carved into it in bas-relief. The creatures ran forward or backward in an apparent series of chases.

There were unicorns chasing dragons, who in turn were chasing goat-footed Pans. Everybody chased laughing nymphs. Who was the hunter and who was prey was unclear; it seemed to depend on your starting point. When he tried to establish the starting point to follow a specific chase, it all got blurry. He found himself squinting to better focus, but the figures would still get mixed up and he had to start over.

What was clear to Daniel was that he was starting to get a first-class headache. As a doctor, he knew it's not wise to focus too long on small, complex figures. In medical school, they teach you to frequently look up from microscopes or risk losing your clarity as well as your perspective.

He moved down the bar to examine a number of bottles resting toward the end. He noted how well the bar's surface was polished, the surface created a mirror effect to showcase the bottles. The bottles were old, ancient really. Their glass had the look of translucent pottery found in archeological digs in Egypt, Persia and Greece. It was incredible that the glass for these bottles was still intact. They had somehow survived millenniums of possible breakage.

Daniel picked up a bottle and discovered it had a fluid inside. Since the bottles were resting on a bar, their contents were obviously available to customers. He recalled the bottle in *Alice in Wonderland* labeled "Drink me", and thought, *Caution is the best approach here.*

Each bottle was a unique work of the glassblower's art. Each stopper presented a carved crystal figure from mythology. His eyes were drawn to one large stopper carved from black onyx. It was a black cat, which was not quite a cat. It reminded him of the knocker on the front door. The cat had well-defined ears that slanted forward. Its eyes were inset green crystal and changed their focus depending how he faced them.

The cat's tail wound back on itself and reminded him of a Mobius strip from his sixth-grade math class. The physical bottle was intriguing; it looked like a rendering of a curving topology surface illustrated by a Klein bottle.

When he attempted to remove the stopper, he found it was tightly sealed. He attributed this tightness to the liquor creating a sugary seal over time. He gently twisted the stopper side-to-side, being careful not to snap it. The stopper suddenly broke its seal and came out. Later he told Virginia he heard a purring sound rather than the expected pop. *Was that weird or what?* Virginia's look said the "or what" was the proper explanation.

With the bottle open, he carefully sniffed the emerging vapors. This initial sniff presented him with a transcendent olfactory sensation. His tongue demanded a taste of what his nose had enjoyed. There was a convenient tasting glass beside the bottles and he proceeded to pour out a small amount of the amber liquid. He took a careful slow first taste, just a small amount on the tip of his tongue.

The taste sensation exploded throughout his mouth and his brain. It was incomparably better than any liquor he had ever tasted. It was a little like brandy, a little like old Port wine, caramel ice cream, chocolate cupcakes, and exotic spices. *If ambrosia, the nectar of the gods exists, this must be what it tastes like.*

The liquor was so amazing he immediately wanted to buy the entire bottle and bring it home as a gift to Virginia, then his practical mind spoke up. *Homeland Security will want a full examination, including a possible tasting. Once tasted it would likely disappear into the black hole of TSA Security. Rats, the perfect present for Virginia is gone,* he thought sadly.

*Since I can't take it home, at least I can treat myself right now.* There was a variety of drinking glasses on the bar and Daniel selected one that fit his Viking adventure. The cup was shaped like a Viking drinking horn. It had a gold rim and a jewel at the base. Daniel filled the horn, offered a salute to the Norse god, Odin, and took a deep sip. *Ambrosia. And not of this world.* Holding his horn, he proceeded to a soft leather chair, sat down, and let his mind soar.

# 3
## The Gift Finds Daniel

While sitting there, sipping ambrosia from his Viking horn, his eyes drifted to the nearby bookshelf. The shelf curved in a way such that each book tended to stand out. Many of these cover titles were in languages he had never seen. There were various alphabets including hieroglyphics and Nordic runes, and some appeared to be Sanskrit.

While skimming the covers, one book drew his eye then his hand. He found himself automatically removing it from its resting place. As Daniel removed the book, he sensed a deep vibration pass through the shop; his instincts told him a surge of power had just been released. For a moment, he was very still waiting for an outcome. After the moment passed, he relaxed and studied the book.

His first impression was that he was holding a warm puppy. His second impression was that the cover was a work of art. The title lettering was Nordic using calligraphy with inlaid gold leaf. Runes surrounded the Nordic letters. All Daniel could decipher was that both the Nordic words and possibly the runes referenced Ragnarok, the great battle between the Norse gods.

The front cover presented an elaborately engraved picture of an old-world version of St. Nick. He was in good cheer in his sleigh resting beside a forest cottage. The side of the sleigh had detailed carvings of Old Norse runes. These rune writings likely represented to earlier people the magic that permitted his sled to fly.

Immediately behind him was the overflowing gifting sack. Poking out of the sack were assortments of hearty foods such as hams, slabs of bacon, fowl of all kinds, decorated cakes and thick hearty breads. Food was obviously the best gift Santa could bring. Of course, simple toys also peaked out from between the surrounding larder.

The back cover was a darker scene with a giant looking down onto deep woods. Resting beside the giant was a large dark cat. The giant and cat both appeared relaxed but watchful. The giant had a stout staff that he was leaning on. The muscles in his forearm and arm were massive and his fingers were sausages.

Daniel looked at the giant and thought, *He's a beat cop doing his job. He looks like a good cop and a tough judgmental cop rolled into one. Maybe his beat is to protect Santa.*

Holding the book, he knew without question that this was Eddie's special gift. He had no idea how special. The book was sentient, he had not found the book, the book had found him.

He had a sudden sense that it was time to leave. He rose up, found the overhead North Star beam and headed back to the checkout counter.

# 4
# Daniel Meets Two Strange Occupants

There was a tall young man standing behind the checkout counter. Daniel briefly wondered where he had been, then considered that he was possibly the cook. *He must have heard me enter and now he's waiting to check me out.* The young man gave Daniel a pleasant, "I live to serve the customer smile," and asked if he had found what he was looking for.

"Indeed," replied Daniel as he put the book on the counter. "I have the perfect coming home gift." The man inspected the book and said, "I concur. This is the perfect choice." He began to carefully wrap the book in protective, thick brown paper.

With just the two of them, Daniel decided to make light conversation as the man slowly wrapped the book. "This is quite an amazing place you have here. I'm a history buff in my spare time. Your book collection is outstanding, truly museum worthy. Is the shop owner a collector?"

The man looked up from the wrapping and stared directly into Daniel's eyes. For a moment, Daniel felt like a prey fixed by a predator's stare. His heart sped up and he felt his blood pressure jump. The man sensed Daniel's changed mood, broke the eye contact, and answered with a relaxed chuckle. "Actually, I'm the owner. Well to be more precise, my friend over there is the owner," and he pointed toward the resting cat beast. "I'm his companion and a permanent resident."

Daniel relaxed after the man's smile and humorous answer, *Sure,* he thought, *the beast owns this place.* Then he said, "I'm a businessman as well as a doctor, so I must ask, how do you get enough traffic to support the store?"

The young man smiled again. "We're not in business to make money. We have independent funding that permits us to pursue our interests. This store is really our personal sanctuary. We carry on our affairs here without disruptions from uninvited visitors. Actually, we have very few visitors."

"So, I'm the unexpected tourist who discovered your sanctuary. Lucky for me that I decided to come down the alley; I was looking for a special gift and I found it. At the risk of making a bad pun, I guess by selling me the book you're rewarding a doctor who still makes house calls." Both Daniel and the man chuckled.

"Anyway, thank you again for selling me this book from your personal collection. What, may I ask, is the damage to buy it?" Daniel mentally braced himself; he knew the sky's the limit in pricing rare books.

"Fifty dollars will settle up just fine."

Daniel was stunned "Really? Are you sure? I feel like I'm stealing it."

"Oh, that's a proper price; we set prices to ensure our books go to their proper homes. Our books have a job to do and they need the proper reader to share their unique content with."

*Weird answer,* Daniel thought, *but the price is sure a bargain. No need for me to look a gift horse in the mouth,* and he smiled to himself at another clever pun.

As the young man was ringing up the purchase, using an old 1920s National Cash Register, Daniel studied him more closely. Being a doctor, Daniel naturally studied people.

On the surface, the man appeared normal yet something about him was off. Physically he was tall with long, straight, dark brown hair, dark eyes, and a strong posture. He had a darker complexion implying a possible Middle Eastern origin. He had a strong chiseled face and exuded both confidence and power. He actually reminded Daniel a bit of himself.

As Daniel studied him, he had an insight. *I know what bothers me. He projects an aura that I've never encountered before.*

This insight had such a strong impact on Daniel, that he described the experience in detail once he was back home. He started by explaining what an "aura" was to his son. "Eddie, all living things, people and animals, have an electromagnet aura that their body generates. It's not visible to the eye but is visible to various medical and scientific measurement devices.

"While I could not literally see his aura, I sensed its unusual presence from my years of observing patients with many different medical conditions. Several of my patents are based on detecting these radiated body fields."

Daniel looked at Virginia and added, "His eyes were strange, actually disturbing. The best way I can describe them is to say they looked ancient. If the Sphinx could really see, that's what its eyes could look like.

"To make matters even weirder, I noticed that the large fireplace cat was watching me. It seemed to be studying me either out of a cat's natural curiosity or as a possible meal. It reminded me of one of the old Egyptian cat sculptures from the time of the pharaohs. Whatever it was, it was quite unsettling."

As Daniel stood by the checkout register, he remained in his thoughts. The man smiled knowingly at him, then interrupted his musing by handing Daniel the wrapped book. Daniel snapped back to the present moment.

His reflections had him intrigued by the man and he found he wanted a little more conversation. "I enjoyed a Viking horn of the liquor from the cat stopper bottle. I left payment on the bar and assume you picked up the payment. Was that payment enough to cover the house tab?"

The man nodded that the payment was fine. "You've made two excellent selections today," he said. "You and your son will find this book is a wonder. You two will have many enjoyable nighttime readings together.

"Regarding your choice of libations, you chose my personal favorite. It's the top-shelf brand, we call it 'Theo's Liquor.'" He motioned toward the resting cat and said, "Care to meet Theo?"

Daniel flinched at the invitation. No way was he going to get up close and personal with the man's pet beast. "Thanks, I'm an animal lover, but not right now. Weather is changing and I'm running late, maybe next time." The man smiled knowingly.

# 5
# The Vanished Shop

Once outside, luck was still with him. He fast-walked to the top of the main street, caught a cab, and was soon back at his hotel. After a fast shower and a room service meal, Daniel was sleeping like a baby.

The next morning Daniel awoke refreshed with great energy. He had a free morning until his afternoon return flight. Because the weather was again favorable for walking, he decided to return to the hidden antique store. He thought that he would try to purchase the Klein bottle of Theo's Liquor for Virginia and risk Homeland Security seizing it.

Following a hearty breakfast of French toast and sausage, Daniel left the rear of the hotel. He was back on the same side street and headed toward the waterfront. He found the branching street and was again the sole person on it.

He walked briskly since he knew the destination and did not trust Boston weather to remain peaceful. He reached Mr. Winthrop's bridge and gave a quick pat to the inscription. Once through the underpass he moved quickly to the village.

It was mid-morning and the village was bustling with tourist traffic.

Daniel immediately started up the left-hand sidewalk searching for the alley's entrance. He got to the top of the street without success. He reversed direction and came back down. When he got to the street's end, he saw the End of Road Maintenance sign.

As he was standing there befuddled, a resident dressed in period clothing came past him. Daniel made a hand motion to the person that he wanted to talk, and the man paused.

"Pardon me, sir. I'm a doctor and I'm having trouble finding a location." Daniel knew that most people respond to doctors with respect, indeed Daniel had the man's full attention.

"I'll try and help if I can," the man said with a warm smile.

Daniel described the alley in detail, the gas light and then the store. The man was listening carefully, and then Daniel sensed that the man was studying him. The man cautiously smiled and said, "Is this a prank? Are we being filmed for a TV show?"

Daniel was puzzled, he shook his head and said, "No prank and no TV show." He removed a business card from his suit jacket and handed it to the man. The man stepped back a pace and carefully read the card. The card was clearly expensive and declared Daniel as both a doctor and CEO of a medical firm.

Daniel saw the man had accepted his credentials. The man shook his head and said, "Doc, I've lived here for twenty years. I can assure you no such alley exists. You must have our little tourist village confused with another place. Sorry." He smiled briefly and entered his house.

Daniel stood on the street feeling like a confused Rip Van Winkle. In the famous 1819 story by Washington Irving, Rip had fallen asleep and woken up twenty years later. Something had changed overnight in this small village. Obviously, he had not slept twenty years; so, what had happened? *Very strange,* he thought. Then he noticed that the weather was changing. He realized he had been given a grace period for his return visit, but the grace period was ending.

Fortunately, the weather lasted long enough for him to catch a cab. Once inside the cab he pondered the vanished store, but no reasonable explanation came to his mind.

Then his mind changed gears and he focused on the pleasant image of returning to his wife and son. He relished the excitement that they would all feel when he walked in. *We have our own special sanctuary*, he thought, *and it's called home.*

# 6
# The King Returns: Hail to the King

Edward was excited and had to burn off energy. He ran back and forth from his mother in the kitchen to the living room. His dad was due to return at any time and great things happened when Dad got home.

Dad's return followed a long business trip and Edward wanted to be the first to meet him. His dad always greeted him by swinging him high in the air and giving him big bear hugs. It was a father–son bonding ritual and Edward loved it. Plus, his dad always had a special present tucked away in his briefcase.

This time, however, Edward knew he should not expect a gift. His mother had warned him that it was just a few weeks before Christmas and that Santa was coming shortly. "Having Dad home will be the best gift we can have," Virginia said. Edward nodded in full agreement.

Both suddenly heard Daniel's car pull up and the garage door open. Edward raced to the door and was immediately swept up into the air. "Eddie, you've grown while I was away.

You're really getting big!" Eddie loved to hear how big he was getting.

Holding his son in one arm and his briefcase in the other, Daniel entered the house and called out, "Virginia, wait till you see what I found." Edward knew that once again his dad had come through with a present.

Virginia came running to greet him with a big hug. "So, you are bringing back more than just your kingly presence?" she said with a warm smile on her lips and in her eyes.

"Indeed, I have," said Daniel, "the returning king has presents for his queen and the young prince." Virginia fell into the playful banter and said, "Please make yourself comfortable your highness. Would a welcome-home libation be in order?"

"You read my mind. Next to seeing you and Eddie, a hot mug would warm this king's body as well as the king's soul. It's miserable outside and the traveling was exhausting."

Daniel put his brown leather briefcase down beside his living room chair, draped his suit jacket over the back of the chair, took off his shoes, and stretched his long legs out in front of him. He settled into the leather recliner that was beside an oversized fireplace and gave a deep sigh. *Home at last!* he thought contentedly.

There was a cheery fire going and he felt an internal glow at how thoughtfully his wife had prepared this welcome home setting. He smiled at his young son and exclaimed, "Eddie, it's really, really good to be home."

Edward beamed at his dad, "It's great to have you home, Dad."

Virginia returned with two mugs that had bright green Christmas trees hand painted on their sides, "Seasonal mulled wine for his lordship."

"Outstanding choice, my queen," said Daniel as he took the first deep sip. He nodded in appreciation and quickly took a second deep sip.

Daniel settled further into his leather recliner throne and motioned for Edward and Virginia to have a seat on the couch in front of him. "I've got something here for Edward that is unique and I'm not using the word 'unique' lightly. Unique fits both the gift and my tale. Believe me, my tale is a show stopper.

"But first, the queen of the manor needs to be recognized." Daniel reached into his open briefcase and pulled out a large golden box. This is a small token of appreciation for all of her lonely duties while the husband is off on a business crusade."

Virginia opened the box of Godiva chocolates, smiled, then offered them to Daniel and Edward. Edward rapidly looked for his favorites, the caramels, seized one and took a large bite.

Daniel smiled at them both and said, "This next gift is a two-part present for both my son and my wife. The first present is the tale of the gift's discovery. The second gift is…well you'll just have to listen to the discovery tale before that gift is presented."

Just as Daniel was starting, Virginia paused him with a hand signal. "Sorry to interrupt before you start, dear, but is this a long story?"

"Yes, it will be. But trust me, you'll never mind the time it takes to hear it."

"Well, please hold up the story for a couple of minutes, my lord, while I get us some fresh baked cookies. While I'm getting them would his highness like more mulled wine?"

Daniel vigorously nodded his head, "You are a sorceress mind reader as well as a master cookie baker and a beautiful wife. I'm a lucky king." Virginia blushed slightly as she rose.

As she headed for the kitchen, she glanced at her son, "Hold off on the chocolates, Eddie, so you can enjoy the cookies." As an afterthought she added, "I'll bring you milk to wash them down."

Once Virginia was out of sight, Daniel grinned at Edward, gave him a small napkin, and said, "Take a few more from the bottom layer, Mom will never notice they're gone." Daniel and Eddie loved sharing little secrets that Virginia didn't know about. Little secrets added to their father–son bonding experiences.

Edward knew all the assorted Godiva candies and immediately found two more caramels in the bottom layer. He quickly slipped it them into the napkin then into a pajama pocket.

Virginia returned with a wooden tray holding the mulled wine, milk, and cookies. "We need our energy to really enjoy this story," she said. "We don't want any stomach distractions. Enjoy them, they're made from scratch."

"They are absolutely delicious," Daniel said as he washed the first one down with the mulled wine. After his second cookie Daniel smiled at Virginia and Edward, "It's really good to be home, it's better than good, it's great! I don't like travel and I hate it over the holidays."

Virginia nodded and said, "We miss you a lot, Daniel... any time you're away."

While eating the cookies and sipping the wine, Daniel cleared his mind. He knew every good tale starts by pulling the listeners into the story right at the start. Daniel reflected on the events that created the story. He placed himself back in time and began his tale of discovering the sanctuary.

"I had an amazing experience. Even though I experienced it, without the gift I bought," and he nodded at the briefcase, "I would question whether it was real. I discovered a mysterious hidden shop purely by accident or maybe it was kismet at work."

Edward looked at his dad, "What's a kismet, Dad?"

Daniel smiled approvingly; he liked the fact that his son was naturally curious. "Kismet is another word for fate. Kismet is when something extraordinary happens that could never have been expected or predicted."

Daniel then proceeded to tell his tale of discovery. He described the shop, with its strange owner and the even stranger pet. Daniel concluded his story with the powerful punch line. "The second time I returned to the village I could not find the shop. A local told me that no such place existed in this village. 'So where is it?' I thought.

"Unable to find the place, I gave up, grabbed a cab, and got back to my room. It was time to pack up and head home.

"Once I was back in my room, I immediately picked up my present. I carefully unwrapped it and confirmed it was intact. If I didn't have this gift, I'd think I had suffered some type of memory lapse or worse, a mild stroke. But I was holding the gift firmly in my hands."

Daniel grinned at Edward and Virginia and said, "So, what do you two think happened? Could I have discovered a magical sanctuary that was gone when I returned?"

Virginia had listened carefully to Daniel's story and was sure he was not pranking her or Eddie, so she gave him a serious answer. "I think one rational explanation is that your Viking horn ran over with some mild hallucinogenic; maybe a touch of Harvard Professor Timothy Leary's LSD. That extra ingredient would explain the drink's relaxation impact and the effect on your mind."

Virginia continued with her Nancy Drew analysis, "Maybe you were in one of the Irish pubs in that village. Possibly, you had a jacked drink and bought this book from a local Irish Paddy who preyed on tourists. The whole magical alley and antique shop could just be a creation of Paddy's tale and your drugged mind. Naturally it was not there when you visited the next day with a clear mind."

Daniel considered Virginia's rational explanation. His scientific mind thought this could be the practical answer. Edward had a different answer, "I think it really was a magical place! Dad, you believe in magic, don't you?"

Daniel considered his answer to Edward's simple, trusting question. Daniel knew that some of these childhood questions and answers would remain for a lifetime. Is the best answer to a five-year-old one that's based on rational science or is there a better answer that will help develop a child's imagination?

Daniel knew that many of his own inventions were the result of his imagination and willingness to think outside the scientific box. He knew science did not have all the answers, not by a long shot. Additionally, Christmas was around the corner, and he wanted his son to feel the magic of that season as long as possible.

"Eddie, everyone has a different view on magic. I have certainly experienced things I can't explain despite all my scientific training. Sometimes you just need to accept the unusual. Call it 'magic' if that seems to fit."

Virginia knew this was the time to dump logic and join the Christmas spirit. "I'm with Eddie, I vote for a magical place!"

# 7
# The Gift

"Well, that story was a long introduction to presenting the gift. Without further ado, here is the early kickoff to our Christmas."

Daniel opened his briefcase and lifted out a package wrapped in heavy brown paper. He handed it to Edward whose hands were instantly in the air reaching forward. "Take your time opening it, Eddie. It's very valuable and very old."

Once the package was in Edward's hands, he followed his dad's request. He avoided his usual rip, tear, and shred for opening wrapped presents and slowly untied the holding string then unfolded the brown paper. As he reached inside the brown wrapping paper Edward felt the leather, it was warm and inviting. He felt he was holding a lovable animal, images of "puppies and bunnies" came to his mind.

Edward lifted out the book, feeling its weight and thickness. Then he examined both covers. Virginia was sitting beside Edward and her eyes opened wide, "Daniel, it's beautiful! May I look at it with you, Eddie?"

"Sure, Mom," and he handed her the book then snuggled next to her.

Something surged up Virginia's arm when she held the book. She felt her mind calm. *Weird,* she thought. She felt like she was walking onto her college drama stage opening night. Jitters disappeared, and calmness swept over her.

She focused on the covers. She saw the front cover had a detailed picture of a beaming Santa sitting in a sleigh in front of a small cottage. There was a light in the upper window of the cottage and smoke was rising from a stone chimney.

The back cover presented a giant leaning on a long thick staff. The giant appeared to be standing on a snow-covered mountaintop looking down at a thick snow-covered forest. Standing beside the giant was an unusually large black cat. Both giant and cat appeared to be friends studying the woods ahead while going for a walk in the winter snow.

Looking at the giant on the back cover, Virginia had a sudden insight. "He looks like a Norse god," she said to Daniel. "I know my mythology but have no idea who his companion is, do you?"

"A Norse god, that's an interesting possibility, dear, and no, I have no idea who his companion could be."

As Virginia opened the book she immediately knew this was not simply an old illustrated book, it was a well-crafted work of art illustrated with beautifully detailed pictures of creatures and settings. The illustrations could have fit into any classic Walt Disney movie.

Daniel watched his wife's reaction to the open book. Clearly, she was experiencing something unusual just as he had. Her eyes had dilated, and her hands were trembling.

*That's exactly my reaction,* Daniel mused to himself. *There's something special about that book, Tim Leary and LSD are not the answer.*

Daniel looked at his son and saw he was now leaning heavily against his mom. His eyes were at half-mast. "I think we should start the first story now, Eddie. Are you ready for bed?" Eddie gave a big nod yes.

Daniel grabbed Edward and said, "Piggyback ride time. Hang tight onto that book. Edward was suddenly giggling and not too grown up for a piggyback ride. He remembered the hidden caramels and knew Dad would let him enjoy the treats while he listened to the first story.

Edward rode his horse upstairs with shrieks of laughter as his horse pretended to buck him off. His dad finally bucked him off on top of his mattress and he landed in bed with a big flourish. He forgot about the caramels and waited for his story.

Daniel sat on the edge of the bed, opened the leather book and began the first chapter. It was a grand opening story. Sadly, for Edward, and fortunately for Daniel, Edward's sugar buzz quickly lost the battle with the Sandman. He tried hard to stay awake, but the day was too long. He barely heard any of the story before his head was lost in dreams.

*We'll get into this tomorrow,* Daniel thought. He shut the thick cover and headed for the door. Then he unexpectedly paused. He went back to a sleeping Edward and slipped the book under his pillow. He had no idea why he placed it there; he just felt it was a right thing to do.

# 8
# Night Time Stories

When Edward awoke the next morning, he was sleeping on his side and was holding the book still tucked under his pillow. He was surprised when he pulled it out, but he liked the feel of the warm leather.

He began a nightly routine with his dad of looking at the pictures, listening to the stories, then tucking the book under his pillow. The book became his North Star for night time Viking dream sailing. The book's presence in the morning became a great way to start each day.

The book's stories were spellbinding to both father and son. Daniel found himself pulled into the subtle, hidden parts of the stories that spoke of courage and moral decisions. Edward simply enjoyed the action and appearance of magic.

Some of the book's stories seemed out of place for children tales. They frequently presented a dark world with dangerous outcomes for the protagonists. Heroes had to make quick decisions and the reader realized that bad things happened, even to heroes. Not every story ended with "and they lived happily ever after."

Some of the stories reminded Daniel of stories from *One Thousand and One Arabian Nights*. Daniel understood the stories from the *Arabian Nights* were metaphor guides to help children and adults make sound choices in their real-world lives. This old leather book appeared to be a similar guide, as well as presenting a collection of exciting tales.

The tales eventually concluded with *The Night Before Christmas*. The leather book's version deviated from the simple classic story. It told of challenges that faced Santa before he was on his merry delivery way. These challenges included an ambush by evil red fire beasts. The beasts were scary; they were described as mutated monkeys with varying size arms, legs, and whip-like tails.

The story finally did conclude with a "happy every after" ending. *Not my parent's version,* thought Daniel as he left the sleeping Edward. *I guess a little scary excitement is acceptable as long as Santa wins.*

The weeks flew by and suddenly it was Christmas Eve and Eddie was wired. After the Christmas Eve story was over, Edward slowly opened his eyes and peeked at his door. He had fooled his dad by pretending to be asleep. The story had stirred his imagination and created a faster heartbeat. He lay in bed reflecting on the story with his senses on full alert.

Finally, as his mind and body relaxed and were ready to shut down, he heard a noise outside his window. Edward sat bolt upright in bed. His covers fell off him and he felt the cold air of the bedroom. He knew he was fully awake and not dreaming.

He looked out the window and saw a large dark shadow pass by. The night was clear, the moon was full, and he knew it was no passing cloud shadowing the moonlight. This shadow had a long black tail, which bumped hard against his window. The bump startled him, and he jerked away from the window; then the shadow with the tail was gone.

Edward knew with a certainty that Santa was on the move outside. He wondered about the tail, the tail was black but seemed to shimmer. Edward knew that black does not shimmer, in fact, black is the absence of color and absorbs light. He also knew reindeer have short, stubby brown tails, definitely not long and black. Then he realized that the reins are black. *I saw a part of the reins hanging down from Santa's hands. Boy, I was this close to Santa!*

Edward stayed frozen in his upright sitting position. His mind was churning. He wanted to get out of bed and tell his parents what he had seen, but first he had to calm down and gather his breathing and his wits.

He waited too long, and the excitement burned off. He suddenly noticed the cold air on his chest and arms. He pulled up his covers to keep warm then laid back. Once he was back in his sleeping position, his mind closed down and Morpheus, the Greek god of dreams and sleep, made a visit. *I'll tell them tomorrow morning,* were his final thoughts. Morning arrived, and Edward had forgotten the visitor from the night before in the rush of Christmas excitement. Later, over Christmas dinner, the memory of the shadow and black tail returned. The magic of last night's event came to him again and he excitedly described the shadow and tail. In his excitement, his words tumbled out like a burst of verbal machine gun fire. Virginia leaned over and smiled a mother's corrective smile, "Slow down, dear, and breathe. Your dad and I really want to hear all about it."

Virginia and Daniel listened to every word. Edward described the black tail in some detail, "I think it must have been a part of Santa's rein hanging down," said Edward. "What do you think, Dad?"

Virginia noticed her husband's face had a distant expression; his mind seemed elsewhere. Virginia smiled at Daniel, "You look like something suddenly popped into your mind. Has the cat got your tongue?"

Daniel came out of his reverie, "In a manner of speaking, yes, a very weird cat may have. For a moment, I let my imagination run away with me. I considered whether that strange Boston cat is real and made a house call last night."

"Could be," was all Virginia could manage as she gave her husband a wink.

# 9
# Goodbye Magic, Hello Science

There were no more Christmas visits from Santa. Nothing ever bumped against his window again. By the time he was a teenager, Edward's belief system had shifted from magic to science and math.

Daniel, the engineer and doctor, was a strong supporter of his son's interest in science. He encouraged the interest by selecting presents that would continue Edward's development in science. He also believed that stage magic was fun, and he wanted his son to have fun to balance the serious study required by science.

On Edward's ninth birthday, he received two big presents from his parents. The first present was a beginner's chemistry set. The second present was a beginner's magic set.

This chemistry set included an assortment of chemicals, a small burner, and a variety of test tubes and curved glass pipes. Edward thought that the equipment resembled the tools shown in fantasy movies about alchemists and mad scientists. He liked the image of himself using science to make mysterious things happen.

The magic set offered an entertaining alternative to the science of chemistry. Of course, the set included the all-important wand as well as a magician's pair of white gloves, a black cape, and a black top hat.

The top hat was particularly cool since it collapsed into a round flat surface and Edward could sail the folded hat like a ninja's death star. His targets varied from empty soda cans to his mother's backside. Mom's backside was an infrequent target since his death star quickly disappeared by mom-magic.

As Edward's interest in the practice of stage magic advanced, he read numerous books about famous magicians. His reading motto became, "Study the greats and learn from them." The more Edward read, the more convinced he became that the only real magic is found in science.

All the great magicians he read about had debunked "real" magic. Houdini in the 1920s threw light into many a spiritualist's darkened room. The Amazing Randi and his associates ultimately offered a one-million-dollar reward for any person who could scientifically demonstrate supernatural abilities. Nobody ever claimed that reward.

By age twelve Edward was advanced in his science experiments. He loved the science labs and used them to bring stage magic into his act. By middle school he was putting on magic shows in his classrooms and challenging his classmates with, "Science or magic? What do you think?"

At first, his classmates were skeptical since they had all seen magic tricks on TV. However, as Edward performed live in front of them they became fascinated. Half the class answered "Magic" to Edward's question. The other half wanted to know the trick. Edward would shake his head and simply answer "I see magic, what do you see?"

His first formal show came in high school. In his eleventh-grade science classroom, he challenged his classmates with, "Science or magic? What do you think?" The science teacher was fascinated with Edward's skill and asked if he would put on a show for the entire school during the Thanksgiving assembly. Sixteen-year-old Edward agreed, and started to plan for the show.

On the day of his performance, Edward peeked out from behind the stage curtain. The high school students filled the auditorium seats. There was naturally a lot of noise and movement, after all it was an auditorium filled with teenagers at the end of the day and ready for the Thanksgiving break. They were busy talking and making noise to burn off months of study.

Edward had expected these distractions. He started the show with a BANG…literally a very loud explosion. The noise stunned the audience into silence.

Ahead of time he had placed a deep iron bowl on the table with a time-delayed chemical fuse. At the approximate start time, the fuse triggered a chemical reaction and the explosion followed. The height of the bowl controlled the created direction of the smoke. A large plume of smoke floated above the bowl as a glowing red cloud.

The auditorium was instantly silent. All eyes were on the stage and the red smoke. Edward had everybody's attention. Edward motioned to the sophomore drama student managing the floodlights. The student pushed a switch and a dark green glow lit the stage.

Edward strode out from behind the curtain dressed in a long black cape with a tall black collar and white gloves. Without the gloves, he could have been a young Count Dracula. He walked confidently to the still smoking container, passed his hand over the red cloud and the air was immediately clear. The auditorium erupted with stomping feet and loud claps.

It was a great opening trick and its timing was perfect. Students had been sitting all day and this was a great excuse to stomp, whistle, clap, and let out their pent-up energy. Teachers winced, but were also caught up in the act.

Standing there, Edward was no longer their classmate; he looked like the real deal from Transylvania. The green light made his high cheek bones stand out and his eyes glitter. His longish dark hair came down to disappear into his high collar. He projected the classic "bad boy" persona and could have ridden onto the stage on a Harley.

While the audience was studying bad boy Dracula, Lisa Sue, the head cheerleader, made her move. Sitting with her squad beside the football team, she declared, "I've got dibs on Dracula."

"Nice try, queen," retorted next year's leader. "We all saw him first so he's up for grabs, and I do mean grabs. Besides, he's Eddie the science nerd when not on stage. I'm in his AP classes and trust me he wants brains first and that definitely puts me ahead of you in the grab line."

While the female claims were being staked out and argued, Edward searched the audience and spotted a very large senior. It was Big Bob, the star of the football team, also known as "Super-Sized Bob."

Edward made eye contact then called out "Bob!" Bob was not sure what was going on, but he nodded toward the stage. "Bob, you're a pretty strong guy, wouldn't you say?"

Bob stood up with an annoyed look on his face. He had his practice T- shirt on that ended just below his shoulders. The shirt presented a dramatic display of his gorilla arms. His name "Big B" appeared on the front and back. He liked to state that, "My opponents know who I am whether I'm coming or going." Teachers often wondered if Bob knew whether he was coming or going.

Bob considered Edward's question, scowled, and nodded. It was a dumb question, "What do you think?" he retorted.

"I think you should join me and demonstrate the strength and skill we all appreciate on the field." Without hesitation, Big Bob did an athlete's walking glide to the stairs and was quickly beside Edward. Bob stood close to Edward and did his best to intimidate by his size.

Edward was tall with wide shoulders but the contrast with Bob was startling. The size of Big Bob's torso and exposed arms created a contrast that Eddie had planned to make the trick more dramatic. "Ready to play?" asked Edward playfully as he stood beside the giant boy. Bob nodded at another dumb question.

On the floor beside Edward was a large dumbbell, "Bob, would you please move that ugly piece of iron out of my way?" Bob looked down and quickly counted the weights, they totaled fifty pounds. It was easy mental math and Bob was a lot smarter than many opponents, and teachers, thought.

Bob could easily do multiple one-arm curls with that weight. Since he was wearing a cut off T-shirt he saw a chance to further inflate then bulge a bicep at the crowd. "Sure thing, Mr. Magic," he said. Bob bent down, placed his right hand on the center of the dumbbell and went to jerk it up. It did not budge.

Bob looked confused for a moment, then he turned a shade of red; he was rarely embarrassed by physical challenges. Before attempting a serious second lift, Bob caught his breath, bent his knees, and braced for a one-arm jerk over his head. He put his full weight and strength into it and snapped with his legs and arm at the same time.

The bar sat in place. The audience was captivated. There were a few snickers from the audience, but most students and teachers remained focused on Edward and Bob.

Bob was now beyond being embarrassed, he was fighting mad. A mad Bob looked more like a charging bull than a person. He put both hands on the bar and yanked. Bob could dead lift over four hundred pounds; the bar did not stir.

Bob got on the floor to study the bar. "It's glued down," he said, as the audience was now laughing. "Bad trick, magician. Maybe I should lift you instead."

Edward knew this response was coming. "You're right! I am so bad, Bob. I gave you the barbell with uranium." Bob got a confused look on this face. "Don't worry, it's safe."

Mr. Samuels, the chemistry and physics teacher grinned and thought to himself, *Bob slept through the periodic table of elements, he had heard the word "uranium" in class many times but never considered it a word he needed to remember. Payback time, Bob, live with it like I do every class period with bored jocks.*

Edward had regained command of the stage again as Bob the bull was not sure of which direction to charge. "I'm sure you remember the periodic table from science class, Bob." There were muffled snickers across the audience. "Uranium, Bob, is over four times heavier than iron. As you remember the atomic weight of iron is 55.8 while uranium is 238. You can see the multiplier effect at work here. Let me use some alchemy magic and change it back to normal iron."

Edward walked over to the bar with his wand. He muttered a few hocus pocus words and tapped the bar with the wand. He made a slight head nod to the lighting student who pressed another button. "OK, Bob, I've changed it back, please try it again."

Bob knew he was being played. He returned to the barbell with a skeptical look on his face. He bent down and cautiously put his hand on the crossbar. As he did, he felt a little motion; he knew he could lift it.

"Can you actually curl that big weight with one hand?" asked Edward, feeding Bob a layup question. This time Bob snapped the bar up and over his head. The bar looked like it wanted to fly to the ceiling.

Bob was back in his comfort zone showing off his superior physical strength. He had so much adrenalin flowing he could have made a fifty-pound shotput out of the dumbbell.

"Easy peasy, Mr. Magic," said a grinning Bob. With that, Bob proceeded to do multiple one-arm curls switching from right hand to left hand. The bar danced in his big hands as he moved it through space. After five reps on each side, Bob's biceps were on display bulging out of his short-sleeved shirt; the audience was cheering, shouting, and stomping their feet.

Bob was enough of a showman himself that he knew when to declare victory. He put the barbell down, then double flexed his biceps. Edward did a bow to Bob who grinned, bowed back, and shook Edward's hand.

Bob then lifted Edward straight into the air with a military press. Again, the students went crazy and shouts of "Big Bob" rang out. The football team all stood and stomped for their hero. The cheerleaders called out Edwards name but with a different purpose than simple praise. "Look at me," was their shout-out.

Edward owned the crowd. He also knew when it was time to bring down the curtain. He did a deep bow to the audience and slid off the stage.

The principal came to the microphone grinning. "I don't know how Mr. Magic did it, but that was terrific. School's over now so have a great Thanksgiving vacation." The auditorium emptied to hoots, shouts, and stomping feet. The principal wished he had magic to lessen the din from the stampeding students.

Later that afternoon Edward returned with the janitor and Mr. Samuels. They disconnected the large electromagnet from under the stage floor.

# 10
# Another Unexpected Gift

Daniel had unexpectedly, and unhappily, received a request to attend a shareholder conference in New York City in the middle of the Thanksgiving break; the meeting was described as a "Must Attend." He tried to get the meeting date moved without success. There were other meetings required of his major shareholders and this was the only available time. Nobody attending was happy, but it was understood that some personal sacrifice was required.

Accepting the inevitable, Daniel put his mind to work to make lemonade out of the holiday lemons. Daniel presented his lemonade as a surprise gift following a family dinner in mid-November. As Virginia was rising from the table to bring in her fresh baked apple pie, Daniel said, "Let's hold off a minute on that apple pie, dear. I have something that I think both of you will be excited about, please follow me."

Virginia and Edward followed Daniel into the living room and took seats in front of the fire. Daniel had earlier placed a large bag beside his chair, tucked out of view. "As you know, business has me out of town for Thanksgiving, but

I want to be with you in spirit, drum roll please!" and he did a fast set of palm slaps on his chair's armrest.

Daniel then brought the bag out from beside his chair and set it in front of the three of them. He reached into the bag and handed his wife and son each an oversized yellow envelope. A truly unexpected gift had arrived, and they were both eager to know what it was. Even at age sixteen Eddie was still a five-year-old at heart when Dad presented a present.

Wife and son reached inside their envelopes and removed the content. Inside each found a scroll, and not just any scroll. These scrolls were not simply rolled-up papers tied with bows. They were constructed from high quality, thick parchment paper. Each scroll had a gold seal over its seam. The scroll's quality and Daniel's presentation were a dramatic way to announce a serious subject.

Both mother and son were holding their respective scrolls and looking at the gold seals. "Please break your seals and let your personal genies out," said Daniel with a big grin. Mother and son slit their seals carefully and slowly unrolled the parchment. There was no ripping and tearing for the older Edward, he knew to take his time.

The top of the scroll had each person's name written, using calligraphy, with gold ink. Below the name came a short message in Olde English lettering, "Prepare for a magical trip." Below the message was a pictorial description of their trip.

The first picture on the scroll was a panoramic picture of downtown Chicago. In the center of the picture was the Drake Hotel decorated for Christmas. Virginia immediately recognized the hotel and her face lit with joy. "Oh, Daniel," was all she could say.

The next picture was a racing train. Daniel knew that the icing on the Chicago trip for his son would be the train ride. Edward loved trains. One of Daniel's earliest Christmas gifts to his son was a Lionel train set for Edward's third Christmas. While watching Daniel's enjoyment as he assembled the track for the first time Virginia had quipped, "Tell me again who that train set is for?" Daniel grinned and began singing "I've been working on the railroad…"

Below the train picture were pictures of a private stateroom. The room had a large picture window that brought the passing views inside. As a big plus, it had its own bathroom. The convenience of the bathroom could not be denied, particularly for nature calls in the middle of the night.

Completing the array of the room's conveniences were two beds. There was a comfortable sofa on the lower level that converted to a double bed. The second bed was a Tarzan-style tree house bunk above the lower bed. This upper bed was built for monkeys who could easily climb a steep ladder. Edward would naturally be the climbing monkey.

Edward and Virginia sat stunned after reading their scrolls. Everybody, whether young or adult, loves a surprise gift and this gift was a showstopper. Virginia jumped out of her chair and vigorously hugged her husband. She continued hugging him until both parents realized their son was looking away. *He's embarrassed,* they both thought.

Actually, Edward was not embarrassed at all; his parents frequently hugged. While his parents were hugging, Edward's mind was already planning the adventures that he would have on the train and then in Chicago.

# 11
# Packing

Edward had almost collected everything to take, and the piles were spread across his bed. Packing everything into one case appeared to be a serious challenge. The travel stuff looked like it should fit in the open suitcase; however, when he tried to pile it in, he found socks, shirts, and underwear had grown a few sizes.

As Edward pondered his packing challenge, Daniel appeared at his bedroom door. Daniel observed the state of packing and said, "I know you're strong, but don't break the suitcase locks trying to cram seventy pounds into a fifty-pound container."

Edward nodded. He found over the years that nodding and saying, "You're right," made his home life much easier. His parents also found that accepting his nods worked well for them. "He's old enough, let him figure stuff out for himself."

Edward surveyed his room a third time, was anything missed? He would typically come in after school or sports and casually drop his stuff. Somehow, wherever it landed, or was kicked to, it was always easy to find. He had clutter radar, his eyes somehow picked out objects that were hidden under jettisoned clothing.

Once he was comfortable that all his travel needs were accounted for, he studied the suitcase. He decided that he really could jam sixty pounds into that fifty-pound case. Strong muscles solved many a problem. As his science teacher jokingly said about boys, "All they need is a bigger hammer to solve any problem."

Edward was now down to making a final selection of a book to read during his travels. Edward was a long-time book-freak. He loved to read even during school classes. While other students were secretly texting on their smartphones, Edward was absorbed in a book.

The teachers cut Edward a lot of slack. Somehow, he always had an answer when called upon, and most teachers still thought reading was an important skill. "Read more and snap or text less" was their advice to students. Students, of course, ignored them.

Edward studied the many choices resting on his bookshelves. Nothing jumped out at him. *American Gods* by Neil Gaiman was a shelf favorite but he had read it three times. He reached behind the facing books. Sometimes forgotten treasures were buried in the back row.

His hand seemed guided to rest on thick old leather. The book was warm and welcoming; sight unseen it called out, "Take me, you'll be happy you did." He took hold of the book and brought it out of the back row for closer inspection.

He was holding the leather-covered book from his childhood. He had not read it for many years, but it felt like an old friend who had just shown up. This was the book his dad had brought back from Boston right before his sixth Christmas. The book was as soft and comforting as the first time he had held it. "I remember you, old friend, you still feel like puppies and bunnies."

He began to examine the beautiful inlaid artwork on the front and back covers. His inspection was like looking at photos from the past but seeing them fresh through the eyes of a young adult.

He immediately remembered the front cover. There was the smiling Santa sitting in an ornate sleigh. The sleigh was in front of a simple country home in the woods.

A small child was peeking out an upstairs window. The child was holding a single candle out the open window looking into the outside darkness. The child's eyes and face were glowing with excitement from the candle's light.

Edward paused as he studied the front cover. Something was slightly different. He did not recall a child in the window. *Small detail,* he thought.

Edward turned to look at the back cover. He jerked straight up in his chair, caught his breath and did a double take. His heart speeded up.

He vaguely remembered the back cover from many years ago. He recalled that the back cover had a giant on it. He seemed to recall the giant had looked peaceful with two blazing blue eyes and a faint smile. There had been a large cat creature sitting beside the giant.

He also recalled there were two large black birds, one on each of the giant's shoulders. His dad had jokingly called them, "Heckle and Jeckle" after the magpie cartoon birds.

Later, as Eddie's dad read stories from the book, he learned their Norse names were "Huginn" meaning "thought" and "Muninn" meaning "mind." The leather back cover still displayed the bearded giant, but Heckle and Jeckle were gone. *Impossible, how could they fly the coop on a cover?* he thought.

While the giant was still standing on top of a snow-covered mountain, his smile was gone. This face was stern and challenging. The giant now had a patch over his left eye. The staff he had been leaning on was gone, and in its place, was a large, wicked-looking spear. The spear had rune carvings running from bottom to top.

Edward studied the runes and thought they reminded him of Egyptian hieroglyphs. Edward loved puzzles, and hieroglyphs were complex puzzles. He had immersed himself in the sixth-grade learning how to translate simple Egyptian hieroglyphs. He practiced his translation skills by using the internet to look at pictures of hieroglyphs carvings on tombs, statues, and sarcophagus covers.

His favorite translations were curses and spells. Ironically, he found he did better translating curses than the typical sarcophagus message that extolled the virtues of the deceased.

His eyes returned to the details of the spear's runes. As he squinted to study the runes, they seemed to shimmer. The artwork was so cleverly done that the runes seemed to move on the spear. *This is disturbing,* he thought.

Edward's scientific mind came up with the explanation. *When I rub my eyes, I see small shapes floating around in front of me. I think pressure on the eyeball creates the effect. While*

*I'm not rubbing right now I am squinting, and that creates pressure on my eyes. The squinting is what makes movement seem to happen.*

He looked away from the runes and saw that the giant's right hand gripped the spear with a threatening purpose. The runes reappeared and seemed to move around the giant's grip and onto his arm. Muscles stood out on the giant's arm that Schwarzenegger, as Conan the Barbarian, would have died for. Despite the giant having only one eye, Edward instinctively knew the giant could hit and kill whatever he threw his spear at.

Flanking him were two slightly smaller giants. The one on his right side was standing in a braced position leaning slightly forward on his left leg. His right hand was behind him and held a two-headed war hammer. His braced position indicated he was preparing to throw the hammer, possible at the same target as the one-eyed giant.

Again, there were runes on the stock and the head of his hammer. These runes also seem to move when Edward squinted to focus on them.

The giant on the left was relaxed and standing totally erect. He held a long sword casually in his left hand. Runes flowed from the swords length up to the pommel and onto his arm. His posture proclaimed, "Try me."

Edward recalled there had been a large cat creature beside the giant. The cat was gone. In its place was a dark cloud in front of the giants. When he squinted at the cloud, he thought he could see eyes inside the cloud looking out.

Edward studied the three giants and the cloud. All four appeared to be looking at a nearby bridge. The bridge shimmered with colors much like a rainbow. *Those three guys look like they want to walk on it, or maybe somebody is walking on it that should not be there.*

Edward was sure these cover details were far different from the last time he had held the book. Then he thought, *Of course that was eleven years ago, and my stuffed bear talked to me. I guess memory is a tricky thing.*

Then a more practical explanation came to mind. *This is a sequel book that Dad bought with the first book. He was going to give it to me but decided it was too scary and stored it away on my back shelf. He simply forgot to give it to me when I was older.*

Satisfied with this rational explanation, Edward's eyes returned to the back cover. Far below the rainbow was a forest of tall ash trees. When he squinted and looked carefully at the ash tree forest, he could see partially hidden bodies with faces watching the giants.

Excitement lit their faces. Their pointed ears looked a lot like Mr. Spock's, except they seemed to be hazy with small flames on the edges. The bodies had a simian appearance and cast a reddish glow.

Their red eyes stared out at the reader with interest. On closer inspection, Edward realized they looked more hungry than interested. His reaction was an immediate, *Yikes. No wonder Dad never gave this sequel to me. I would have had nightmares for months.*

*That was then, and this is now. I bet the stories and pictures inside are all new and exciting. There's certainly no problem handling scary stuff at age sixteen. The scarier the better, I eat scary for breakfast.* Edward knew this book was his traveling companion and said, "You're heading to the big city, friend. Show me your new stuff."

# 12
# Ready for Travel

Edward liked to plan ahead. He practiced this in school by reading his textbooks in advance of the class. He found that a little advance effort helped him get the most out of class. When he knew about the Chicago trip, he immersed himself in planning his sightseeing agenda.

He started his planning with the history of the Drake Hotel and this led to many interesting facts about Chicago. A landmark event in the city's life was a great fire in 1871. Few buildings survived, the fire almost wiped Chicago off the map.

He read that one surviving structure is called the Water Tower. It is a small, stone water pumping building originally built in 1869. It still stands today as a survivor of the great fire. *It's an easy walk from the Drake, gotta see that early on.*

Across from the Water Tower monument is a high-rise shopping center, aptly named Water Tower Place. It offers eight floors of shopping as well as a movie theatre and restaurants. Edward expected his mother would spend significant time there. *She can shop till she drops, then easily walk back to our hotel.*

At the top of his "must see" list was the Chicago Museum. He was particularly interested in the museum since it had a new, world-renowned display from the Middle East. The new exhibit was an ancient portal that predated the earliest Egyptian kingdoms.

The portal was on a long-term loan from the Syrian government. It was a physical link between man's earliest civilizations in Mesopotamia to the beginning of the first pharaohs in Egypt.

Edward had a longstanding interest in the history of ancient Egypt. Part of his interest in translating hieroglyphs was to see if he could decode hidden science knowledge.

He believed that the priests that served the Egyptian pharaohs for close to three thousand years would have acquired amazing insights into the forces of the universe. He knew the priests were picked for their intelligence. He thought, *Smart men and three thousand years to study and record; what a powerful combination for discovery.*

Edward believed that the writings, paintings, and hieroglyphs inside pyramids and stone tombs were more than recordings of religious beliefs. He believed they placed their scientific knowledge inside structures like pyramids and stone tombs to ensure their knowledge was safe forever.

Edward was certainly correct that ancient priests and scholars knew how fragile the physical storage of knowledge was. The great library at Alexandria held the accumulated knowledge of thousands of years. Julius Caesar accidentally burned down the library in 48 BC.

Caesar had invaded Egypt, and became trapped by the Egyptian army in the port of Alexandria. Caesar set fire to his own ships, so his men would not try to escape. The fire got out of control and spread to the great library. The accumulated knowledge of thousands of years became, in the words of the band Kansas, "Dust in the Wind."

Secure with his sightseeing itinerary, Edward's focus came back to the train schedule. He worried about breakdowns in schedules. Virginia knew he worried, so she reassured him each day that the trains were running on time and everything was going to be OK.

The night before their departure she said, "Eddie, you'll love this. There is lots of snow in Chicago! It's such a great city at any time, but the Christmas season with snow is just magical.

"Here are a few facts about Chicago you'll appreciate once we're there. Chicago is called the 'Windy City.' Some say it's because of the windy politicians but I think it's the fierce winds coming off Lake Michigan. Our Charlottesville winds have a bite in winter, but Chicago winds could freeze Eskimos. You must bring heavy clothing for protection. Bring a scarf, a heavy coat, thick socks, and importantly earmuffs. Now sleep tight and don't worry; our train will leave on time."

Edward appreciated the "on time" message but tuned her out at "earmuffs." No self-respecting teenage boy would be caught dead wearing earmuffs. Edward nodded and smiled back, "OK, Mom, I'll leave my swimsuit at home."

Edward was normally a great sleeper, "Morpheus and I are best friends," he told his parents when they worried about his getting enough sleep. This departure morning Morpheus apparently had better places to be. Edward was wide-awake at five o'clock. He climbed out of bed, dropped his pajamas on the floor, and went into his bathroom for a wake-up shower.

He knew their train compartment had a shower, but he also knew from its size it favored smaller passengers, certainly not tall guys like him. He suspected the hot water would be limited and he enjoyed very long, very hot showers. *When you need to shower up, make it a great experience,* he thought.

This morning he took a longer than usual shower. He kept his head under the showerhead and held his breath but kept his eyes open by squinting to control the pupils. He could still see even with water cascading over his face.

*Maybe I have some DNA from the Moken island people.* He had just read about the water-born Moken islanders. He was fascinated at their ability to see twice the normal distance under water and to hold their breath twice the normal time.

He chuckled at their water talents. *They must have been late arrivals in leaving the water to crawl on land. They will rule the earth after global warming raises the ocean levels.*

He stepped out of his shower and presented himself to his full-length mirror. When he hit his second growth spurt at age twelve his mother upgraded his mirror. "A tall mirror to capture all of a fast-growing boy," his mother said.

Edward was pleased with his height. Starting at age twelve, he began to rise above his classmates. *I'm above the herd,* he thought with an ego-stroking chuckle. By age sixteen, he was indeed well above the classmate herd, and more than a bit full of himself.

"Mirror, mirror on my wall, who's the baddest dude of all?" he said to the steamed glass. "You are a definite contender," he mimicked the mirror saying. He flexed his biceps and got them to jump. Weight lifting had added muscle as well as definition.

"I see a future terminator, beware Arnold!" He then stretched himself as high as possible on his toes. "Standing tall and strong at a bit over six foot three inches, and probably more where that came from. Thank you, Dad."

He toweled off his body then his hair. He ran his fingers through his thick mop of brown/black hair. *Hands make the best combs,* he thought. *Thank you, Mom, for the full head of hair.* Edward had just read in science class that hair comes down the mother's side. Fortunately for him, both parents had full covers, "No Mr. Cleans in this family," he said smugly.

He dressed in his pre-selected travel outfit. He climbed into dress jeans. He had considered wearing his stonewashed jeans with holes in the legs and knees but knew his mom would immediately demand a change. Next came a black turtleneck sweater followed by shoes. These shoes were built from sturdy, water resistant, dark leather. *I can do my Chicago walkabout and never worry about my feet.*

Edward was well aware that having "marching ready" footwear was essential for warriors who walked long distances. Napoléon had famously said, "An army marches on its stomach," but Edward knew that footwear was also essential for a successful march.

He knew that the honored VII legion of Caesar, marching through Gaul, could only go as far as their footwear permitted. With secure sandals, they could easily march thirty miles a day and launch surprise attacks on their enemy.

He reviewed his open suitcase a final time. His mental checklist assured him everything was in its place. He pressed down hard and snapped the two locks. "Success!" he declared. When he lifted it to go downstairs he thought, *This puppy weights a ton.*

Edward's case naturally had wheels. However, he was too proud to use them. His mom and dad would say, "too vain" to use them. *Wheeling is for women, children, and old people,* he assured himself. *I'll hand carry mine as a strength exercise. I'll switch hands to keep my body in balance and work out both arms equally.* He had it all figured out.

"Time to go, Eddie," his mom called up to him.

"I'm ready, Mom. Can I bring your cases down now?"

"Yes, thank you, dear. They're at the top of the stairs. Please put them all in the trunk and we're out of here."

Edward chuckled to himself. His mom's tone of voice was that of a young girl going on a vacation trip. *She's trying to act like a cool adult, but I can see she's excited. Dad is The Man; he scores big time.*

"Mach schnell!" he said out loud to himself. This was one of his dad's favorite expressions, meaning "move fast" in German. His dad liked to use the expression when the family needed to speed things up. Following his own advice, Edward quickly took the bags to the car and placed them in the trunk.

As they pulled out of their driveway Virginia said, "Time for a travel prayer." Their family travels always started with a travel prayer. Both Virginia and Daniel believed rituals are one of the glues that bind a family together.

She proceeded with the short prayer for the family. Edward the science cynic, stoically accepted the prayer, but noticed when he added the obligatory, "Amen," that he somehow felt more relaxed.

Once underway they headed south on Route 20 and passed the Stony Point Elementary School. This was the rural school where Edward had started kindergarten. Virginia felt a strong wave of nostalgia. *My little Eddie is almost grown up and I feel like it was just yesterday I was in the car line dropping him off.*

They continued south on the scenic rural road into Charlottesville. In less than twenty-five minutes, they were approaching the Charlottesville train station parking lot. "I'll let you out by the front of the station. You can take the cases inside and I'll go park the car."

Edward was quickly out. He removed the three cases from the trunk and thumped the car's side door. His mom headed off to find a convenient long-term parking space.

*Man, it's cold,* he thought. He tried to make it a one-trip carry but found the suitcase handles and weights did not allow it. "Rats," he grumbled aloud, then accepted that it was a two-trip load.

When he entered the station the second time his mother was already inside talking to the agent. *How did she beat me?* he thought. He rubbed his cold sore hands together, *Should have used my gloves. Dumb.*

Virginia returned from the agent with a big smile. "Everything is on time, Eddie. The train will be here in about twenty minutes. There are no problems expected between here and Chicago. Winter is all over the north, but we will be comfy inside our suite. I'm so excited Eddie, this will be a grand trip," and she gave her son a big hug.

Edward flinched at a public hug from his mom but instinctively hugged her back. He'd heard that hugs are good karma and he did not want to jinx the trip. Plus, Mom was pretty enough that he was not totally embarrassed. "I'm going outside," he declared.

Virginia nodded; she could see he was really wound up. *And so am I,* she thought. *It's cold out there, but it's good for him to get some exercise before we board.*

Edward was outside looking down the tracks when the loudspeaker announced the incoming train. "The Cardinal is arriving at the station. Train 51 to Chicago! Please take your luggage and move to track three now. Passengers with reserved rooms should stand by area twelve, all others please board between six through ten. Have a great trip. Enjoy the winter scene from inside our warm, magic carpet."

The loudspeaker's announcement broke Virginia's musings. She panicked for a moment as she looked down at the three suitcases and no Edward. Then on cue, he was suddenly there, with his nose and cheeks colored a nice pink.

"It's definitely winter outside," he said grinning. "Relax, Mom; I'll take my bag and your heavy bag. You can manage your light bag pretty easily. Follow me and try to face away from the wind." With that, he was out the door heading for boarding area twelve.

Despite the warning, a cold wind startled Virginia as she went outside. *Boy,* she thought, *I've gotten soft living here in Virginia.* She then put on a pair of earmuffs. *I don't want to catch a cold right now, and besides I look darn cute.*

Even carrying the two heavy cases, Edward walked fast. He was now well ahead of the other reserved room passengers and was first to the boarding area. *He always wants to be first,* Virginia thought, *even though the train doesn't leave until everyone is boarded. He's just like his dad; it must be in their DNA.*

Virginia joined Edward, put her case down, and looked down the tracks. In the distance there was a soft light that reminded her of a dimming flashlight. Then the waiting platform began a soft vibration. The vibration increased until the engine appeared from around a curve.

The dim flashlight was now a bright beacon lighting the steel tracks ahead. The waiting passengers froze as the iron beast rumbled toward them. It was powerful, majestic, and dominating. Its presence made each passenger feel insignificant.

The engine was now moving at a slowing-down pace. It reminded Virginia of an enormous cat that was picking where to place its paws before curling up. It was controlled power in slow motion.

The engine continued forward until the reserved sleeper suite car was exactly across from the number twelve on the platform floor. There was a deep sigh from inside the beast's belly, it gave off a whistle of steam, rocked slightly, then was quiet. The cat was curled up.

# 13
# All Aboard

A conductor opened the sleeper car's door and a set of steel stairs automatically lowered. He stepped out with a small, one-step stool and placed it in front of the lowered steel ladder. He smiled and motioned to the passengers that they could board.

Edward politely let his mom go up first. Virginia showed both tickets to the conductor, who smiled and said in a deep southern voice, "Please step right up. Once you are onboard turn to your right, your room is halfway down." He took Virginia's case and set it inside.

Edward handed up the first of the two heavy cases. He watched how easily the conductor took each case and set them inside. *Strong,* Edward thought with respect. After the second case was on board Edward was quickly up and inside.

Edward carried the two heavy cases and followed his mom down the aisle to their room. The aisle was a bit narrow, so Edward awkwardly held one case in front and one case behind. He noticed his hands were quickly sore again. *Really heavy bags, should definitely have worn gloves,* he again reprimanded himself.

Virginia opened the compartment door and stepped inside. Edward left the two heavy cases in the walkway, so he could determine where to put them. He knew the room's floor plan and immediately confirmed the overhead luggage rack. "Right where the luggage storage should be," he confirmed to his mom.

"Mom, would you step outside for a moment, so I can get these cases stored in the overhead?" Virginia ducked outside and watched her son take charge of luggage storage.

He took his mother's case first since it was the heaviest. He did a military press and put it into the storage space. Another military press and his case joined it. Virginia's third case was small and stayed on the floor.

Virginia watched how easily he managed the cases and thought with pride, *Occasionally, we modern women still need some brute male strength. Eddie's just like his dad, blessed with that male muscle. I never could have gotten those heavy cases up there.* "Very well done, Hercules," she said, and Edward accepted the praise with a modest grin.

With the cases stowed away, Edward and his mom could start to relax. They shut the door and closed the door's curtain. "It's so nice here," said Virginia, "our own private little castle."

*Let's get this train on the road. Mach schnell,* thought Edward. His dad's expression fit so many of Eddie's situations.

They sat facing the picture window and watched the continuing passenger movement outside. The late arrivals were rushing to board the waiting train. Virginia could see the efforts the latecomers had to make dragging cases behind them while resisting the biting wind. She thanked the fates for having a son who made the boarding effort easy.

Finally, there came the classic railroad call of "All aboard that are coming aboard. The train will be pulling out shortly. All people who are not continuing on should depart at this time." They watched as a few people hurriedly exited the train and backed away from it. The cat was ready to move and the mice instinctively sought distance from it.

There was a noticeable snap as the entry doors closed and locked. They felt a tremor, followed by a mild jerk as the engine made its initial move forward. Edward could feel the vibration from the growing power of the engine as it strained to move forward against resting inertia. A long call on the train horn announced its departure to anybody near the tracks.

The view through the picture window started as a series of snapshots of the outside. Then the snapshots began shifting into a slow-motion movie. As the speed of the train increased, the outside views began to resemble a movie running at a natural rate.

The train's rhythm was also adjusting to the increasing speed, a soft vibration accompanied a gentle rocking motion. The sound of steel wheels moving on steel tracks settled into a soothing background hum. Passengers felt the tensions of boarding and settling drifting away with the comforting vibration.

The moving scene outside the window captivated Virginia. She watched as the familiar buildings of downtown Charlottesville passed by. In a short time, the view was shifting from downtown to the surrounding suburbs and then into the rural Virginia countryside.

She recognized the countryside and many of the farms and horse properties. "Watch for our house," Virginia told Edward with excitement in her voice. "The trees are bare, so I think we may see our fields and house."

Edward focused on the passing countryside but with little luck. One field and set of fences looked the same to him. *Boring,* he thought, but tried to appear interested for his mom.

"Up there!" Virginia exclaimed and pointed. Suddenly Edward saw their home high up on their personal ridge. The red brick and large center chimney presented a commanding presence. Edward felt a surge of pride that his family had a high castle dominating their own surrounding land.

Once their house disappeared, Edward was quickly bored with the passing countryside. The real action to him was inside the train and he wanted to explore. Just as he stood up to leave there was a knock on the door. "Come in," his mother said and slid the door to the side. Standing in the doorway was a porter.

"Tickets please," she said.

After a quick check, she handed the tickets back. "What time would you like dinner this evening? First class seating starts at five o'clock and coach seating begins at half past six. Of course, you can come whenever you wish."

"It's been a long day for Eddie and me, so we'll be there at five sharp." The porter made a note of their reservation time.

Then with a smile, the porter added, "There are usually three or four people seated to a table, so you will likely meet other guests. Our passengers often tell us that they enjoy the new people they meet. I bet you will too. Shared dining is all part of the railroad adventure. It's much better food and conversation than any plane can offer."

Virginia nodded in agreement. "You are so right! My husband and I love to travel by train. We have had many great experiences and have met a lot of terrific, interesting people."

Edward the Explorer was twitching. He politely interrupted, "Excuse me, but can I walk look around and check out the common areas?"

"Of course, honey. Amtrak just added a new young-adult entertainment car. It's after you go through the bar car. It has individual seat stations with a wide choice of current movies and video games. Check it all out, but watch out for the pretty young ladies when you go through the bar car," she gave a wink to Virginia.

Edward started a slow blush but recovered and said, "Mom, I'll catch you in the dining car at five. It's time for me to explore, see ya."

# 14
# Edward Explores

Once outside their compartment, he paused for a moment. He memorized the room number and picked a coffee station as a landmark. Like every good Boy Scout, Edward understood the importance of having landmarks. He knew you could easily get lost anywhere, even on a train. How many people had he seen in parking garages and parking lots wandering around with a look of frustration on their faces?

He decided to first head down the aisle toward the back of the train. He wanted to see how many sleeper cars were behind them. The aisle made a short dogleg curve that ended with a set of sliding doors. Edward hit the door's entry pad cushion and it opened with a quiet whisper. He stepped through.

He took his time as he moved down the long aisle. He noticed that the normal rocking motion seemed to be nearly gone. *They must have added better stabilizers in this car,* he thought. As he walked down the aisle, he realized there were no entry doors or windows on the right compartment side. Apparently, this was a single private car.

The left side exterior windows had darkened glass and reminded him of the tinting done on private VIP vehicles. Edward pressed his face to the window glass and could barely see outside. What he could see appeared as a fog of sorts or possibly heavy snowfall. *Boy, has winter darkness arrived fast,* he thought.

As he proceeded up the long aisle Edward noticed the material that covered the side of the long compartment, it looked like old stone. Edward knew enough physics to know it had to be artificial and thought, *No way it's real stone. That would be way too much weight for the springs. It has to be one of the simulated materials that architects use to make exteriors look like real brick or stone.*

As he continued down the aisle, he dragged a fingernail across the assumed fake stone. *Boy is that a good replica, it feels just like the real thing. Even fake it has to be expensive; the owner sure is rich. I bet this car is for the president of the railroad.*

Edward reached the end of the aisle and had to stop. A door was blocking his way. A sign across the top of the door stated, "Very Private. By Invitation Only". Edward studied the lettering on the sign; it was similar to the fancy lettering in his leather book. *Now there's a coincidence,* he thought.

The top of the door curved into an overhead arch. Beside the door was a flickering gas lantern. The door was made of a dense, dark wood. A heavy antique knocker rested in the center of the door.

The knocker looked like old cast iron. It was in the shape of an unusual cat's head. The cat's ears stuck out at a sharp forward angle. Its eyes were some type of green crystal. It reminded Edward of the Egyptian cat god, Bast.

Standing outside of the door he knew he was at the last car. He looked back down the aisle he had just walked and saw the hallway was completely empty. He also found that it was unusually quiet. The normal train sounds of wheels on rails were muffled. *Spooky,* he thought. *More advanced technology for the president.*

He noticed there was no window in the door like there was in his own suite. *They certainly don't want people looking in on their activities.* Edward's explorer curiosity taunted him, *What would this very large compartment look like inside? It's got to be very cool.*

The door was challenging to the explorer in Edward. The iron knocker seemed to be asking for a hard pound. Edward looked up the hallway again and confirmed nobody was around. *Is there anybody inside? Why not just knock and see what happens? Where's the risk in that?*

*Before knocking he recalled there was a better way to get the lay of the land inside.* As a Boy Scout, he had learned that a common drinking glass put against a wall acted as a snooper scope. Once your ear was firmly against the bottom of the glass, the glass magnified any sound on the other side of the wall. While he did not have a glass with him, he knew an ear pressed hard against a wall also worked.

Edward pushed his long hair to the side of his head. *I need the best-sealed contact I can make*, he thought. He spat on his left hand and wiped his left ear, this gave him a better seal. He wiped his hand on the back of his jeans then carefully put his left ear to the door.

He slowly pressed his ear against the door, being careful not to rattle the door. This position also permitted him to see any person coming down the hallway. *I am a train-ninja,* he thought to boost his confidence.

After a minute of listening he moved his ear away, there appeared to be total silence inside. He waited a minute and tried again. There was still no sound. *It's empty,* he assured himself, *time to use the knocker. If somebody comes, I'll put on my best, "Help me, I'm stupid and lost" face.*

He felt his body tense up as he lifted the heavy cat knocker. He released the knocker and it fell hard against the door. Even outside he could hear the sound echo inside down the long compartment. Nobody appeared, and he relaxed. *That would have woken Rip Van Winkle. It's time to explore this treasure car.*

He placed his hand on the iron lever that served as a handle and very slowly pressed down on it. "Open Sesame!" he commanded. The handle went all the way down. *Yes! It's open. I bet the occupants are in the bar car, maybe talking with Mom. That would be ironic.*

He slowly pushed against the heavy door and cautiously called out, "Excuse me," in a strong voice. Still no response. *Houston, we have lift off, all systems are go.* He pushed the door open and stepped inside.

Edward the astronaut froze. Sitting in a large leather chair, calmly watching him, was a young man of indefinite age. He could be eighteen, twenty-eight, or one hundred and eight. Edward was speechless. There was a frog in his throat, his glib explanation slipped away.

The man smiled at him, "Lost?" he asked, "or just exploring?" Edward knew a layup question when he heard on.

Edward immediately puts on his sincere face. The frog disappeared, and his prepared explanation returned. "I knocked and I'm sorry to intrude. I feel really stupid. I'm looking for the entertainment car and seem to have gone in the wrong direction."

Edward realized the man was looking at him with a slight smile. *He knows I'm lying, but doesn't seem mad. Let me try a little truth.*

Edward gave a weak smile and said, "Actually you caught me. I'm exploring the whole train and started with this car. I got interested in the stone exterior and followed it to the cool wooden door. I knocked and thought if it were empty, I'd peek inside. There are no thieves in my family. I'm just naturally curious, that's all."

The young man nodded with an understanding look on his face, "I'm a bit of an explorer myself. I believe it's good for a person to wonder what's around the corner or what's inside the next room. Everybody should have some explorer in their blood; it's how we discover more about our world."

Edward knew he was off the hook. The man was not going to tell his mom what he had been up to. The onboard railroad police, known in the 1930s to train jumpers as "bulls," would not be throwing him and his suitcase off the moving train. Edward also knew he needed to make a graceful exit. "Thanks for being so nice about this," he said, and began to back out into the aisle.

As he was stepping back, he froze again. Beside the man, on top of an elevated bunk, a set of eyes was marking him.

Edward could not breathe as the large cat eyes continued to hold him. *I'm a mouse and the cat has me under its spell.*

The eyes were large and slanted. The part of the head that was visible was far too large for any normal cat. Edward thought, *Please don't yawn, Mr. Really Big Cat. I really don't want to see the size of your fangs.*

Then he saw a little more of the animal and he became further spellbound. Its size was hard to determine. It had high ears that seemed too large but maybe were the right size for the head and body. There was a twitching motion behind the head, which looked to be a tail. The problem was that the tail was too long, unless the rest of the body belongs to a black Bengal tiger.

The man broke Edward's trance with a calm voice and said, "Ignore Theo up there. He is quite civilized. An old soul, so to say. I promise he will be well-behaved." Then he kiddingly added, "He rarely eats anything that doesn't deserve it."

The large dark head disappeared back onto the bunk and Edward was suddenly able to breathe, move, and say, "I'm really sorry for the intrusion. I'll not bother you again." Then a witty exit line came to him, "Happy tails to Theo."

As he was shutting the door, he heard the man reply, "Theo says, 'Happy trails to you, your mom, Roy Rogers, and Trigger.' I'll see you at dinner."

*I don't think so,* Edward thought. *Very cool guy but definitely very strange, with a super-strange pet. Both belong in a zoo in another galaxy.*

# 15
# Bar Talk, Music, and DOTA

Once outside the strange guy's compartment, Edward's confidence came rushing back and he headed out to explore the rest of the train. He passed his own room first and continued forward. He proceeded to the bar car on his way toward the entertainment car.

The bar car was a serious adult entertainment car. Its décor created an ambience that was an elegant throwback to an earlier age of sophisticated train travel. The car had various seating arrangements with overstuffed chairs and marble-topped tables.

At one end of the car was an ornate bar that made an L shape across the back and up one side. Behind the bar, a bartender dressed in a tuxedo was serving the passengers. People were drinking cocktails from a variety of elegant glasses. Champagne was offered in long-stemmed fluted glasses. Cocktails were served in cut crystal glasses.

The men were dressed in suits; some wore ties while others wore cravats. The women wore a variety of cocktail dresses with classic designs. Pearl necklaces were common and diamond earrings made a style statement as well as a wealth statement.

In the center of the car, an older man in a dark suit played a piano. The tunes were vaguely familiar to Edward. Beside the piano was an attractive middle-aged couple. They were asking the pianist if he could play certain classics. The man nodded in agreement at their choices, and began playing.

Edward had never heard these songs, but he knew from their melodies they pre-dated his generation's rap, hip-hop, and new age rock by many decades.

The pianist announced the next request song, "'Stardust', created in the late 1920s by the composer Hoagie Carmichael." The audience nodded appreciatively at this request.

Edward was captivated. He was drawn into the haunting melody and lyrics. He sat down to listen. The "Stardust" melody and lyrics washed over him. *Music does soothe us,* he thought, *and this song works for me.* The strange cat and the strange guy were rapidly fading memories.

After "Stardust", the player moved into another smooth melody called "Moonlight Serenade." The piano man introduced the song as being popular during the war years of the 1940s and its composer was a famous bandleader named Glenn Miller. Edward thought he had heard about the composer. *I think there was a movie about him that Mom and Dad liked watching.*

Again, the melody was relaxing and spoke of an earlier time of formal elegance and manners. Men opened doors for women, stood up when women entered a room, and swearing in public was frowned upon. It was another world, but not a world completely forgotten. His mom and dad would have fit comfortably into that world.

*I have to go back and tell Mom to come to the bar; she'll love this music and the dressed-up people.* He hurried back to their room. As a courtesy, he knocked first on the door. He heard his mom telling him to come in.

Edward opened the door to find Virginia was already dressed for dinner. *She looks great,* Edward thought with pride. *Older women, at least my mom, can still look terrific. Lucky Dad.*

Edward described the scene at the bar car and recommended his mom pay it a visit before dinner. "That's a splendid idea, Eddie, thanks for coming back. I'll meet you in the dining car at five, you continue to explore."

With that, she stepped past him with a twinkle in her eye and a strong forward step. *Woman on a mission,* Edward thought. He immediately dropped that thought and replaced it with, *There are no good party-missions for Mom without Dad.*

Alone in the room, the day's pressure caught up with him. *This is a good time to visit the throne room. Mom's gone and nature calls. I'm a lucky bear with my own private woods to do my business in. Thanks again, Dad.*

Once inside his private bathroom Edward had a weird thought. *Where does that guy's big cat find a litter box on this train? That would be one giant litter box, and who would clean it? Not a pretty picture.*

Before leaving, Edward decided he needed to dress up. *If Mom's looking that great I need to show a little effort,* he thought. As he was lifting his arms to bring down his suitcase, he whiffed a nasty fragrance around him. He promptly did what all young men do, he sniffed under his arms.

"Hmm, I detect a manly odor. That cat beast really made me sweat, and who wouldn't have? Time for a fast wash-up." He lowered the room's fold out sink from the wall. Once put down, the sink's bowl offered a fresh washcloth, hand towel, and a wrapped cake of soap. *Efficient use of space,* he thought.

Once washed off, he applied deodorant and declared odor victory. He opened his suitcase and selected his best slacks, sweater, and a corduroy jacket. Finally, he ran his fingers through his mop of hair. Admiring himself in the small mirror he announced, "The casual man, but still well groomed; looking darn presentable if I do say so."

Edward left the room and proceeded to the bar car a second time. He felt quite the mature young adult wearing his coat, slacks, and sweater. *I fit right in with this crowd, clothes do make the man.*

When he entered the bar car he noticed his mom talking with other passengers by the piano. Several passengers were attractive older men. Older was anybody over forty to Edward. Virginia was holding a champagne glass in one hand and making a small gesture with the other. Edward saw she was animated and clearly having a great time. *The belle of the ball,* he thought.

A mischievous thought came to him, *Should I leave her alone or go ask her how Dad and the sick babies back on the farm are doing?* and he laughed to himself. *No, why rain on her parade? I'll be the good son and stay invisible. Besides, as her watchdog son, I'll be camped by her side at dinnertime;*

*it'll almost be like Dad's there. Feet do your stuff. Let's check out the entertainment car.*

As he was passing through the dining car, the wait staff was cleaning and setting the tables for dinner. The service people gave him the look that said, "Please keep moving young man, we're busy." One harried serving person looked at him and commented, "We don't open till five."

"I know, I'm just passing through," and he continued toward the back-exit door.

As he got to the last table he saw a menu on the tablecloth. He paused for a moment to scan the evening's choices. The menu looked great. It had many dishes Edward loved including spaghetti, roast chicken, and broiled New York strip steak.

His eyes darted to the desserts at the bottom and noticed the hot fudge sundae. *Oh yeah!* He made a mental note to order it at the same time as his dinner, and then he noticed the continuing frowns as waiters watched him. He put the menu down and went out the door.

Once past the dining car he was in coach class. Now he was in the Wild West. Kids were shouting, and babies were crying. Exhausted parents were trying to calm the kids or were quietly arguing.

Edward thought, *Must get out of Dodge fast. Happy trails are up ahead but not in here. Where's Trigger when I need him?* Edward left the chaos of Dodge City as quickly as his pony feet could move him.

He went through two more chaos cars until he hit the new game room car. As advertised, it was filled with teenagers.

The girls were watching movies while the boys were clustered around various video games; the sound of gunfire was nonstop. Shouts of "Die zombie," spoken with German and Russian accents declared their side was mopping up the other side. Team players were calling each other idiots over missed kills.

Edward knew this competitive gaming world well. He was an accomplished *Defense of the Ancients* player and his team was a strong force within the Charlottesville and Virginia gaming community. He lingered for a while to watch a DOTA team lose its initial advantage. It crumbled as the opponent team called out "Die" in unison. *So, goes the life of a DOTA warrior. No sympathy or respect in defeat,* he thought. *My team would annihilate these rookies.*

He stayed in place watching the flow of several games. After another team was crushed, he considered replacing one of their weak players. *I could carry this whole team to victory myself.* As he was picking an opportunity to deal himself into a game, he looked at his watch. It was 5:07 p.m. *Yikes, I'm late!* He turned and sped back toward the dining car.

With the last Wild West car behind him, he breathed a sigh of relief and opened the dining car's door. Pleasant dinner aromas called out, his stomach growled an answer back and he considered again his menu choices.

These pleasant thoughts stopped on a dime as the connecting door shut behind him. His view into the dining car ruined his mood big time.

# 16
# Company for Dinner: Three's A Crowd

He was looking at his mother's back. She was sitting by the window, clearly engaged in an animated conversation. Across from her was the strange young man from the private car. He heard his mother's laugh and saw the good-natured smile on the man's face as he acknowledged something witty Virginia had said.

*Unbelievable,* thought Edward. *Of all the possible table guests, how did I draw the short straw?* Then the man spotted Edward and waved. Edward's mom immediately turned around and sent hand signals motioning her son to join them.

Edward put on his best poker face as he walked to the table. "Honey, let me introduce our dining guest, Mr. Mert."

"No formalities please, 'M' will do just fine."

"Well in that case, M, call me Virginia and this is my wonderful son, Edward."

Edward winced. How embarrassing for your mother to refer to you as her wonderful son. *At least she didn't call me Eddie,* he thought. Edward acknowledged M with a neutral nod, sat down and sent an eye message that declared, "This is my private space not yours."

Edward tried his best not to pout, but still he refused to join in the table conversation. To join would be giving tacit approval to the strange guy's presence. He looked past his mom out the window and watched the darkness rapidly creeping across the Virginia countryside.

*That's odd,* he thought. *When I was in this guy's private car, it seemed totally dark outside. Now it's still a little light out. Everything about him is weird, maybe he has the windows tinted black because he's a vampire.*

The waiter appeared and presented a dusty wine bottle for inspection. As the waiter wiped the bottle clean he said, "I never knew we had this label and vintage on board, sir. I looked where you told me and sure enough, there it was. I never knew there was a built-in wine cabinet behind all the normal stock, I can see from the dust that it's been hiding a long time. May I ask how you knew it was there, sir?"

M smiled and said, "Of course you may ask, there's no secret here. I've ridden this train many times. A number of years ago I saw this bottle being served. I recognized the vintage as a classic, so I asked if it was on the menu.

"The wine steward at the time told me, with a wink I would add, that if I asked for it by its secret location then indeed it was available. Apparently, it's the top shelf selection and it is kept hidden for VIPs. I'm pleased there was still a bottle safely tucked away."

Virginia was nonplussed for a moment. How has a man so young ridden this train for years? Edward thought the same thing. *"Vampire" is the best explanation*, he mentally affirmed.

The waiter inserted a corkscrew into the bottle's neck and began to twist it down. The screw tried to dig into the cork but suddenly froze in place. The waiter reset the pointed screw but could not get it to penetrate the hardened cork. It was a standoff between modern man's tools and an old cork.

"Permit me to do the honors," said M, "these old vintages can be tricky to uncork, and we don't want the cork to break up inside the bottle." The waiter readily agreed. He knew the wine was expensive and he certainly did not want to damage the contents.

Edward was intrigued to see how Mr. Vampire would get the bottle open. He knew from chemistry class how old corks get brittle and tend to crumble when being pulled out.

He hoped to see Mr. Vampire get wine all over himself. He anticipated having a big laugh at the expense of the unwelcome table visitor. *Okay,* he thought, *let's see you make a fool out of yourself.*

Surprisingly, M ignored the offered opener. Instead, he covered the top of the bottle with a white table napkin and rested the covered bottle between his legs. He reached under the napkin with both hands, made a small jerking motion, removed the napkin and presented the intact cork to Virginia.

Virginia, Edward, and the waiter were stunned. "Professionally speaking, sir, how did you do that?" asked the waiter.

"It's an old bar trick I learned in one of my travels to southern Spain; it has earned me my share of free drinks. All that's required is a strong grip using the palms to hold the neck of the bottle and then a sharp upward twist and snap with the thumbs. Quite easy once you get the hang of it."

M poured a small amount into Virginia's glass and invited her to do the tasting honors. Virginia was flattered; fortunately, she had learned the protocols for approving wines from an elective she took in her senior year. College electives should be fun as well as informative and this one was a big hit.

First, she swirled it in the glass and did the initial "nose" test. Next, she held the glass at eye level and studied the color. She blinked, as the color seemed to turn from a dark red to a reddish blue then back to a deep red with blue and green sparkles inside the swirls.

*I need to have my eyes examined when we get home. Maybe the champagne at the bar hit me a tad more than I realized,* she thought.

She lifted the glass and sniffed more deeply. This time the fragrance brought up memories of past holidays at home with her parents, parties with best friends in college, and special events with Daniel and Edward. She took the first sip and let it flow over and under her tongue. "Wow!" she said.

M smiled, "I'll assume it's fit for our consumption," and he poured a glass for Edward as well as himself.

Virginia's face began to register an objection to Edward's glass when M anticipated her. "Young men coming into adulthood need to gain experiences in all facets of life. I believe your son is certainly of an age that has him ready to expand his dining repertoire."

"Well he's still a little young for expanding into alcohol," said Virginia, "his birthday is coming up in February and he will just turn seventeen."

"Amazing," said M. "He carries himself with the ease and confidence of an older, mature young man. What say we take a small risk and introduce him to the wine?" Without hesitation M added, "Bottoms up!"

Before his mom could register more of an objection, Edward took a tentative sip. *My God,* he thought. *It's ambrosia, nectar of the gods. This would be what Odin and Zeus would drink.*

He took another sip and felt the wine flow through all parts of his body. He had never felt stronger or more in control of his senses. He suddenly felt much more accepting of M at the table. *I was hasty in my first impression; vampire or not, this guy is all right.*

The waiter brought bread and appetizers while the wine worked its magic. Virginia was animated and aglow; her mind seemed on hyper-drive. She had a strong desire to talk and discuss a variety of topics from politics to the live theatre. As if reading her mind M asked, "Are you a student of the theatre?"

"I love it. I was a drama major in college," answered Virginia. "Live theatre is much superior to taped shows. It's real life, you can feel the human side of the actors. You can tell when they are nervous and when they are exuberant. Their energy flows out of them and into the audience."

M nodded in agreement then turned to Edward and asked, "What live shows do you like, Edward?"

"Magic, no question. I prefer close-up hand magic over the disappearing elephants. The elephants are all tricks created by using cameras. Hand magic, properly done, feels real." Once again, M nodded in agreement.

"Who are the most impressive magicians you have personally seen?" asked M.

"Penn and Teller are the best I've actually seen. They do close-up tricks that are amazing. They have a show where they let other magicians perform and try to fool them.

"After the magicians perform, Penn, the tall one, explains to the challenging magician how the trick was done. Penn speaks in magician code, so the trick's secret stays hidden from the viewers. The magicians are all great but only a few ever fool Penn and Teller."

"So, you don't really believe in magic I take it?" asked M.

"I'm a science guy, I believe in the human mind. But I think everyone secretly wishes there was real magic. As young children, we believe in Santa and magic and it's exciting. Then school starts, and magic disappears."

Edward found himself unable to stop taking about a favorite subject. "Even though I know it's just tricks I still love it. My dad brought me a set of magic tricks when I was just nine years old and I became captivated. I've read a lot and have mastered many complicated tricks.

"I can modestly say that I'm quite good myself with close up magic, particularly card tricks. I can usually see how even the best trick is done. I can figure out more than half of the tricks I see on Penn and Teller."

M listened and nodded his head. "If you think about it, TV itself would be considered magic to even the best minds a hundred years ago. It does makes you wonder where magic ends and science begins. Some would argue it's the other way around."

"Well," said Edward, feeling very mature and a bit full of him, "I believe everything is explainable with science. We may not yet know the scientific explanation for certain happenings but it's just a matter of time before science finds the answer."

M listened and gave Edward a strange smile. Edward could not decide whether he was being humored or agreed with.

While Edward was talking, the main course had arrived and was sitting in front of him. Edward was oblivious to it until Virginia interrupted him, "Eddie, honey, you want to eat your food before it gets cold. Your roast beef looks delicious, but it cools quickly as do the potatoes and veggies."

Edward was immediately annoyed with his mom. She was addressing him as "Eddie" as though he were a six-year-old. He considered several retorts but bit his tongue. He begrudgingly took a bit of the beef with some mashed potatoes. *Rats,* he thought, *she's right, the food has gotten cold.*

M was watching Edward, "Virginia's quite right, Edward. Cooled food is the price we pay for engaging in dinner conversation. Indeed, my beef has also gone to room temperature. I think it needs a bit of heating up. Would either of you like your plates heated?" Edward immediately nodded an affirmation.

"Yes, I would," said Virginia. "But I don't want to send it back to the kitchen. We were talking too much so it cooled, but the wait staff needs to serve other tables."

"Let me see what I can do," said M. "There is a bit of heating magic I picked up on another trip; let's test it on our plates. Would each of you please cover your plates with your linen napkins?"

Without thinking, both Virginia and Edward covered their plates. M paused for a moment then reached across and held the side of each plate for a long moment. "Now try it."

When their napkins came off, steam rose from each plate. Both Virginia and Edward stared at the steam. "Try a bite and be sure it's not too hot," said M.

Both Virginia and Edward cut fresh slices of their beef and added a little potato to their forks. They both used their tongues to confirm the heat was exactly right.

"It's perfect!" exclaimed Virginia. "How in the world did you do that?"

"As Edward said, it's all in the science. I used some basic rules of applied thermodynamics. You will notice that the ice in your water glasses has nearly melted. The ice energy was transferred to heat the plates. Hot and cold are just two sides of the same energy coin, quite simple really."

*Simple, my left foot,* thought Edward. He was mystified; how did that happen right before his eyes? He had studied the law of conservation of energy in physics at school. This apparent energy exchange happened in real time as fast as the napkins were lifted. It had to be a well-planned trick.

*But why trick us?* Edward thought. *Unless he's a con man and was going to dupe whoever sits with him. He's after something; I'll play along until I figure out his deal.*

As he ate, Edward decided to pursue a line of investigative questioning. *He must have arranged in advance somehow to pull that heat trick off. Let's see what this guy can do when I set up the challenge.*

Edward began to consider the various traps he could lay for Mr. Vampire. While he was plotting his attack, his mom and M were locked in a serious conversation about theatre plays.

"How good do you think the ancient Greek plays were compared to modern plays?" Virginia asked. "When we performed classic Greek tragedies in college, such as Oedipus Rex, the same play got interpreted in totally different ways depending on our director."

M gave an understanding nod, "What we miss today," he said, "in understanding the intended messages of those old plays, was what real life was like for the common man and woman back then. We think we can understand them based on academic research, but we cannot. Time erases far too much.

"For example, we think we understand the reasons behind building the pyramids and the Sphinx, but our best scholars are simply wrong. We view the Sphinx as a temple but that's not at all why it was constructed."

M's perspectives mesmerized Virginia. She felt she was back in one of her advanced college philosophy classes discussing the meaning of life. "That's an interesting way to view history," she said. "It's like saying we don't know what we don't know but I guess that's always true," and she laughed. "It almost sounds like you were there and really saw what the builders of the Sphinx and pyramids intended."

M nodded at her conclusion and said, "You are close to the truth. Our ideas and judgements of history are a mix of facts with a large dose of academic opinion, exaggeration, wishful thinking, and cultural bias. Police will tell you that two capable observers will describe a shared event in quite different ways."

Then he laughed, "By the way, how in the world could I ever have been there with the Sphinx? I don't have any gray hair and that is an observable fact. But I will tell you that I have it from a very good authority that the Sphinx was actually built in one night as a fortress to hide in."

Virginia laughed back, "Sure it was. A giant Egyptian boy built it using Legos. Now I know you're pulling my leg."

"Maybe," was M's reply.

The wine was continuing to work its magic and Edward decided on a challenge for the hosting vampire. He said, "Let's get dessert, and after maybe you can show some more thermodynamic tricks."

"That sounds like a solid plan, Edward, dessert first, then a little abracadabra."

"For dessert," said M, "may I suggest a little something special that's not on the menu?"

Virginia immediately nodded, "After that spectacular wine I'm game for whatever you suggest."

Edward was slower to agree because he had the hot fudge sundae in his mind. "Sure," he said, with a tone that implied, "Don't mess up my dessert."

M motioned for the waiter to come to the table. He whispered in the waiter's ear. The waiter's reaction implied surprise but then he nodded in agreement.

About five minutes later the waiter returned with a silver tray. On the tray were three deep china bowls, each with a generous serving of ice cream. There was also a large china pitcher filled with a dark sauce. "Another hidden compartment, you know this train better than I do, sir."

M took the waiter's compliment with a smile, then said, "Virginia, Edward, I think you'll like the ice cream. It is a blend of a special vanilla recipe mixed with ripe cherries. The topping should satisfy any chocolate craving. Trust me, it's better than the train's hot fudge."

Edward immediately took the pitcher and poured a Mississippi river of the hot chocolate onto the ice cream. Virginia poured a dainty stream on her ice cream. M looked at Edwards's river, said, "I like your style, Huckleberry," and then poured his own Mississippi.

Each of them took a spoonful. Both Virginia and Edward had stunned looks on their faces. "This is beyond delicious," said Edward, "I know my Godiva chocolates and hot fudges, and this is way beyond anything I've ever tasted."

Virginia looked at M, "How exactly did you get this on the train? Amtrak could never have produced this. I don't think Godiva has anything close to matching this sauce. This ice cream and the cherries are beyond description. The cream content must be forty percent butterfat or more. The cherries taste like they just came off the tree. Any gourmet magazine would kill for the recipe."

M had a Cheshire cat grin, "I'm so happy you are enjoying this dessert, Virginia, I agree it is quite remarkable. From my previous travels, I knew there was a hidden cache at the bottom of the freezer for both the ice cream and the cherries. We benefit tonight from the high culinary standards set by past VIP rail travelers."

The three of them settled into their desserts. Edward was serious as he leaned over his deep bowl. He repeatedly ate in small bites. Normally, he ate ice cream in big spoonfuls; now he took much smaller bites and savored each one. His mother had often told him to slow down on his mouthfuls, but this was the first time it made sense. He definitely did not want to rush through this dessert.

# 17
# Table Abracadabra

M had finished his bowl and sat with a very satisfied look on his face. "I feel quite fulfilled," he exclaimed. "Great food and great company, what more can a person ask for?

"Would this be a good time for a little close-up magic, Edward? Can I attempt to fool you and Virginia as I would Penn and Teller?" Edward immediately nodded and thought, *Fool away, Mr. Vampire, I'm ready.*

"Edward, I'm short of energy transference tricks, but I know you appreciate card tricks. Would a few of those tricks meet with your approval?"

"Bring it on and magic me, M," he said with a challenging grin. "But I'll warn you, I have been performing sleight of hand tricks since I was nine years old."

Virginia affirmed, "Yes, he is quite good, M, and not a bit modest about his skills. I'd love to see you fool him."

"The gauntlet is thrown and accepted," answered M. In fact, he looked extremely pleased at Edward's warning. "Thank you for your professional honesty, Edward.

Forewarned is, as they say, forearmed. I love playing to a capable critic; it brings out the best in me."

Edward felt compelled to ask, "If you're so good, did you ever think of challenging the Amazing Randi? You could win a million dollars if you convince him you have powers he cannot explain."

"Indeed, I did consider taking him up on his challenge, he has a bit too much hubris. However, I decided against it. Randi was getting up in years. I would not want to take his money nor unsettle his fixed views of the universe."

Virginia nodded her approval at M's answer; *He is such a classy young man to be that considerate of an older person. I hope Edward understood his answer as his just being concern for Randi and not being afraid to challenge him.*

Edward thought, *That's a definite, I cannot fool Randi, so I'll hide behind caring for him. That caring answer is a big smokescreen that Mom doesn't see through.*

"So, my question still stands, M. If Randi's physical health or his mental health or his economic health were not considerations, would you accept his challenge?"

"Edward, why don't you decide that for yourself? You know a magician's actions speak much louder than his words. Let's get started with a bit of table abracadabra.

"Edward, please remove the deck of playing cards from your jacket's upper right inside pocket." Edward was startled. He knew what was in his jacket since he had checked it twice before leaving the room. He knew he was not carrying a deck of cards in any pocket.

M smiled and repeated, "Try the upper right inside pocket." Edward put his left hand up to the pocket and felt an object in there. He reached down into the pocket and, sure enough, there was a card deck.

"Well done, M," Edward graciously acknowledged, while he thought, *OK, round one to the con man. He did a clever misdirection over dinner and stuck them in while we were eating. Maybe he's a pickpocket in addition to being a con man and a vampire.*

Virginia gave a small clap to show how impressed she was by this simple trick. "I never saw you do that M. Very clever, I'll hold tight to my purse," she said grinning. M acknowledged her compliment with a slight nod.

"Edward, please give the deck to your mom. Virginia, would you please examine the deck and confirm it's properly sealed from the factory." Virginia took the deck from Edward and examined it.

"All sealed up," she confirmed.

"Please open it up now." Virginia used a fingernail to split the cellophane.

M looked at Edward and said, "Women carry a built-in tool kit. Their nails are like a Swiss army knife, they can solve a lot of problems." Edward grinned back at M and Virginia acknowledged this fact with a sweet smile.

"Now, Virginia, will you please inspect the deck? Look for any funny business." Virginia proceeded to look at the open deck by keeping it in her left hand. She slid the cards over one at a time to inspect them; it was a slow process.

"Mom, let a pro do that inspection," said Edward. He politely took the deck from his mom. Edward wanted to inspect the deck but also to show Mr. M some of his own skills.

Edward fanned the deck across the table. He took the end card and made the spread deck stand up. He then generated a wave across the standing cards. As he moved the wave, he quickly saw each individual card. If there were hidden patterns, they would appear using the fan technique. He also looked for classic card gimmicks such as very small notches on edges.

"What's your expert opinion?" asked M.

"It appears to be a normal deck of cards," said Edward. "Do you want me to shuffle them?"

"Of course, but before you shuffle please remove the two jokers and return them to the empty box. Shut the box after the jokers are back inside and give the box back to your mom for safekeeping.

"Virginia, after Edward gives you the box, please tuck it into your purse and hold onto it for dear life. There may be pickpockets around us." He gave Edward a sly look as he said "pickpockets."

Edward quickly removed the two jokers from the deck and put them back into the box. While doing that he rubbed the inside of the box to ensure there were no fake walls in which to hide cards. He sealed the box and handed it to his mother.

Virginia took the deck, shook it to hear the cards inside, then put the box into her purse and snapped it shut. "Totally secure," she announced.

Edward proceeded with a few elegant shuffles. He did a reverse ruffle with each shuffle. Then he put the deck in his right hand and did a series of fast, one-handed cuts and shuffles. Finally, he took the shuffled deck, bent it slightly and propelled the cards through the air from his right hand to his left.

"Does that seem like enough shuffling?" asked Edward with a smirking challenge in his voice. The challenge was a warning; do not treat me like a rube on card tricks.

This time Virginia gave her son a few claps. M smiled and said, "Indeed, those were superb shuffles. Your hand control is excellent. Penn and Teller could not improve on it."

"The next two tricks will involve some mind reading. Virginia, please pick a card from the deck. As we magicians always say, 'Any card will do.' Now concentrate on the card without letting me see it."

M put his hands over his eyes, paused and said, "It's the king of hearts." Virginia put down the king and immediately clapped.

Edward knew how to do this trick. There was a mark on the card's face that M had seen in the brief time it took for his mom to hold the card in her hand. This trick requires very fast recognition on the part of the magician, but that's how it works.

Edward also knew that "hands over the eyes" are a pure fraud. Magicians learn how to place their fingers to give them vision while appearing to be blindfolded.

"Mind if I take a shot at your telepathy?" said Edward.

"Of course not, I would expect nothing less from you or from Randi if he were here."

Edward paused for a brief moment as he studied M's face. *Is that a look of confidence or smugness? Either way I'll wipe that look away.*

"I'm going to change the rules just a tad," said Edward. "If you don't mind I will put the deck behind my back, pick my card then keep the deck behind my back. Is that OK with you?"

M nodded, "Your hands, your deck, your rules."

Edward picked up the deck and did several fast one-hand shuffles. He covered the deck in his right hand and put it behind his back. He pulled a card from the middle of the deck and kept it completely covered by his left hand.

He kept the deck behind his back, brought the left-hand card to his eye for a covered peek then moved his left hand back behind him. He slid the card back into the deck.

"OK, Mr. Magic, I have the card in my mind's eye," said Edward.

"Well done Edward. Indeed, you are a pro at this card game business. You know how to keep the magician honest."

"Well, let's have your answer," said Edward. "You have one chance in fifty-two." Mimicking the movie legend detective Dirty Harry, Edward grinned at M and added "Are you feeling lucky?"

"Actually, luck has nothing to do with it," said M. "It's the three of diamonds."

Edward was stunned, that was his card and that was impossible. "Once more?" he asked.

"Of course."

Edward knew he now saw a definite smirk. Edward repeated his shuffle and the eye peek, but he surreptitiously slid the card into his lower left side suit pocket rather than back into the deck. He put the deck on the table.

"Go fish! Please find my card in the deck."

"Two questions I see. Find both the card's location as well as the card's identity. Fortunately, I was always lucky at fishing. It's the five of clubs and it's in your right-hand pocket."

*Wow! This guy is over-the-top good. How did he know it's in my pocket?* Then he said, "Not bad M, but only half right."

"Humor me please and check."

Edward stood up and reached into his left pocket. It was empty. Both his mom and M were grinning at him. He reached into his right-hand pocket and found the card. *That's impossible*, he immediately thought. "Bravo, M," was all he could say as he sat down.

M was now in complete control of the show and clearly enjoying himself. "Edward, please put the card back into the deck and give one of your impressive shuffles. Keep the deck in your hand." Edward did as requested.

"Edward, you know how sneaky cards can be, you know how they like to move around. Would you please put the deck back down on the table, fan the deck and find the five of clubs?"

Edward spread the deck and fanned it. Both he and Virginia looked for the card. Neither could find it. "I know I put it back in," said Edward. Virginia's head was nodding; she had seen it go back into the deck.

"Missing in action, is it?" said M. "You know cards always want to return to their home. In this case, home is the original package they came in. Virginia, would you please check the home container?"

Virginia reached into her purse and opened it. She removed the closed card case, opened the lid and shook it upside down. A single card came out, the five of clubs. Virginia froze. Her face had a blank look on it. "No way," said Edward. "That is absolutely impossible."

"Excuse me, Mom," Edward said as he took the card case and reached inside. It was empty. "Where are the jokers?" he asked.

"Well, my best guess is that since they are jokers, and jokers are unpredictable, they returned to their starting location."

Edward considered this and asked, "Where is the starting location if not in the case?" A possible answer suddenly came to him. He hesitated and said, "I don't believe this will happen." He again reached into his top right-hand suit coat pocket. He put his left hand down into it and pulled out the two jokers.

Edward stared at M. "I have seen, but I do not believe. I think Randi was very lucky he never accepted a challenge from you. You would have blown his mind as well as his bank account!"

"Indeed, but as I previously said, I did not want that responsibility on my conscience. In life you need to consider whether your gain is worth the other's loss."

Virginia had recovered and was quietly clapping and laughing. "That was simply wonderful, M. I have to tell my scientific husband this story. He won't believe it, but he will have his wife and son vouching for what happened."

"It has been my experience in life," said M, "that the scientific mind resists any event that does not fit its model of the universe. I endorse science, but I also believe we need to consider the universe as a wonder not to be stuffed into mathematical models."

M continued, "One of my favorite science stories is how Einstein argued against quantum happenings. 'Spooky action at a distance,' he called them. Einstein could not accept the weirdness that happens at the subatomic level. He famously said, 'God does not play dice with the universe.'

"Niels Bohr's rejoinder to Einstein's skepticism was, 'Einstein, stop telling God what to do.'"

With this exit line, M stood up, bowed to Virginia, and shook Edward's hand. "I expect our paths will cross again. I have a magic shop in Chicago, Edward; you may want to stop by if you find yourself with some free time. Coincidently, it's a comfortable walking distance from the Drake Hotel."

For a moment Edward thought, *how does he know we're at the Drake?* Then he realized his mother must have mentioned it before he joined them.

"That sounds like a solid plan. How can I find your shop, is it in the phone directory?"

"No, I choose not to advertise, it's by invitation only. Here's my card with the address." Edward glanced at the card then put it into his suit coat pocket. "Virginia, if Edward does find the time to drop by he will find a very interesting shop to browse in, trust me."

"I absolutely do trust you, M," replied Virginia. "Thank you for a wonderful evening."

Virginia and Eddie rose and followed M toward their respective cars. When Virginia and Eddie reached their room, M waved and continued ahead. "I didn't know there were more compartments behind our car. I hope he has a suitable place to spend the evening."

"Don't worry about him, Mom. He can take care of himself."

"I was going to have a nightcap in the bar car," mused Virginia, "but I think what I need now is a good night's sleep. You need a good night's sleep also, Eddie. Tomorrow's a big day. We have to be up for a seven-thirty breakfast and we arrive in Union Station at ten."

When they got back into their room, they found the porter had made up both beds with fresh sheets and multiple pillows. Edward gave his mom first use of the throne room while he put on his PJs.

Once he was in his nightwear, he did a monkey-swing up to his loft bed. "Monkeys don't need ladders, Mom." Virginia admired the easy way he swung himself up. Comfortably in place, he stretched out, relaxed, and let his mind do its own walkabout.

He naturally started with M's magic show. *He is beyond anything I have ever seen. If I was not right there, I would never believe it. I really wish Dad could have been there. Maybe with all his science background he would have figured it out.*

M's show triggered a memory back in time to magic in his bedroom. He was five again and it was Christmas Eve. He was in bed holding his leather book when he saw the shadow cross the clouds and heard the black rope slap against the windowpane.

*It would certainly be fascinating if magic actually existed,* he thought. *Of course, the obvious question is, "Would it be good or bad, and who would get to use it?"* That question was his last thought before his mind closed down for the night.

# 18
# Hello Chicago

Edward awoke with a start. The gentle swaying of the car overnight demanded he make a fast trip to the throne room. He carefully came down the ladder to avoid stepping on Mom. To his surprise, Mom was gone.

He found a note taped to the mirror in the bathroom with a smiley face. "Woke up early and feeling great. Join me for breakfast. Love, Mom."

Edward looked out the window and saw a bright clear day with lots of snow. He quickly dressed. He put on his walk around clothes and shoes. In a matter of minutes, he was out of the compartment and moving down the aisle toward the dining car. He passed through the club car and noted there was no sign of the festivities from the prior night. Nobody was sleeping under the piano.

When he opened the dining car door, he spotted his mother. She was sitting alone by a window with a book and coffee. Edward could not tell if he was disappointed or relieved that M was not there. He plunked himself down across from his mom.

"Just you and me today, Mom, guess it will be an M-free breakfast. Don't feel too let down, I have magic of my own; watch me make French toast disappear."

Virginia grinned, "Last night was certainly special, but I feel beyond special coming back to my old stomping ground. The waiter said we'll be there in about an hour and a half so there's still plenty of time to enjoy the French toast and bacon and the view coming into my city."

Edward settled into his breakfast and watched the approaching Chicago skyline. Giant skyscrapers appeared as dots on the horizon. Then they rose from the flat midwest earth to declare the "second city" was second to none.

Despite the heavy snow, the waiter was correct, and the train arrived on time. Edward manhandled the suitcases down from their storage loft. He carried one in each hand through the train's narrow corridor.

When they reached the waiting area by the exit door, he set them down and felt his muscles were pumping up. While standing beside the bags he continued to use them as a set of barbells and got in some early morning exercise.

Virginia watched her son with a smile on her face. She began to hum the *Rocky* theme song "…Getting Strong Now." Edward was oblivious to his mom's humor. *If Mr. Magic used drugs on us last night they have sure pumped me up. I feel terrific. Look out Chicago, there's a new kid in town.*

Other passengers arrived with bags and soon the exiting area was packed. The conductor entered, stood in front of door and announced, "Next stop, Chicago!"

In the close quarters Virginia noticed how the conductor used his body to subtly calm down the crowd waiting to exit.

People were instinctively pushing toward a locked door. *We are such herd animals, and dangerous in crowded places,* she thought.

With a hiss, a snort, and a jerk the train slowed and stopped. The beast settled into its berth. The conductor opened the door, went out, and put down the one-step stool.

He kept crowd control as he helped passengers down one at a time. Edward and Virginia were first off. The conductor took their cases and handed them out to Edward. As Virginia stepped out, she smiled at the conductor and thanked him.

Edward took the two big cases and they headed for the station's main room. "We need to move fast," said Virginia. "With all the snow we want to grab a cab before they all get taken." Edward squared his shoulders and lengthened his stride.

When they entered the main room, Edward recognized much of what he had read about. He knew that Union Station was constructed in 1925 at great expense. It was even more impressive than the pictures. The ceiling was a work of art. Its barrel shaped convex curve with inlaid geometric patterns was stunning.

The main floor presented a wide variety of shops offering books, magazines, souvenirs, and sundries. There were numerous coffee and pastry shops as well as a range of restaurants. People of every ethnic background hurried along. The effect felt like being in a Middle Eastern bazaar, everything was there except the camels.

They paused in front of two statues resting along a top balcony. There was the goddess Night. She held a wise-looking owl in her hand. Beside her was the goddess Day. Day was holding a rooster who looked ready to greet the morning sun. The statues were from the railroad's glory years. They were gods looking down on the scuttling human ants.

"This feels a lot like being in a cathedral," Edward said to his mom as he pointed out Night and Day. As Virginia studied the two goddesses she simply said, "You're right, Eddie, it does feel like a grand cathedral, or an ancient Greek temple. It's humbling."

Once outside the terminal they hurried to the cab line. Due to Edward's fast pace there were plenty of waiting cabs and they went to the head of the line. Edward hoisted their bags into the oversized yellow cab trunk and they headed for the Drake Hotel.

Edward was fascinated as they moved from the train station through traffic to Michigan Avenue. Skyscrapers of varying heights and styles created corridors for cars and people to move. Sitting in the cab looking out Edward had a sense of driving at the bottom of a manmade steel-and-glass Grand Canyon.

Michigan Avenue announced that the Christmas season was in full swing. Street lamps were decorated with pine wreaths, red bows with ribbons, and oversized silver tinsel bells.

Many street corners had a jolly Santa with a donation kettle beside him. The Santas were vigorously ringing their hand bells both to keep warm and to catch a passerby's donation. The ringing bells added to the street's festive decorations and encouraged people to enjoy the season.

It was holiday information overload. Edward stopped trying to focus on individual impressions and just let the city roll over him. It was an exciting kaleidoscope of ever-changing sights, sounds, colors, and movement. He had found a big city and it was big. Very big.

# 19
# Hello Drake

The cabbie slowed and stopped in front of the Drake Hotel. A formally dressed doorman appeared wearing a stovepipe top hat. He was instantly at Virginia's door, "Season's Greetings and welcome to the Drake. I'll take your bags."

Edward realized his pack mule duties were over, *I can live with this.*

As they came through the revolving door into the lobby, a full-on Christmas scene greeted them. A large Douglas fir tree dominated one corner. The tree rose over eighteen feet and was festooned with a variety of ornaments. The tree's lights reflected on the ornaments and the tree boldly shimmered even in daytime.

Around the tree, a steam locomotive pulled a variety of passenger cars. Several children and parents were watching the train maneuver through the challenges presented by stacked presents close to the tracks. One present stack formed a long tunnel and the engine sent out a warning call as it went in and out of the tunnel.

There were small villages settled around the tracks and packages. Various action displays were activated as the train passed by. Flagmen raised small lanterns, signalmen raised their hand signs, and crossing-gates raised and lowered. As Edward studied the scene, he kept finding new enchantments hidden among the tree's boughs, tunnels, and small villages.

Virginia proceeded directly to the reservation counter and handed the confirmation slip to a smiling clerk. "Welcome to the Drake," the clerk said and seemed to actually mean it. The clerk confirmed the reservation and commented. "A very nice suite of rooms, I think you will be very pleased."

The clerk motioned to a nearby bellman. "Room 718 please," and handed him a key. The bellman had a cart ready and began to stack the cases on it.

Virginia noticed that Edward was again a five-year-old captivated by the train setup. *How sweet,* she thought. "Eddie, we can go up to our room now. The bellman will bring our bags." Virginia and Edward headed to a bank of elevators. They entered an empty one and pressed floor seven.

As the elevator ascended, they looked around at the cozy compartment. The elevator's décor mirrored that of the lobby. It was lined with rich dark wood. A polished bronze railing wrapped around the three sides and reflected the light from the Erte-designed lamps. The lamps projected light and warmth to the space.

"Snappy lift," commented Edward, displaying his use of the British term "lift" for elevator. *Elegant,* Virginia thought.

There was a soft ping and the doors opened to the seventh floor. A sign in front of them directed them to go right down a wide corridor. Their room was at the end of the long aisle, a perfect location to minimize hallway sounds.

Edward sped ahead with the entry key card. He zipped the card down the slot beside their door and pushed down on the polished handle. He held the door for his mom to enter first. "Thank you, Eddie," Virginia said as she entered the main room.

They stood together in the entryway taking in the spacious living room. Picture windows presented the view of downtown Chicago in all its holiday glory. "Dad has nailed this," said Edward.

"Yes, he certainly has," agreed Virginia. She wished Daniel were with them.

Edward immediately found there were separate bedrooms, each with its own bathroom. "Which one is mine, Mom?" Edward asked.

"I'll take the one with the big bathtub dear. You take the one with the big shower."

"That works for me," replied Edward.

The doorbell rang, and Virginia opened the heavy door for the bellman. He placed the bags on a holding rack on one side of the entryway beside a large closet. Virginia thanked the bellman and tipped him. She walked to a large picture window and let her memories of the city wrap around her.

"I'm going to unpack later," said Edward. "I'm starting my walk around now if that's OK, Mom, or do you want me to stick around?"

Virginia laughed, "Please head out. I'll be Brer Rabbit and just hide out here in my luxurious briar patch. Please be alert to traffic, honey. The streets are slippery, and many drivers are already enjoying their spiked eggnog.

"What's first on your tour? I bet it's the museum, right?"

Edward was already at the door, "Yep, I'm heading for the museum. I expect I'll spend most of the day there. What time do you want me back for dinner?"

"Let's say around six. Let's keep tonight simple, room service and a movie. How does that sound?"

"Sounds like a great plan, Mom. Let's toss a coin to see who picks the movie."

"No zombies please, how about a nice Hallmark Christmas movie?" Edward nodded affirmative.

Virginia called after him, "Wear your earmuffs, dear." Edward gave the usual nod, "Sure, Mom."

# 20
# The Museum

Edward was quickly in the lobby. He took another look at the steam engine as it tooted and traveled. *Time for me to get moving also.* Outside the wind hit him hard in the face. *Welcome to Mom's Windy City,* he thought as he lowered his head into the wind.

The walk to the museum was bitter cold and longer than he had thought. Halfway there, he slipped the muffs out of his pocket and put them on. *You're right again, Mom. I sure don't want an earache on day one.*

He continued until he saw the wide museum steps. He strode up the steps and noted they were swept clear and salted. *Smart,* he thought. *Avoid injuries and expensive lawsuits.*

He recalled his dad's dinner table comment, "No matter who's at fault, the lawyers always win." As a doctor and business owner, his dad had a lot of experience with lawyers.

Upon reaching the top of the stairs, he quickly took off the muffs. *Don't want to look like some loser geek.* He pushed on one of the rotating entry doors. The door did its job, rotated and ushered him into the welcoming main hall. Standing inside the museum lobby, he noted he was surrounded by a wide variety of display stands; each display promised an exotic exhibition.

Edward proceeded to the ticket counter where he found himself at the back of a seventh-grade class. *Was I ever that that loud?* he thought. "Louder!" his seventh-grade teachers would have answered.

With ticket in hand, he proceeded to the largest display stand. This display presented visitors with the museum's newest exhibit. The featured exhibit was an ancient stone arch, supported by its original twin columns. An artist rendering presented what the exhibit would look like with a temple behind the original portal.

The display showed visitors passing under this ancient arch and entering a reconstructed temple. The display pointed out that the exhibit's temple was a replica of what the original temple might have looked like. The original temple was lost in history.

The narrative below the rendering explained that the portal was on long-term loan from a major museum in Syria. It stated that while archeologists were still dating the portal, it seemed likely that it predated the earliest Egyptian structures, including the pyramids.

Attached at the bottom of the display stand was an open container of pamphlets. The pamphlets presented a short history of archeological finds over the last hundred and fifty years. This relatively recent period of discovery was a golden era for archeology; the arch was another major discovery.

Edward took out a pamphlet and walked to a quiet alcove area close to the wide staircase that led up to the exhibit. The pamphlet was in two parts and Edward settled in to read both parts.

# 21
# A Portal Through Time
# Dr. James Smith, Curator
# Part 1: The History Behind the Science of Archeology

Ironically, archeology, the history of the distant past, only joined the major sciences fairly recently. Its emergence was partially a consequence of a major war in Europe. The Franco-Prussian war took place between a coalition of Germanic states and France between 1870 and 1871.

Prior to the war, there were twenty-six independent Germanic states. Each state resembled a small country with its own ruler. Some states, such as Prussia in the north, had powerful armies and a long tradition of warfare. Other states such as Bavaria in the south were relatively peaceful with pride in their beers. To fight the French, the separate German states combined their forces.

The German commander over the collective armies was Baron von Bismarck. Bismarck was a visionary for a united

Germany and used his power base of Prussia to create a united coalition.

Bismarck cajoled, pleaded, and threatened any hesitant German state to join the military coalition to defeat the French. His argument to reluctant states was something like, "You can join your fellow Germans and fight the French, or you can fight Prussia and its allies after we defeat the French." Bismarck made an offer that none of the Germanic states could refuse.

When the war was successfully concluded, Bismarck kept the coalition together and converted the states into a single country. We know this country today simply as Germany. The leader of the newly created nation of Germany was called a kaiser. Each kaiser was an emperor who had control over all twenty-six of the member states.

Bismarck's unification of the separate Germanic states was similar to the result of the US Civil War when the northern states ultimately prevailed over the southern states in 1865. Subsequently, the power of the individual states was subordinated to the power of the national government.

Many northern states were surprised to find that they had lost a great deal of their own independence. For citizens and political leaders in many northern states, this was not the outcome they had expected or wanted.

With the creation of the newly formed nation of Germany, there was an explosion of German patriotism and national energy. The new German nation strutted like a giant on both the European stage and the global stage. With its newfound power, Germany was intent on establishing itself as the most scientifically advanced country in the world.

One area of scientific leadership they moved into was the emerging new science called archeology. German archeologists were not just academics studying relics in dusty university labs or lecturing in classrooms, they were explorers. They were a gang of German Indiana Joneses looking for fabled lost artifacts.

As explorers, they pursued legends of history. They sought physical evidence to validate ancient stories. They had startling success. In 1870, a German archeologist named Heinrich Schliemann discovered the remains of the legendary city of Troy. This was the same Troy written about by Homer in his epic story, *The Iliad*.

Several years later in 1876 Schliemann again struck historic gold, literally gold. His next major discovery was a gold death mask.

When famous kings died in these early times, it was common to create their physical likeness from a mask of their face. While their faces were also put on coins, the death mask was much more detailed. For the very rich, the death mask would be made from a precious, malleable metal, notably gold.

Based on the intact golden mask, Schliemann determined it belonged to King Agamemnon. Agamemnon had declared war on Troy after Paris, a Prince of Troy, kidnapped Helen, the wife of Agamemnon's brother. As the expression goes, "Helen was the face that launched a thousand ships."

Schliemann concluded that the bearded death mask was of Agamemnon's face. His logic was based on the fact that there were only six people of sufficient Greek stature who would deserve such a death mask. Since the mask presented a man with a beard and since Agamemnon was the only one of the six with a beard, Schliemann concluded the gold mask was of Agamemnon's face.

The world was stunned. It now knew Troy had existed and that King Agamemnon was a real man and further what he looked like.

With the discovery of a real Troy and the golden mask, there was an outpouring of public excitement over archeology. Money followed the public's excitement and modern archeology was born.

Archeological efforts and funding continued until they were again interrupted by another major war. This was the First World War. Nations put their resources into the military conflict. Science progressed mainly by advancing the tools of war. Following the end of the war in 1918, archeologists again put on their hats, gloves, and boots and began to explore.

One region that benefited from this exploration was the Land of the Pharaohs. Egypt with its pyramids, the Sphinx, and the gigantic statues in the Valley of the Kings had long held the public's interest.

It was a mysterious land, long associated with gods and ancient mysteries. If there was an ancient afterlife, it had to be known by the Egyptian priests. The Egyptian *Book of the Dead* gave instructions for the rituals, chants, and offerings that would direct souls into the afterlife.

The ancient Egyptian world burst into the modern world in 1922. The British archeologist, Howard Carter, found an undisturbed, intact tomb of the young pharaoh Tutankhamun. The tomb dated to 1323 BC.

As Carter peered into the open tomb his associate Lord Carnarvon asked him whether he could see anything. Carter is famously quoted as saying, "Yes, wonderful things!" All the world now knows the contents were indeed magnificent.

The highlight of the tomb was a gold death mask of the young pharaoh. This mask, just like the mask of Agamemnon, brought the pharaoh to life as a real person. The artifacts in Tutankhamun's tomb still travel the world and excite modern people.

Schliemann and Carter brought the lives, times, and events of ancient people to the modern world. Their discoveries put actual faces on kings and pharaohs who lived over three thousand years ago.

# Part 2: Discovery of the Portal

Our museum is proud to have one of the earliest of these ancient artifacts. The portal is the entrance to an ancient temple. We have not yet determined its age, but believe it predates the earliest of the Sumerian and Egyptian structures.

The portal was discovered in 1917 toward the end of the First World War in a remote region of Syria. German infantry stumbled upon it as they advanced through the desert and mountainous terrain.

As the soldiers advanced, a German sergeant observed a carved rock sticking out of the sand. Fortunately, he recognized that its shape was manmade.

The sergeant reported the find to the major in charge of his unit. Once more, we were fortunate that the major had an interest in the new science of archeology. The major examined the protruding stone and recognized it as a relic from the distant past. As he made an initial clearing of the surrounding sand, he confirmed it was a keystone for an arch.

As his men began carefully removing the sand of thousands of years, the keystone was found to be part of a wide arch. The full arch was intact under the sand. The major concluded that the sand had protected the portal from the elements for thousands of years.

The major observed elaborate carvings on the arch and down the sides of each pillar. He drew copies of a few of the symbols. He thought they could be Sanskrit or hieroglyphs and would excite linguists as well as antiquity historians.

On a personal note, the major kept a detailed diary of the discovery. He knew that he had made an important discovery. He commented on the similarity of his discovery with the Rosetta Stone discovery, probably the single most important discovery in archeology.

The major reflected on how the Rosetta Stone, discovered in 1799 by a French captain during France's invasion of Egypt, led to the deciphering of hieroglyphics. Prior to the stone's discovery people no longer knew how to read hieroglyphs. Three thousand years of Egyptian knowledge was lost.

The stone provided a physical written language bridge. It gave a message in Greek and Egyptian as well as in hieroglyphics. Even with the two known languages it took two brilliant linguists, Thomas Young an Englishman and Champollion a Frenchman, to figure out the meaning of hieroglyphs. Champollion completed the translation by 1824 and founded the science of Egyptology.

The major was well aware of these facts. We know from his diary that he hoped for personal recognition for the find. He comments in his diary, "Life is short, but 'name fame' is lasting."

At the same time, he was a practical man. He cynically wrote, "No way will a low-grade army officer be credited with this discovery. Credit will go to a high-ranking army general or an expert like Schliemann." We can hear him accept being forgotten as he writes, "But I have contributed to my country and I'm proud of that."

His cynicism was misplaced. When his report was received at the German Central Command for the Middle East, the senior staff immediately knew the major had made an important discovery and rewarded his initiative. The major was promoted to colonel and his name was associated with the discovery. He had secured his name's place in archeology.

At the same time, there was no recognition given to the sergeant who had initially spotted the keystone. As the old military adage goes, "Rank has its privileges."

Please proceed to our Exhibit Room.

# 22
# Passing Through Egypt

"Onward and upward to ancient Egypt," Edward declared aloud. He left the alcove and chose to take the adjacent staircase rather than the elevators. *Real men climb, they don't ride,* he thought as he ascended. As he climbed, he enjoyed feeling the power in his legs. *I'm one strong guy,* he thought.

When he hit the top floor, he found real men also get out of breath. He paused then turned right and followed the signs for the portal exhibit. The broad aisle led first into a room filled with displays of artifacts from a time before the pharaohs. During this earliest time, Egypt was a sparsely populated land occupied by nomadic herders.

The herders built simple tent villages along the vast Nile River. Since they could never predict when the waters would rise, they had all their possessions ready for a fast retreat to higher ground.

Across the top wall of the exhibit room was a long mural depicting early life beside the Nile. The mural presented women at cooking fires and children chasing small animals in playful activity. On the river, men stood upright in reed boats fishing with long spears.

Edward paused to study the details of the mural. He quickly spotted the evil eyes and long snouts of sly crocodiles; the reed boat hunters were also being hunted.

Away from the men and the crocs, a large mother hippo was paddling along with a baby at her side. It was clear that neither the boatmen hunters nor the sly, hunting crocs would offer any challenge to the behemoth hippo mother.

Edward slowly walked past the displays of pottery, jewelry, and carvings. Most visitors ignored the displays of small objects and headed for the big stuff in the Egyptian exhibit. Edward, however, enjoyed examining the small objects that brought real day-to-day life into focus.

Of particular interest to him were small carvings of various gods. Some of the carvings were very detailed. One glass display case contained two elaborate figures, confronting each other in a mock battle scene.

One carving made from black obsidian was a cat god with elongated ears and a whip-like tail. There were small jewels embedded in the obsidian head creating the cat's green eyes. The eyes sparkled and seemed to look out at both Edward and the enemy in front. The cat god was crouched in a posture to defend or attack; it was not clear which.

Confronting the cat god was a carving of a simian-like god. The figure was formed from red clay and then glazed. There were deliberately blurred features for this monkey-like god. The monkey god had various appendages that extended at strange angles and with differing lengths and thicknesses.

Either the artist was a poor molder, or the figure presented a god changing its shape, possibly to attack or defend.

*Well, I recognize good old Bast,* thought Edward, as he studied the cat god. *My favorite among all the Egyptian gods. I'm not sure who the evil red monkey god is, he almost looks like he's on fire. Mr. Fire Monkey had better not mess with Bast or he'll be monkey stew for lunch.*

Edward proceeded to the next series of rooms and was now in the time of the early pharaohs. On display were many objects of art including jewelry and carvings. The objects were a physical testament to the advanced skills of these early artisans.

Next were the ever-popular mummy cases. Some cases had their owners inside and available for inspection. The mummy cases were physical statements of Egyptian art as well as their belief in the afterlife. Inscribed hieroglyphs on the caskets were the best public relations the deceased could make to have his many virtues presented to the gods.

The gods, however, did not bother themselves with the self-declared worthiness of the deceased. The gods had many other duties, so they relied on one god to be judge, jury, and gatekeeper to the afterlife. That god was Anubis.

Resting in the center of the room was a giant statue of Anubis, god of the dead. The marble statue stood nearly fifteen feet high and was a dominating presence. The ancient god stood on human legs with a human torso and the head of a jackal. The head was carved from black marble; the color black was associated with the dead. The eyes appeared as red rubies and spoke to a final judgment.

Edward read the text below Anubis, which declared that jackals were associated with the god since they were frequent visitors to Egyptian cemeteries, and Anubis was the god who looked over the dead.

Anubis held a golden scale in one hand. The scale measures the worthiness of the deceased. On one pan of the scale was a feather. On the other pan was the deceased's heart with its weight of a lifetime of deeds, good and bad. If the feather pan went down, the deceased was worthy and passed on. If the feather pan rose, the deceased was an immediate Scooby snack. There was no jury trial with Anubis. No clever lawyers could try to reinterpret the facts and ask for a retrial.

Anubis had responsibilities similar to the Norse god, Heimdall. Heimdall was the gatekeeper to Asgard, home of the Norse gods and appeared as a giant man. Both gods were ultimate judges and neither put up with lies or unwelcome intruders.

Once Edward was finished in the mummy room, he headed for his ultimate destination, the recently arrived ancient portal.

*It's interesting,* Edward reflected, *that the portal's age was still being studied. The poster on the first level declared that the portal was being carbon-dated, but so far had not yielded its age to science.*

# 23
# A Locked Door

An overhead red arrow directed visitors to the exhibit's entrance door. Edward followed the arrow and arrived at the display room door. It was shut and locked. A sign announced, "Exhibit is temporarily closed due to exhibit changes."

Edward felt a surge of disappointment, which quickly morphed into anger. *Unbelievable! This is false advertising. I paid to see this display.* Another surge of adrenaline hit him, and he felt justified in getting inside anyway he could.

Without further thought, he hit the horizontal locking bar with his forearm. "Open Sesame," he declared. He slammed the bar a second and a third time. He put his body behind his hammer blows. On his third hit, he heard a snap inside the door's locking mechanism.

He had a satisfied reaction to snapping the annoying locking bar. *All any good explorer needs is a bigger hammer or a strong arm.* He pushed on the door and it easily swung open.

For a moment, he felt a tinge of guilt over breaking in, but then he rationalized his behavior. *If they had explained this in the lobby display, I would have been disappointed, but would not have gotten angry.* He quickly put any guilt behind him. A more mature Edward would later understand how people delude themselves to get what they want or to justify their bad actions.

He cautiously looked inside for museum staff, and confirmed the room was empty. A bonus, he thought, was that he could study the display without having annoying seventh graders distract him. He ducked into the room and pulled the door shut behind him. From the hallway, the exhibit appeared closed to visitors.

Safely inside, he examined his personal exhibit room; he found it to be grand. It was ballroom size with granite floors. A high domed ceiling rose over thirty feet above the floor. Built into the ceiling was an array of louvered windows that admitted natural light.

In the center of the room was a crane. *How did a crane get inside this room?* was his first reaction. He then thought of a ship inside a bottle. He realized that, just like the ship, it was assembled inside the room.

The top of the crane approached the top of the ceiling. The crane's apex stopped about five feet from the windows. *If the crane operator messes up, there's going to be a sea of window glass on the floor along with lots of Chicago ice and snow.*

The crane had steel bracing legs that extended fifteen feet out from each of its four corners. The legs braced the crane when it strained to lift heavy objects. Each of the legs ended with three-foot square steel plates that functioned as feet. The steel feet rested, in turn, on thick wooden planks to protect the granite floor.

As he studied the crane, Edward recalled from his physics class, Archimedes' famous statement in 225 BC about moving heavy objects, "Give me a lever long enough and a fulcrum on which to place it, and I shall move the world." *Sure,* thought Edward, *maybe the moon is your fulcrum, but where do you stand? On Mars?*

As Edward walked toward the crane, the portal emerged from behind the crane. It was magnificent. Its grandeur matched the elegance of the room. There were two columns about fifteen feet high.

An arch connected the columns. Edward saw that the arch was missing the critical keystone. For support, there were vertical steel posts supporting each of the unconnected ends of the arch.

Edward walked toward the arch and then saw the missing keystone lying on the floor. It was a massive stone block. Opposing sides slanted toward the bottom. The slanted sides of the keystone appeared to match the slanted sides of the ends of each arch.

Edward realized why the exhibit was not yet ready for public display. *Now I understand the need for a crane. The crane was necessary to get the vertical steel support beams in place. Now the crane can lift the keystone into its resting place and secure the arch. What an impressive feat of crane operator skill.*

Edward walked forward to go through the portal and examine the temple display behind it. Edward knew there was no original temple found with the arch; the display was the museum curator's best idea of what a temple from that time might have looked like.

He considered the possible demise of the original temple. *Maybe a rival tribe with a different deity had seized the original temple and used the building materials to construct their own temple. On the other hand, maybe the conqueror used the temple's material to build a personal palace.*

Edward knew that even the original white Tura facing stones of the great pyramids had been removed for other uses. *Even the ancients believed in recycling when it was convenient. I wonder what the shelf life of a god's temple was back then.*

Edward was starting to pass under the arch when he heard a commanding voice call out, "Please do not go there; it's not ready for visitors." The voice added, "If you had read the sign outside you would know that."

Edward turned to see a man studying him with an angry look on his face. The man was middle-aged, medium height, and lean with close-cropped hair. He stood ramrod straight and had a strong stride as he approached Edward. *He looks ex-military,* thought Edward, *I'm so busted.*

"What's your name?"

"Edward, sir."

"Edward, follow me. My office is down the hall." Edward felt like a ten-year-old being walked to the principal's office. He wisely decided to keep quiet and take his punishment.

The man stopped in front of an elegant wood door that led into his office. The door had an arched entry and reminded Edward of castle doors and more recently the door on the private train car. A sign beside the door declared the office belonged to the Dr. Smith, curator of the museum.

"I really like your door, it feels very Tudorish," Edward blurted out. The curator turned and studied Edward for a moment. "Actually, it is exactly that. The museum had an opportunity about eighty years ago to acquire Tudor period doors and this is one of them.

"Well, sir, you are in the antiquities business." He sensed he had said the right thing. The man nodded and motioned Edward into his office.

"Have a seat, Edward," the man said, pointing to a leather chair in front of his desk. "Before I call security, explain to me how you got in." Edward's mind was scrambling for possible answers.

A lot of facile lies came to his mind. *I found the door open, sir,* was his first thought. Who would know if his lie was true or not? Then he decided on the best answer, the honest one. This approach had proven itself on the train with M.

"I live in Charlottesville Virginia and read about the portal exhibit on the museum's web site. My mom and I just got here a few hours ago by train and I immediately came here. I was totally pumped up to see the exhibit.

"Once in the museum I picked up the pamphlet from the display sign and read it in the alcove by the staircase. After reading it, I was even more excited. I followed the red arrow to the exhibit. When I got to the entrance, I discovered it was locked. Yes, I did read the sign.

"I was disappointed, and then got angry. In my frustration I banged hard on the door to see if somebody inside would let me in. My frustration had me worked up and I hit down hard on the entry bar."

"How hard and how many times?" asked the curator.

"I know it was three times," answered Edward. "I hit three different places on the bar using my forearm and body leverage. The third hit on the right side was the one that opened it. When I heard the snap inside the door I realized I had broken the lock.

"At that point I knew I had to either leave or go inside, I decided to go in. Truthfully, I figured I would be in and out without being caught. I really wanted to see the portal and the temple behind it." The director remained silent and watched Edward, then he nodded that Edward should continue.

"Once inside, I was captivated by the room. The granite floors are a work of art. I looked up and saw the louvered ceiling windows; they're another work of art. Of course, I wondered how they were opened and cleaned that high up. I figured out they were opened by a panel on the wall, but I still wonder how they get cleaned.

"When I looked at the crane I thought about the skill the operator must have to not punch out the windows while placing the steel support beams. I also saw the crane is set up to place the keystone. I guess that's the holdup to open the exhibit."

The museum curator visibly relaxed as Edward talked. He was both surprised and pleased that Edward had actually read the pamphlet. The curator had written the pamphlet himself and knew that few visitors ever took the time to read about exhibits.

He was also impressed that Edward had noticed the room's elegance and had figured out how the windows operated. Most of all he appreciated Edward's comment on the crane operator's skills. Mike, the crane operator, was a top professional and the museum had to call in favors to get him.

"All right, Edward, I believe you are telling me how you got in. I appreciate your being truthful; it's a disappearing quality today." Edward stayed quiet. He sensed the curator was only going to give him a reprimand and would not call security.

"You understand my most important responsibility is for the safety of our visitors as well as our workers. The door was locked because we are almost ready to place the keystone into the arch; when we place that stone, things can get quite dangerous.

"The keystone, as well as the arch stones, is extremely heavy. While these stones appear solid as a rock, no pun intended, they may actually be very fragile. Over the years, internal cracks can develop, when they are stressed they can literally explode like a grenade. Do you understand the potential danger I'm talking about?"

Edward rapidly nodded his head, he did understand. The curator stood up and motioned toward the door, "I appreciate your interest in the display and I appreciate that you read the pamphlet. We have many school classes coming through. For most students, and sadly many teachers, the field day is just an outing away from classroom studies, few read the pamphlets."

The curator paused in the doorway a moment then asked, "Would you like to go back and complete your tour with me as your guide?"

Edward was stunned then broke into a big grin, "Yes, sir. I would love that."

"Well, follow me back. The good news is I don't need to find my key to get in." Edward gave the curator a sheepish smile.

# 24
# Cursed Portal

The two walked back to the exhibit hall. Once inside the exhibit room, the curator began a lecture about the discovery.

"The Syrian museum kept the portal in a long-term storage locker for many decades. Money and politics prevented the portal being put on display. Finally, when funding became available, the museum announced the portal as a world class archeological discovery that is part of ancient Syrian history.

"When the museum announced it was going to exhibit the portal, all types of craziness broke loose. There was a strong backlash to displaying the portal from people who lived in the region where the artifact was found. They claimed the portal was cursed and a source of demons. Many village elders traveled to the exhibit city to warn about the cursed portal. They made their case in mosques, in parks, and on street corners.

"Of course, city people can be just as superstitious as rural people can. The elders' warnings were believed. There were marches and street protests opposing the museum's effort for a display. Confronted with a populist rebellion, the museum had to back down. The portal remained in long-term storage."

Edward was fascinated that in this modern world villagers would still believe in black magic. "What were the villagers afraid of? I mean, this piece is really ancient. How could modern people even know about some ancient curse?"

"Well that's where the tale gets interesting," said the curator. "Supposedly, there was an event during the Second World War that created the legend.

"The portal had remained in its place in the mountains after the First World War. The Germans had documented it after its discovery but had not attempted to move it. Remember there were only twenty years between the First World War and the Second World War.

"German efforts and funding after the First World War were focused on their military buildup. All non-military funding was restricted; consequently, funding to move an ancient artifact across half a continent was a low priority.

"Once the Second World War started, Germany desperately needed oil. It again invaded this region looking to secure oil refineries. Certain officers were aware of the portal's location. While they were in the region of the portal, they decided to visit it. Beyond their curiosity, they may have had a self-serving political motivation.

"Der Fuhrer, Mr. Hitler, was fascinated by tales of objects that commanded unearthly powers. The officers may have felt they would earn his goodwill by a visit to the portal. My guess is that they were already in the region, were curious about the portal, and used the visit as a break from the war.

"Naturally the mountain people were watching the Germans. Their region and their mountains were being invaded. They maintained a close surveillance on the Germans, so they could alert neighboring villages if a military threat seemed imminent.

"When the Germans arrived at the portal site, they set up camp, and then proceeded to uncover the sand from the portal. Once it was free of sand, they examined it. In total, there were around thirty soldiers and officers examining the portal.

"The watching villagers said that they saw the Germans running their fingers over the raised glyphs. Supposedly, some of the Germans appeared to try to chip off glyphs from the columns, possibly as souvenirs or gifts back to Hitler.

"The watchers all reported the same event happening. According to them, a number of simian-like fire demons came out of the portal. The fire demons passed over and through the individual soldiers. They described the attack as a blotter passing over ink. The demons were the blotters and the soldiers were the ink.

"Each time a soldier was absorbed there was a momentary shadow of the soldier on the demon's exterior and then the soldier disappeared inside the demon beast. Some watchers claimed that the inside of the beasts changed colors as soldiers were absorbed, it reminded them of a digestive process.

"Naturally the Germans fired their weapons, but to no effect. Others ran, some tried to hide, however nobody escaped. These fire demons absorbed every German in less than a minute.

"Their story, as told to me by the Syrian curator, reminded me of an early Hollywood horror movie from the 1950s called,

*The Blob*. In this case, there were a number of blobs and they moved very quickly.

"The curator and I agreed that the rational explanation is that the tribesmen ambushed the Germans, probably out of revenge for the last German invasion. They created the fire demon's explanation within their villages to maintain the secrecy of their killings.

"Because the Germans were all killed, there was no official German report. The German high command assumed the tribesmen were responsible, but it was impossible to send in a larger force. The German army was having its Waterloo at Stalingrad.

"So that's the legend behind why the portal was never displayed by the Syrian museum. Great story, wouldn't you say? I think Hollywood needs to redo *The Blob* a third time, but place it in those remote mountains."

Eddie loved the story and nodded in agreement at the possible *Blob* remake. "I've gotta ask, how did we get lucky and get it here?"

"As it happened, I was at a conference last year with the curator of the Syrian national museum. He and I have known each other for many years. As we were discussing future exhibits, he brought up the stored portal, its history, and the problems with showing it. I was fascinated by his description of the portal and asked if I could visit it.

I remember that he looked like lightning had struck him. 'I am inspired,' he said. 'A better approach is to have your museum create a major display. You Americans are not superstitious and there will be no problem with our rural, indigenous mountain people objecting to the display being in

America.' Then he laughed, 'Many of our politicians would love to send America a care package of demons.'" Edward joined in chuckling over demons in a shipping box.

"He, of course, wanted a quid pro quo for lending the portal. He suggested that we should discuss revenue sharing from the exhibit's income. That would make it easier for him to facilitate releasing the artifact. I quickly agreed. It was a fair request.

"He also said that after the Second World War, when the museum was in the process of bringing the portal back to the storage facility, they found the keystone on the ground. They assumed the villagers had probably removed it. He said it appeared unharmed and we could easily place it back into the arch once it arrived here in Chicago. Of course, placing it back is far from easy, but that's our problem to deal with.

"Now you know the story and understand why we needed a little more time to complete the exhibit. You can see how close we are to being finished. We're scheduled to insert the keystone tomorrow afternoon and we'll have a full crew on hand. Mike, our crane operator, will be in charge and he's a genius with that powerful tool."

"If I may ask a technical question, sir. Why doesn't radioactive carbon dating get you pretty close to its age?"

"An excellent question, Edward, and usually it does. For some reason our usual dating methods don't seem to be working. They are giving us an age for the portal that doesn't make sense. The various tests date it as being far too old."

"How old do the tests say it is?" asked Edward.

The curator laughed and said, "Around a hundred thousand years old. Unless early Neanderthals had a civilization beyond long spears and fire, there is no answer right now except that our dating methods are flawed in this case. Possibly the stones contain a contaminant that's throwing off the readings."

Edward knew he had taken up quite a bit of the curator's time and goodwill, it was time to move on. "Sir, thank you so much. This has been a grand time for me. I'm heading back to the Drake Hotel to tell my mom all about the display and my great teacher."

As the two of them walked back to the staircase, the curator thought to himself, *Not only smart but polite, he has had a great upbringing.* At the front exit doors, the curator turned and shook Edward's hand.

"Thank you for your interest, Edward. If your mom decides to visit us, please feel free to introduce her to me." With that parting comment, the curator headed back to his office. Edward headed down the outside front steps and into the challenges of the harsh Lake Michigan winds.

# 25
# Edward Finds the Sanctuary

Standing outside the museum, Edward looked at his watch. It was two o'clock. Too early to go back for dinner. As he walked up Michigan Avenue, he pondered how to kill a couple of hours. It was getting colder and a harsh wind was at his back. Even the trees looked cold. Reluctantly, once again he took out the earmuffs.

Out of nowhere, an idea struck him. He reached into his pocket for the card he had gotten from M, the train magician. The back of the card had directions starting at Water Tower Place, so he headed there. Once at Water Tower he began to follow the map.

The map took him down a major side street then continued onto a series of ever-smaller streets. The streets shifted from a blend of larger commercial stores into ethnic restaurants, specialty shops, professional offices, and private homes. Edward made a mental note to remember landmarks for returning to the Drake, it would be too cold to wander around once the sun was gone.

He followed the card's map until he found the map ended with a long quiet residential block. There was no address for the shop on the map and he wondered how he was supposed to find the place. *M's shop had better be close and obvious or I'm heading back. There better be a big neon sign flashing, "Get your Magic Here".*

He looked down the street for any sign of a shop, but nothing stood out. Then he glanced back at the card in his hand. A small dotted line had appeared on the card replacing the street directions.

*These dots were not there a minute ago. There must be a navigation system built right into the card. Now that's very cool M! I guess the message is to follow the dotted line.*

Edward walked slowly up the residential block holding the card in his left hand. In the middle of the block, he saw the dots suddenly disappear. *Rats, the navigation system just went down. Victim of another battery failure.*

While standing in the middle of the block, shivering and deciding what to do, he noticed a small alley to his left. *Well, I never saw that coming at a distance; pretty clever architecture to camouflage a side street so that it's not noticeable until you're right on it. It must be for those who don't want to be bothered by uninvited visitors, and that sounds like M.*

He looked down the alley and thought, *Is this a situation I should get into? Mom would have a cow if she saw me going in. Probably nobody uses it except vagrants, robbers, and serial killers.* As he stood deciding whether to go down, a warm inviting light appeared halfway down the alley.

*Nothing ventured, nothing gained,* he thought. He turned into the alley and proceeded toward the light. When he got to the light, he saw it was an old gas lantern beside an entry door. He studied the door; it appeared as a thick oak door with iron bars across the front. It was recessed into a stone arch. In the door's center was a carved iron knocker. On inspection it was a black cat's head, the cat's green quartz eyes stared out at him.

*This door and knocker look like copies from the train,* thought Edward. *So, this must be M's place.* Before knocking, he took a final look up the alley; he could still walk back out. He saw a few people passing by the front of the alley, but none looked down.

"Hello, Mr. Theo," he said to the knocker as he lifted it up high then dropped it down. He was deciding whether to knock again when the door opened. He cautiously stayed outside and looked in.

All he saw was a pair of long bookcases on each side of the hallway, then he was greeted by an inviting draft of warm air and pleasant cooking odors. *What the heck?* he thought and stepped in. The door closed behind him.

He walked past the bookcases and found himself in an amazing room. Ahead of him was a two-story fountain with water cascading down from a top statue. There was a table beside the fountain with high-backed leather chairs. Across from the fountain on the opposite wall was a roaring fire.

The fireplace was one typically seen in Hollywood's versions of castles. The height of the opening went up six feet and the width was at least eight feet. *You could burn a tree in there,* he thought. *The only thing missing is the lord of the manor wearing a long sword with mastiff dogs at his feet.*

Edward froze. Instead of mastiff dogs there was a large black cat resting in front of the fire. The cat was studying him. *Oh my god. It's the beast from the train. I'm a mouse again and that thing has me back in its sights.*

At that moment, a familiar voice called out a warm greeting. "Welcome, Edward, you've come to the right place! Don't worry about Theo over there; he's as easygoing as a tabby cat. He's a big lug who enjoys sleeping by a nice fire, and he hates to get up. He just watches everything and enjoys having company."

With the familiar voice and welcoming greeting, Edward found himself relaxing. "Good to see you again, M. By the way, that card with the built-in navigation system is really cool. I didn't figure you as a tech guy."

M nodded, "It served its purpose, and here you are. I'm pleased you followed the yellow brick road, or in this case, the dotted line road. I expected no less of you. By the way, how is your delightful mother? Is she happy in her suite at the Drake? Has she headed out shopping yet?"

"Yes, on both counts. She's a happy Chicago girl, she thinks she's twenty and in college again but with a big credit card."

"Very good," laughed M. "She is a delightful lady, I thoroughly enjoyed our dinner conversations. Speaking of dinner, don't worry about tonight, you'll be back as planned."

The thought of dinner made Edward's tummy rumble. As if reading his mind M said, "I think an afternoon snack is in order for my special guest. I have been baking some of my cold-weather muffins, I'll let you judge how they go with a freezing Chicago day.

"Please make yourself comfortable while I retrieve our muffins. Have a seat by the fountain or, if you prefer, by the fire with Theo."

"Right here works fine for me, I love this fountain." He glanced over at the beast. For a moment, he thought the beast grinned at him like the Cheshire cat in *Wonderland*. *That's crazy,* he thought. *Cats don't make expressions except when they hiss and cough up hairballs.*

He sat down in a deep leather chair beside the fountain and settled his long frame into a relaxed position. He let his eyes roam and begin to take in the room. *Where are the shelves with the magic tricks?* he wondered.

# 26
# Edward Meets an Ice Princess

As M headed for the kitchen entry, he paused and looked toward a back part of the room. He called out, "Glenda, please tear yourself away from your books and join us. You need to meet Edward. I'm bringing in a tray of my hot winter muffins and hot cider."

*Who's he talking to?* thought Edward. Then, from a distant alcove, a figure stepped out. Clearly a girl. As she moved toward the fountain, Edward found himself staring at her. She was very tall and lean with long, reddish-blond hair. As she got closer, he noticed her emerald green eyes.

*Oh my god, she's stunning and moves like a gymnast,* was all he could think. *But she's too tall to be a gymnast. Maybe she was a gymnast until she got too tall.* His mind was racing, and his mouth was dry.

As the girl approached the table, Edward had a strong second reaction. *She sure does not like me being here. Those eyes are shooting green icicles at me. What did I do?*

Fortunately, M appeared with the muffins, cider, and introductions. "Glenda meet Edward, Edward meet Glenda. You two settle in and I'll be right back."

Silence settled around the table like a thick fog. Edward was scrambling to break the ice and tried to think of a clever greeting, but none came. His mind was pinned in place by green icicle arrows.

The girl stood there looking down at him and examining him in the same way the cat beast had done. Since his mind and voice had failed him, Edward needed to get in motion. He stood up, stretched to his full height, and pulled out a chair for her. She rewarded him with a frown.

*Now she's annoyed. She resents gentlemen as well as unwelcome guests. Maybe she resents guys that are taller than her.* Edward took a slow, deep breath. *Relax, I'm M's guest not hers. She may be the castle's ice princess but she's sure not my princess.*

He swallowed, found his voice, and said, "My dad taught me to always rise and pull out a lady's chair; he still does it for my mom. He told me at an early age that good manners are always appreciated, even when they're not acknowledged."

"Well," replied Glenda, "thank you for being the good little son. Did he also tell you that today's woman is quite capable of managing for herself?"

"I assume that's a rhetorical question," responded Edward. The two were now staring each other directly in the eye.

Edward straightened his back to elevate himself as much as possible. He found himself arching his feet off his toes.

With a feeling of satisfaction, he saw the girl was annoyed at being forced to look up.

*Welcome to my world,* he thought, *I'm taller than you are and I'm a young gentleman, but are you a young lady?* Glenda looked like she was ready for another exchange, but changed her mind and sat down. Edward wisely avoided pushing her chair in and sat down himself.

Edward bolstered his confidence thinking, *I'm surprised her looks don't freeze the water in the fountain. I bet the Chicago temperature falls even further the minute she hits the street.*

*Stalemate exchange,* thought M while standing in the kitchen doorway and chuckling to himself. *These two will learn soon enough to stop sparring and work together.*

M casually approached the two young people. "We need to enjoy a little afternoon refreshment time. Edward, you've had a full travel and sightseeing day, and Glenda, all that hard study takes energy. Dig in while they're hot. Bon appétit."

Edward saw that the girl was going to play it cool and pass on the food. *Shoot yourself in the foot if you want,* he thought. *I've had a much busier day than you have and I'm hungry.* He proceeded to butter a muffin and take a large bite.

The buttered muffin melted in Edward's mouth. There was an explosion of goodness on his tongue. He took a gulp of the hot cider. "This is the best muffin I have ever tasted! It's amazing. Really! You should sell these and get rich. Instead of Famous Amos you can be Muffin Man M."

M grinned and said, "Thanks for that. These are my own recipe and a big secret. Only special friends get them."

*Now I'm a special friend,* thought Edward. *Sounds good to me.* He finished the muffin in two more bites. "Seconds OK?" he asked, and M nodded encouragement. Edward took another muffin and covered it with butter. Glenda sat quietly in her chair with a condescending look on her face. Edward ignored her.

"Let me guess, your fire cat is another special friend. Will he be joining us?" asked Edward trying to be social.

"Yes and no. Theo is indeed a very special friend, but the muffin and cider are not for him." M buttered himself a second muffin and proceeded to take a large bite.

Edward enjoyed watching the girl squirm. Clearly, she wanted to eat but wanted to avoid joining him in a pleasant activity.

M watched Glenda's standoffish attitude, took pity, and casually said, "Glenda, please help me out and have a muffin or two. I overbaked and don't want to waste them. As you know, they taste best while warm."

With M's asking her to help out, she immediately took a muffin and ate it without pausing for butter. Edward made it a point to look at M and ignore the girl while he finished the second muffin. He acted as if he did not see her joining in, or he saw but did not care. Then he said, "I have no pride; will I embarrass myself with a third?"

"I take that as a big compliment, please help yourselves; these are here for us to finish off right now." As Edward reached for a third, he was pleased to see the girl had quietly taken a second and covered it with a slab of butter.

After the three of them had washed down the muffins with hot cider, there was an uncomfortable silence at the table. M stood up and said in a soft but directing voice, "Glenda, would you please do the hosting honors and show Edward around. You can formally introduce him to Theo on your tour."

# 27
# Edward's Tour

"Of course," said Glenda standing. "Follow me to the study area. This is where most of your time will be spent."

*Most of my time?* thought Edward. *What is the artic princess talking about?* "I don't mean to sound rude, but I'm only here for maybe another hour then I'm returning to my hotel. My mom expects me back at the Drake for an early dinner." As he followed her, Edward tried to be pleasant and added, "You may be confusing me with another guest that's coming in. Probably M hasn't filled you in on everybody he's invited."

Glenda glanced back at him, "No, you're the only invited guest." Her tone and facial expression added, "Sadly." For some reason he felt both annoyed and disappointed over her tone of voice.

"Well, let's not debate my schedule, but I'll be braving that Chicago winter shortly. Give me a quick tour then I'm out of here. Feel free to skip the cat introduction."

"His name is Theo," said Glenda, "and he is definitely not a cat. He is the most important person here, or in Chicago, or anywhere else you could imagine. Theo will certainly meet you and size you up."

*Size me up for what?* thought Edward. *Dinner?*

"We'll see whether you measure up. If somehow Theo approves of you, then M will explain what's going on. After all, I'm just the tour guide," she added in a miffed tone of voice.

Edward chose not to say anything else. He thought, *She must be M's wacko younger sister. Good-hearted M is probably charged with raising her. She can either live with him or live in a place for the mentally disturbed. She probably still talks to her dolls and thinks the cat is some fairy tale creature.*

Glenda stopped and pointed straight ahead. They were standing at an alcove that curved into the far end of the great room. There was a medium sized dark oak table with carved legs. Two heavy leather chairs were on one side of the table.

A small fire was burning at the back of the alcove about fifteen feet away from the table. The fire produced a cheerful atmosphere as it illuminated the mosaic tile that framed the hearth. A welcome amount of heat was coming from the fire that kept the alcove cozy without being overly warm.

"This is your study chair if you become a student. It will adjust to fit your body perfectly for the long hours you will sit in it.

"Study books are in these two cases. Notice there is a blank nameplate on that case. If you happen to become a student, your name will appear. You may notice my name appears on my case," and she pointed with pride to her bookcase. Edward saw that, sure enough, there was an iron nameplate. Engraved into it in old English lettering was the name "Glenda."

"If you happen to become a student here, your books would be the ones I've already finished and put into the unnamed case. My advanced studies would not make sense to you, so never take a book from my shelf; you could hurt yourself by attempting to use them."

*Books are my buddies, Princess,* he thought, *and I've read more than my share without injury. She's a definite wacko.* "I'll certainly remember that Glenda, and thanks for the warning. By the way, I don't see a calculus book in either my case or your case. Since I've finished calculus AB and BC, I don't need one. Out of curiosity, which textbook did you prefer to use? Personally, I liked the classic one by Thomas from MIT. He wrote it in the 1960s, but I think it holds up well."

For a moment, Glenda looked nonplussed and a faint tinge of pink appeared on her cheeks. *Could that reddening be a little "I've been put in my place" embarrassment?* thought Edward. *Surprised you, Miss Smartee, didn't I?* He fought to keep a smirk off his face.

"You do not surprise me," she said, as if reading his mind. "One thing I know is you're smart or you would not be here. Of course, I don't know why you're here at all." *Maybe to teach you some humility,* she added to herself.

"To answer your rhetorical question: no, I have not studied calculus. There is far more serious content to study here than simple math."

Edward bit his tongue. He wanted to say, *Yeah, that's what all the art, music, and language majors say when it comes to math. Math is all below their genius talents.*

Then another thought sprang to mind, *I've got it! M is a master magician and she's learning his craft. This is a school to learn gimmicks, misdirection, and hand control but not math, no wonder she's a math idiot. I bet her main role is to get cut in half. She's probably confused over fractions, so M has to place her in the exact halfway spot.*

Glenda continued the tour without looking at ego boy. "Most of our time will be spent in only three places: here in the study alcove, in our bedrooms, or by the fountain." The word "our" registered with Edward. For a moment, it sounded pretty good.

"Let's look at what may be your personal room." Edward walked behind her and tried not to notice the natural bounce in her long gymnast legs. *She walks with the same bounce as Tigger,* he thought. *No way could Tigger bounce up the museum staircase for seven levels. She would be sucking wind with a side ache by floor four.*

Edward noted that the hallway had doors on the left side and right side and then ended with a stone wall. *This tour must be almost over,* he thought. "Your room would be here," said Glenda as she pushed the door open. "Please step in."

"Ladies first," Edward said. Glenda chose to ignore the sarcasm in his voice.

"Wow!" came out unexpectedly from Edward. The room had a large poster bed in the corner. Across from it was another welcoming fire. In front of the fire was a deep soaking bathtub. The tub was solid granite with multiple large faucets.

"The bathroom is through that door. In it, you will find a rather special shower that makes you feel like you're under a tropical waterfall. It's voice activated for the desired temperature. Of course, there is the usual throne for the rest of your business. I'll let you explore the bathroom by yourself."

Edward again noticed a slight blushing on her face. *I guess the ice princess is human after all. She's just my age so I'll cut her some slack on her limited social skills with boys. Maybe she doesn't get out much. Probably a study nerd, despite her good looks.* Edward's male confidence had reestablished itself.

Glenda was back at the door ready to exit. Edward followed her out and noticed the door across from his. There was an ornate name set into the door that read Glenda. Edward said, "I notice there is no name on 'my' door. That tells me I'm not a permanent resident like you."

Glenda just looked at him and said, "Maybe your name will be there, maybe not. M will discuss that possibility with you shortly." She turned and headed back to the great room.

As they passed the alcove, Edward stopped. "Hold up a minute, Glenda. I've got a couple of questions for you," his face made it clear he was asking a serious question.

"Yes," she said, "what's on the gentleman's mind?"

"Is this place set up as a mini-university for apprenticing stage magicians? Are you training to be M's stage assistant?" Then he added, "By the way he is the best I've ever seen by a mile. He is brilliant, his tricks appear as real magic, but I guess you know that."

Glenda gave him a serious look then started to laugh. "No, to everything you're thinking. Especially 'no' to my being the cute girl in the skimpy dress that gets sawed in half."

Edward thought, *Exactly what am I doing here? I don't see any tricks for sale and I'm certainly not becoming a stage magician. I think it's time for me to exit this crazy place.* "I'll skip the kitchen tour and the Theo introduction if that's OK with you. It's time for me to move on and head back to my hotel."

"That's fine with me," answered Glenda, "we rarely visit the kitchen anyway, that's M's 'go-to' area for cooking and relaxing. It also leads back to his personal quarters." With that comment, Glenda proceeded to sit down beside Theo. "Join us or not."

Edward picked the "or not" and headed back to the fountain where M was sitting with a mug of steaming tea. Edward the planner eyed the entry door. *The coast looks clear, but I may need an exit plan. If I need to get out of here fast, I'll pull down one of the hallway bookcases as I run out. I'll be out of here before anyone can touch me. I'll slam the door immediately so that big cat cannot follow.*

# 28
## Theo Illuminates

"M, it's time for me to head back to my hotel; the sun's almost down and it's a freezing slog going back. Maybe I can visit you again while I'm here."

"I certainly understand," agreed M. "You may head out whenever you're ready. By the way, did you enjoy the tour?"

"Absolutely," said Edward, and he meant it. "You have a cool castle right here in the middle of the city. I think Glenda has a terrific place for her to do her studies and it's clear she is a serious person."

M nodded at this, "Yes, she certainly is a serious student. The reason for her studies is what makes her so focused, some would say socially aloof. She doesn't have time to be a normal young lady like her peers, but that's a life choice she's accepted.

"Before you leave, Edward, would you have a seat and give me a few minutes to explain why I invited you here? It's a short but engaging story and something you can take back to the hotel as my early Christmas present to you and Virginia."

Edward knew that the best response was to humor M, so he sat down beside him while keeping an eye on his escape route.

"Edward, I know this place must seem strange, maybe a bit crazy. Believe me I experienced the same thoughts when Theo first brought me here. I've lived much of my life here and have had experiences and been shown understandings few would ever believe.

"Glenda is new here. Like you, she was very cautious about what I was inviting her to experience. I had to earn her trust over a number of months before she agreed to a visit.

"Ultimately a deciding factor for her and for me to stay here with Theo was that we were both orphans. Theo brought us to his home and we really had nothing to lose by staying with him. Once here, he opened an alternative world to us.

"You, of course, have both a home and great parents. If you decide to join us here, you will find that you are not losing your parents but gaining special friends and allies."

Edward politely listened, but internally shook his head. *This is crazy city here. This guy is talking about the cat creature adopting them instead of the other way around. Maybe M and the girl have eaten the catnip and hallucinate. I had better ask a few simple questions but get ready to bolt out the bookcase exit.*

To keep M's goodwill in place, Edward accepted this story with a sincere nod of his head. "I certainly see why you and Glenda love this place. I assume that Theo was left a trust fund for his lifetime care when his owner passed.

"I know rich people often love their pets so much they make sure they are cared for. You and Glenda are the lucky people the trustees chose for his care and maintenance. I think that's a terrific outcome for both of you."

Glenda had joined them and smiled at Edward's insightful analysis. *Clever boy,* thought Glenda, *totally ignorant about us and our sanctuary, but clever enough.*

"One question before I pack it up?" asked Edward. "What do you mean by allies?"

"Yes, that is the sixty-four-million-dollar question," said M. "Rather than my trying to explain, I think Theo would be the best to handle that answer."

On cue, the large cat beast rose and softly walked across the floor. The beast called Theo was now standing beside Edward with its head on a level plane with Edward's head. Its eyes were looking directly into Edward's.

Edward was instinctively scared. Fight or flight came to mind, but neither was an option. *No way can I make it to the door with the beast next to me, I'm a trapped mouse. I'll play along and find my chance to escape when it appears.*

"Now, Edward, please bear with us for a couple more minutes, then you can head back to your mom. We are going to perform a simple ceremony that will answer the questions you are not asking. Trust me and have no fear.

"Edward, please hold Glenda's left hand with your right hand and my right hand with your left hand." M's voice was soft but commanding and Edward immediately complied.

When Glenda took his right hand, he felt himself relaxing. There was a sense of comfort holding her hand that surprised him. What Edward did not know was that Glenda was having the same experience, much to her surprise.

Theo now stood immediately in front of Edward. He seemed taller and larger in the shoulder than a minute before. He now loomed over Edward and stared into Edward's eyes. Then he slowly brought his head forward until it was gently pressing against Edward's forehead.

M placed his left hand on Theo's shoulder. "Glenda, please put your free hand on Theo's other shoulder. Glenda felt her heart racing as she placed her hand on Theo.

The moment the loop was complete, images passed through all their minds in the same instant. The images flashed by as clear as a high-speed video game. The images showed Edward's father in Boston eleven years ago. It showed him moving under the Winthrop Bridge to the village. Next, he was coming down an alley toward a gas light. Now he was in the room with the fountain and fireplace. There was Theo by the fireplace looking at Daniel but also at M.

Edward watched his dad select his drinking horn and fill it with the liquor. He saw his dad sipping his drink in the leather chair then pulling out his Christmas book gift.

Time blinked forward, and Edward was five years old in his bed on Christmas Eve. He saw and heard his dad reading the leather gift book. Once again, he jumped in his seat when he saw the black tail bump against his window. Glenda jumped at the same time.

Now there was a new set of images. There was a battle raging between dark cloud creatures that resembled Theo and red simian fire beasts. Theo's kind was under attack and losing. M, Edward, and Glenda all felt Theo's fear, grief, and anger. Then Theo was alone in a sanctuary he had constructed with his mind.

M dropped his hand from Theo, as did Glenda. Theo went back to resting in front of his fireplace. He was still large but smaller than minutes before. With Theo gone, all hands returned to their owner's sides. Edward glanced at Glenda as he released her hand, but she seemed lost in thought.

Several minutes passed while the three absorbed the visions, then M spoke. "Like you, I needed time to compose myself. After all these years, he still surprises me. The three of us have just shared a powerful message and certain personal experiences. One experience shows us how Edward's father was led to our sanctuary and found the book. Now we all understand how the book, over the years, has led Edward to be here at this moment.

"We saw that while Theo is a powerful ancient being, his kind was under attack. Possibly only Theo escaped. Theo's survival matters more than we can imagine. He has been in hiding for millenniums. To survive he needs allies, without allies he will be destroyed. Without Theo's presence, everything we know is at risk.

"It's strange," mused M, "that Theo and I found both of you about the same time. Glenda arrived here just five months ago and Edward here you are today.

"Neither Theo nor I understand why, over the many millenniums of searching, we found two potential allies at the same time. I guess it's the universe's version of kismet." Edward's head jerked at the memory of the word "kismet." He had a sudden flashback of his dad explaining the word when he was a five-year-old. It was a sweet memory.

"The only question now, Edward, is will you choose to become an ally with Theo, Glenda, and me? This is entirely your choice. You should agree only if your head, heart, and instincts all tell you this is your path." Glenda quietly watched Edward and thought, *The moment of truth.*

M gave Edward an encouraging smile and added, "If it helps, Edward, think of the American founding fathers as they had to individually decide whether to sign the Declaration of Independence. By signing they put their lives, their families, and all their worldly possessions at risk. Benjamin Franklin gave them a simple admonition: 'We must all hang together, or assuredly we shall all hang separately.'

"With that cheerful adage to guide you, Edward, what do you want to do?"

"M, please cut me a little slack, I'm stunned right now. This feels like real magic but I'm a science guy. May I ask a couple of questions?" M nodded.

"First, if I choose to leave, what happens? This experience is too weird for me to ever forget. What if I talk to people about it?"

"Nothing happens if you leave. All events associated with today will be gone from your memory. Neither you nor your mother will ever remember meeting me on the train. You will join your mother for an early dinner, watch a movie, and have a good night's sleep. You will wake up at the Drake tomorrow and continue with your Chicago vacation."

"Fair enough," said Edward. "My other question is: if I choose to stay, do I lose contact with my mom and dad?"

"This question is easy and fortunately has quite a happy answer. If you decide to stay and begin your studies, you will wear this ring that controls the time dimension for you and the outside world."

"Please explain exactly how this time ring thing works," Edward said with a skeptical look as he fingered the ring.

"The ring is a receiver of sorts that is connected to this sanctuary. Theo controls the sanctuary's master clock.

"The ring you wear operates on several levels of time. For you, the ring stops time from aging your body, regardless of whether you are inside the sanctuary or out in the external world."

Eddie slipped on the ring then said with a grin, "So now I'm immortal! Does that make me a kind of god?"

M laughed and Glenda snorted. Then M took on a serious tone. "No, you will not be a god. The ring's effect on your body may be thought of as being cryogenically frozen. You are fully awake and functioning, however, the cellular deterioration is akin to being frozen."

"Of course, you may choose to have your body advance to some alternative age. Personally, I chose to remain a ten-year-old for quite some time before I decided to have the body of a young man in his twenties. Being ten has many advantages depending on when and where you live. At age ten you are no threat to anyone and people tend to be helpful. However, after enough time passes, being Peter Pan gets tiring.

"The ring's second control is that outside time remains fixed until you enter it. You can choose the time you desire before entering that time world. Think of the external world as staying in a stasis until you enter it. When you leave the sanctuary, time will be whenever you want it to be. You can have long periods of study inside the sanctuary but can return to this afternoon's time and see your mom. There is no loss of time with your parents.

"The physics of all this is far beyond my capacity to understand. Somehow time is manipulated by the sanctuary and ultimately by Theo."

Edward looked skeptical, "Excuse me for doubting; but to repeat, I'm a science guy. What you said sounds a lot like the movie *Groundhog Day*. From my study of physics, it's impossible. Are you saying Einstein is wrong?"

"Einstein's thinking was not wrong, simply far too simplistic and very far from complete. He was correct in the four-dimensional world he studied and accepted. Einstein's genius was how he used 'thought experiments' to discover relativity. However, even Einstein could not begin to do thought experiments in a multidimensional universe. There are many more dimensions available to Theo than what Einstein and string theory have ever imagined. Does that help with your decision?"

# 29
# Decision Time

Edward suddenly realized how tense M was. Unlike M, Edward was beyond calm. He felt outside of himself. He was beyond the strongest runner's high he had ever experienced. He felt confident and in total control of himself. He knew his best decisions came from his intuition and following his instincts.

He looked both M and Glenda straight in their eyes, "Sounds like you and the magical cat really need me as an ally. I accept there is a dangerous challenge to all of us, and that I'm an important part of meeting that challenge. I've never backed down from a hard challenge before and this is not the time to start. Count me in."

Then to loosen the tension he added, "Plus, I want more of those muffins!"

When Edward answered, he saw a look of transcendent relief pass over M's face. *For once, he's lost his all-knowing poker face. I got him for the first, and maybe the last, time.*

He saw Glenda nod, then she added, "If an old-world gentleman can step up to a challenge, the modern woman can obviously be counted on," and she gave him a little wink. Edward felt a warm glow pass through him.

M stood and put an arm across each of their shoulders. "Bravely said! As allies, our shared fate begins at this hour and this minute. We will surely hang together.

"Now to officially start our shared journey, we need to place a name on your bedroom door and on your bookcase," said M.

"My name is easy," said Edward. "It's E-D-W-A-R-D, spelled just the way you would think." As an afterthought he added, "Definitely not Eddie."

M and Glenda smiled at him, "Not quite," said M. "You will now have two names. The name in your current time world will remain 'Edward' or 'Eddie' as some prefer," and he grinned. "However, in this alternate time world you must select another name.

"What name do you feel will best describe you? Don't ponder this, answer what comes to your mind right now. Follow your instincts."

Without hesitating Edward answered, "Traveler." M nodded.

"Why Traveler?" asked M.

"Because I will be a time traveler and 'Dr. Who' is already taken."

M shook Traveler's hand, "A wonderful choice, and quite fitting."

Traveler looked at Glenda, "Turnabout is fair. What was your original name and how did you pick 'Glenda'?"

Glenda frowned, "That's a rather personal question since we barely know each other."

"Well I told you mine, I think it's only fair you tell me yours."

*Boy, this guy can really be pushy,* thought Glenda. "OK, Mr. Traveler, fair is fair. My original name was Sally."

Traveler grinned, "I can't help myself. Did you consider choosing 'Sallyforth' as your new name? After all, she's your modern woman role model."

*He's not only pushy, he's always half a step away from being insulting.* "No, I never considered 'Sallyforth,' as you know she's a cartoon character. Our names are serious. They help define who we are."

"Relax, I was just kidding about Sallyforth, but why Glenda?"

"I named myself after Glinda, the good witch from *The Wizard of Oz*. She had magic powers and was a positive force against the dark forces." Glenda mentally added, *And of course, she was beautiful.* "I just made a small change in the spelling to 'Glenda'."

"That's a great name and it suits you."

For a moment, Glenda was caught off balance and was annoyed at herself for liking his compliment. "Well thank you, Traveler, for your vote of confidence, I guess I'll keep it."

M smiled to himself. *They are jousting, but in a way, that will lead them to accept each other as equals.* M's upbeat mood continued as he thought, *At last, after all these centuries Theo has his allies and I have companions. Now the training begins for all of us.*

# 30
# Training Begins

With M gone, both Traveler and Glenda were again uncomfortable. They felt like Marine recruits who find themselves in a barracks with total strangers. Their tensions did not transfer to a relaxed Theo who yawned, stretched, and rolled on his side. For a moment, Traveler thought of the comic strip tiger Hobbes stretched out in total bliss.

Neither Traveler nor Glenda knew what to say and the air seemed to chill further. The silence was deafening. Traveler broke the silence with, "Can you show me my starting study material?"

Glenda was relieved, "Good idea, Traveler. Follow me back to our study alcove." Traveler found he had mixed emotions about her response. He liked her calling him by his new name. At the same time, he was mildly annoyed that he was told to "Follow me." He bit his tongue and followed.

As he trailed behind, he again noticed her walking motion. *She seems to bounce a lot. I wonder if she has kangaroo blood in her, maybe a little Tigger the Tiger.* He gave himself an internal high-five.

At the alcove, Glenda opened the glass door to Traveler's bookshelf while pointing to the nameplate, "Is that the correct spelling of Traveler?" Traveler nodded "Yes," while thinking, *How did they do that so fast?*

There were only two books inside Traveler's case. His original Christmas book was resting on the left side of the top shelf. Glenda moved it to a lower shelf, "It's done its job, time for it to take a rest."

A second book was beside it. She pulled it out and handed it to Traveler. It was also leather bound but without illustrations on either cover. *This one must be serious,* thought Traveler.

"This will introduce you to ideas that lie far outside your normal math and science readings. For you, science boy, it will seem wrong about many of its teachings. Trust me, it's correct.

"The content is the most important and challenging you will ever read. The book requires you to train your mind to accept ideas that will seem impossible and counterintuitive."

Traveler opened the book to find it had no preface and no table of contents. He discovered that the book could only be opened to the first page. "I think the pages are stuck together. Did you glue them when you were finished just to annoy the next reader?"

Glenda gave him a subtle smirk, "The book is a bit more advanced than your conventional textbooks. It only permits you to move ahead as it determines you are ready. You can consider the book as having some similarities to one of your interactive video games. You cannot advance until you achieve certain objectives."

"Are you trying to tell me this book reads my mind? Are you messing with me?"

Glenda expanded the smirk as she answered, "I think I already know you well enough to say: I won't try to tell you anything. Find out for yourself." With that retort, she left Traveler and headed back toward the fountain area. She carried a thicker book with her.

Traveler bristled at the departing smirk then thought, *OK, maybe accusing her of messing with me was a bit out of line. Sorry, Princess.*

Traveler sat down and looked at the opening page. *Let me get on with this one-page-at-a-time reading. I'm at the top of the reading curve, so it should only take me about three minutes to finish page one. Let's see what deep secrets are being presented that my "poor" science background can't comprehend.*

Three hours later Traveler was staring at page two, he had just gotten to it, page one had taken every minute of that time.

Once he started the first page, he lost all track of time. The first page had stunned him, and Glenda was right. The content was unlike anything he had every read. He found that part way through the first page he suddenly had to go back and start over. The book seemed to be controlling his reading to ensure comprehension before permitting him to continue.

As Glenda promised, the content was an enigma. It contradicted much of his strong math and science background. Sometimes it seemed to agree but frequently it went in opposite directions. Sentences and paragraphs did not follow the usual logical construct; one sentence or idea did not naturally segue into the next.

Edward was startled when a hand rested on his shoulder. M was looking down at him. "You must be starving. You will need to keep your body well fed and rested to stay the course in these early weeks."

M looked at the page number, "Ah, I see you are on page two, nicely done. Don't tell Glenda, but she took almost five hours to move onto page two."

Then he added, "Of course her pace picked up a lot after the first few days. She became a very quick study once she committed herself. I think she initially wanted to argue with the book. Personality matters somewhat as you absorb the book's teachings."

*Yes!* thought Traveler. *Looks like I came out of the starting block a bit faster than the Ice Queen did, and I am built for distance running. I should catch up with her sooner than she thinks. Can't wait to ask her if I should slow down.*

M understood that competition between the two was both natural and desirable. *One sword will sharpen itself on the other sword. They need to compete against each other until it becomes counterproductive. When challenged by an adversary, they will need to instinctively come together as a seamless team.*

Traveler walked with a purposeful stride to the fountain table. He sat down and made it obvious he was on page two. Glenda glanced at him then his book. *Great, he's moved past page one already. He will be even more full of himself, if that's even possible.*

# 31
## First Day

The end of the day dinner was not only a feast but also a time for relaxed conversation. With a little prodding M got Traveler and Glenda to talk about their upbringings.

As Traveler talked about his home life, Glenda realized what a nurturing pair of parents he had. Traveler was clearly bonded to both parents. He spoke with equal enthusiasm about both parents' achievements. She felt regrets welling up inside her over the early loss of her parents.

While he described his dad as a science and business success, he described his mother's achievements in equal terms. Glenda liked his presenting both parents as different but equal.

Additionally, his parents appeared to have a mutually rewarding life together. Glenda knew that was unusual in today's modern world. Glenda particularly enjoyed the story of Daniel the gift giver creating this Chicago trip for his wife and son.

Traveler listened quietly as Glenda described being raised in a Norwegian orphanage. Her life clearly required a lot of self-discipline and self-confidence. Without the benefit of a stable and supporting family, she was alone in determining who she would be.

"How did you pick your role models?" asked Traveler. "I assume they were strong modern women like Amelia Earhart, Madame Curie, or Eleanor Roosevelt. Did you have a favorite?"

Glenda gave an easy laugh. "This may surprise you, Traveler, but my role model was King Arthur. I was drawn to his virtues and his vision. I saw myself as a female knight rather than a pampered princess. If you watch *Game of Thrones,* I would be the female knight who pledged to protect the Stark daughter. Does that surprise you, Traveler?" she asked as she watched him squirm.

Edward found himself getting red in the face. *Has she learned to read minds from these crazy books? Does she know I think of her as an ice princess and full of herself?*

"That does not surprise me at all, Glenda. It's an amazing coincidence because Arthur is one of my greatest heroes. I guess we have a bit in common after all. Hindus, with their belief in reincarnation, may say we were both knights of the round table in another life."

M smiled at both. "Indeed, you can both consider yourself knights committed to a shared quest. The four of us, with Theo as King Arthur, are indeed a round table. Like Arthur's knights we follow a shared honor code as well as being pledged to support each other when needed."

M stood up, stretched and declared, "Dinner's over, and this is a good stopping point. I have learned it is best to leave a good conversation or a good party with everyone looking forward to the next one.

"Traveler, you can catch up with your mother now. It's always around five o'clock her time. Alternatively, you can spend the night here and catch her tomorrow at five o'clock, your choice."

"This definitely feels like the *Groundhog Day* movie. Are you sure if I sleep now my mom won't be anxious about me?"

M smiled. "I am absolutely sure. Trust me, I have quite a bit of experience with the time patterns of *Groundhog Day*."

"I'll stay then. I'm stuffed from dinner and I could not eat another meal. Plus, I'm exhausted, the book wore me out. If it's OK, I would like to go to my room. May I take my book along for some final reading?"

M nodded. "Spending the night here and reading are both good choices. One suggestion about the book, try sleeping on it, you may be surprised."

"After today I don't think anything will surprise me."

With that farewell, Traveler walked back to the alcove, picked up his book and got to his room. As he opened the door, he again noticed his name as "Traveler" inscribed on old iron. It was positioned the same as Glenda's nameplate and was written in the same old English script. *Pretty cool,* thought Traveler.

After he had stripped off his clothes, he looked at the oversized soaking tub by the fireplace. He wanted to try it out, but found himself too exhausted. He put on his PJs and climbed into the bed. The bed seemed designed to support his body in the most relaxing way possible.

He intended to read page two again, for the third or fourth time but found his eyelids had weights attached. At the last moment, he tucked the book under his pillow. Once under his head he found there was no physical sense of it being there, he was asleep within seconds.

# 32
# Books Live, Books Rule

Traveler woke up to the smell of breakfast. He had no idea of the time, but then time was different here. He stretched to his full length then rolled to the side of the bed. He sat up and considered his options. The first option one was no option, *must visit the throne.*

Once he was ready to move on, he noticed the shower. *I probably stink, and besides I want to test-drive this rain forest shower.* Edward noticed a sign set into the side of the stone wall. "Control the temperature by voice. Say Hotter or Colder as you desire."

"Hotter" he commanded and smiled when the falling water obeyed him. Soon it was a perfect temperature for entering. Edward stripped off his PJs and stepped into the shower alcove.

He saw how the cascading water came down from an overhead rock. The rock protruded out so that the bather could stand under the falling stream. The rock also offered a grotto behind the waterfall. The grotto offered a warm padded seat for sitting as you lathered up or just relaxed.

On the seat were several natural sponges and open vases of various bathing gels. Naturally, Edward experimented with all combinations of water temperature. He did the hottest he could stand and scrubbed with determination. Once he was twice scrubbed he let the cascading water wash him as clean as a surgeon's hands.

His final command after he was soap-free was to make the water progressively colder. He took a polar bear dip, and this had him huffing and puffing before he got out.

A rack of warm towels rested on another bench. He dried off and went back to the bedroom. Fresh clothes were on his bed. They were his usual choice of jeans and a black T-shirt with half-sleeves to his elbows. *I could really adjust to this place,* he thought.

He dressed quickly and was just leaving the room when he remembered the book. He reached under his pillow and took it out. On his way past the study alcove, he placed the book in front of his chair. His nose led him to breakfast.

M and Glenda were just sitting down as he arrived. "Perfect timing," said M. "I made the same muffins as yesterday. I suggest you try some of the honey today as well as the jams and butter. The egg and bacon omelet has a few additional ingredients, trust me you'll enjoy them."

"The fruit today is a Crenshaw melon, it's fully ripened, firm and delicious." Edward was a fruit lover but had never tried a Crenshaw melon. M cut thick slices of the melon and placed them on a platter.

The meat of the melon was a golden color. Edward took a slice and carved out a generous portion to sample. It was amazing. The melon's flesh was sweet, firm, and chilled.

"Wonderful," was all he could say. The three commenced to fill their stomachs as they prepared for a long day.

"I have some chores to attend to," said M after he finished his own plate. "You two know the study drill. Before I forget, Traveler, you can visit your mom anytime you want, it will be five o'clock her time when you get there."

Traveler nodded. He was feeling a bit guilty about skipping Mom-time, but he really wanted to get back to that book. He was also interested in how Glenda would act today now that she knew he was not going anywhere.

As he arose, Glenda looked up, "I'm going to study here today. I like the sound of the fountain, it helps me concentrate."

*Well, it looks like my study companionship is not necessary for the princess,* he thought. *Probably for the best, since I don't want any interruptions or corrections from her.* With that rationalization, Traveler headed to the alcove.

When he arrived at the alcove, it seemed a bit barren and he felt a little disappointment about being alone. His chair however, seemed excited to see him. "Hello chair, my new best friend. We are going to spend a lot of time together. I know you will always be here to fully support me and you won't give me any sarcastic grief."

Traveler settled into his chair and pulled the book into his reading range. He opened it to page one and looked at the content. It's always good to back up a little when starting to study. It seemed like ages since he had faced the book's opening page challenge.

He skimmed page one and turned to page two. He was ready to read it fresh this morning. *What's this?* he thought.

He had briefly tried to read page two in bed but had quickly fallen asleep.

This morning the book permitted him to move past page two onto page three. He reread page two and found he understood it. He thought, *I must have gotten more out of my late reading than I remember. Sometimes a read right before bed sticks with us the next day.*

He started to read page three and found he could now proceed to page four. *I know I never read page three, so how can I already be on page four?* He turned back to page three and began to read it. *I know I never saw this before, yet I understand it. This does not make sense.*

He picked the book up and fast-walked to the fountain where Glenda was reading. She was sitting Indian style on her seat with her book resting on her knees. *What an awkward study position,* he thought as he approached her. Then he noticed that her legs were so flexible that they acted as a reading stand to rest her book on. *Benefits of a gymnast's body,* he thought.

"Glenda, excuse me, but something weird has happened." Glenda looked up, gave a noncommittal nod, and asked, "Exactly what is the weird thing that has happened to you? Did you find your clothes were all fresh after you showered?"

"Yes, that was weird, but this is seriously weird. I was only on page two yesterday when I fell asleep. When I started reading a minute ago, I found I could go to page four. I had not mastered page two, much less even started on page three. When I looked at pages two and three it was amazing. I found that I understood them. How did I go from lockdown on page two last night to page four this morning?"

Glenda gave Traveler a knowing, superior look. "Did you follow M's instructions and sleep on it last night?" she asked.

"Of course, I did, it was tucked under my pillow all night. It was a bit strange that once it was under my head I didn't really notice it. You would think you would notice something like that under your head. Of course, I was out like a light, so maybe it would have bothered me if I were less sleepy."

"The explanation is simple; the book continues to instruct you while you sleep. The book demands that you do your part while awake and studying, then the book does its part once you're asleep. Think of it as study momentum continuing in the brain. How it does that is beyond me, but I know it does.

"The more effort and time you put into your study while awake, the more the book does for you when you sleep. The book rewards you based on the amount of conscious effort you make. The book is a metaphor for many things in life; the greater the effort, the greater the result.

"By the way, you cannot fool the book. If you sit staring at it and only pretend to study, it knows. You may fool a teacher in the class by looking like you're working hard while actually daydreaming, but you cannot fool the book. If you begin to backslide in your effort the book will take away previously learned pages while you asleep. You must move ahead at all times."

"How did you discover all this?" asked Traveler.

"Painfully, and with serious setbacks. M let me learn the hard way. The book backed me up several times just when I was about finished. I was eager to finish it and go to a new text. I tried to bluff through the last few pages. You cannot bluff the book. It determined I had not earned the right to move onto the next text and penalized me for trying to fool it."

Then Glenda made a begrudging compliment. "If you are now on page four the book likes your effort and your talent. It took me two full days to reach page four while you seem to have gotten to it in one day. But remember, you cannot rest on your laurels."

Traveler appreciated her sharing her hard-learned experiences. "Thank you, Glenda, you've given me a serious study tip. Maybe I'll be able to help you at some point."

Glenda knew a sincere compliment followed by an equally sincere offer. She gave Traveler a genuine smile. "I think that's what Theo and M are hoping happens. I think we can make it happen if we're on the same effort page."

The next few days passed with both Traveler and Glenda immersed in their studies. Glenda worked by the fountain and Traveler in the alcove. They ate separate quick lunches and then pressed on with their readings. Both visited their rooms as nature demanded, then immediately returned to their study areas.

As she returned from a late afternoon break, Glenda passed beside Traveler's chair. She was mildly curious about which page he was on, but also found she would like a little casual conversation. She paused by his chair saw he was unaware of her presence, they were two ships passing in the night. For a moment she was slightly annoyed and wasn't sure why. She immediately put it out of her mind and continued to her fountain chair.

Traveler found that he had mastered pages four, five, six, seven, and eight but only after five intense days. *This is really slow going,* he thought. *I hope the book rewards me tonight. I must have spent twelve hours and only went through pages seven and eight. I'll be ancient before I finish.*

Both students found they were exhausted from the concentration by the end of the day. Neither needed prompting to retire. Both collapsed into their beds, tucked their books under their pillows, and fell into deep slumbers.

# 33
# Mind Intruders

As the weeks of study passed, the students felt their mental powers growing. There was an increasing absorption capacity to their minds when they were awake and when they slept.

The depth of their immersion into the ocean of knowledge continued to increase. They felt similar to high divers leaping off rocky cliffs into a deep ocean far below. Holding their books, they readied themselves for the leap. With each leap, they entered the knowledge ocean to greater depths. The deeper their dive took them, the greater their exhilaration and awareness of a vaster, complex universe.

In life, many positive developments can also have a downside. There arose a downside to their developing mental strengths. As their minds developed, they crossed a threshold and began to experience strange dreams. While the dreams were not exactly nightmares, they were far from pleasant. The dreams were disturbing to their subconscious minds, but once they woke up they could not recall the reason for their unsettled sleep.

Once asleep, each sensed a mental probing from an outside source. Something wanted to get inside their thoughts. The probing was a late-night animal scratching at a front door. It was similar to a hacker trying to enter a computer or a virus invading a living body.

Fortunately, their books recognized the intruder threat and double-bolted their minds' entry doors. No ninja-intruder viruses were allowed into their sleeping minds. While sleeping both Traveler and Glenda could sense when the scratching had stopped, and their sleep became restful and refreshing.

Once awake, each of them discounted the dreams as the result of over study. Neither of them wanted to acknowledge the dream stress. They considered the stress a sign of mental weakness and did not want the other to laugh at them. Each kept up a strong front with the other.

Over breakfast one morning, M asked them how their sleep was going. With this leading question, they both began describing the dream stress. M listened, nodded his head, and began an explanation.

"There are adversaries in this dimensional world that are searching for Theo. They sense your presence as your mental powers grow. You offer them a potential map to finding our sanctuary. The books are your guardians, they will protect you until your minds have developed their own defenses.

"Think of your studies as getting shots from the doctor. You received a lot of shots when you were young to protect you. The books are not only knowledge guides, they protect you while you are vulnerable to mental attacks."

"Is there any specific training we can take now for greater mind protection?" asked Glenda. "Would reading faster help?"

M shook his head. "That's an excellent question, but sadly the answer is 'No.' Permit me a short explanation.

"First, accept that the books are just as motivated to protect your mind as you are. The books are at risk themselves. If your minds are infiltrated, then the invader will have access into the books. Like all living beings, the books have a strong survival instinct. They protect themselves by protecting you.

"Now, reading faster is not possible in your studies. The word 'reading' does not describe what you and your book are doing. Yes, you physically sit and look at a book. You advance the page when you know you can, but you are not reading in the usual sense of that word.

"The books are building a complex learning platform into your physical brain. They are changing the basic architecture between your mind and brain. You may consider that they are literally upgrading the hard-wiring you were born with. They are permitting you to develop learning capabilities to understand the universe.

"Even if the books' contents were transferred into a modern vocabulary of words and symbols, they would still be an enigma to the most advanced human mind. Einstein or Hawking would mentally melt down attempting to understand the contents of the books.

"There is a *Far Side* cartoon that illustrates what I'm saying. In the cartoon, professor dogs wearing white lab coats are working in a classroom. Several professor dogs are studying a schematic drawing of a simple doorknob on a whiteboard. The cartoon's caption says, 'Knowing how it could change the lives of canines everywhere, dog scientists struggled diligently to understand the Doorknob Principle'."

Traveler and Glenda roared with laughter over the image of the struggling professor dogs. Glenda said, "We sure don't want to be scientist dogs. We get the message, trust the books to develop us as well as teach us." M nodded an affirmative.

Message accepted, both students excused themselves and headed back to their alcove.

# 34
# Traveler's New Skill

As the days and weeks went by, each of them felt an increase in some latent capability developing, what the capability would be was not clear. Their awareness was similar to a child's on Christmas Eve; there will be gifts arriving, but what they are is the mystery.

The first gift arrived for Traveler. He discovered he had greatly increased reaction speed. Finally, there was a tangible pay-off to his study and he was elated. He imagined how he would dominate on a basketball court stealing the ball or as a baseball player hitting home runs. His male ego remained connected to sports and he visualized winning state high school championships. He could hear the cheering crowd.

He thought about how to demonstrate this new skill to Glenda, naturally he wanted to show off. He had an epiphany about how to impress Glenda with his newfound talent. He grinned to himself as he imagined Glenda as Big Bob being surprised and humbled just a bit by Mr. Magic.

They were taking an afternoon study break when Traveler casually said, "Let me show you something. Try this," and took a dollar bill out of his wallet. "Spread your thumb and first finger so they are a couple of inches apart. Now keep your elbow on the table and no moving your hand."

Glenda was curious about the demonstration, so she went along. "Now what?" she asked.

"Simple. I'll hold the bill between your fingers then drop it. If you catch it between your fingers, you keep it."

"Easy dollar," said Glenda.

Traveler dropped the bill and she snapped both fingers together. An embarrassed Glenda watched it pass between her finger and thumb. "Sorry, no prize for Princess Glenda," said Traveler, with the annoying look of a high school boy who just pulled one over on you.

"Not fair, I was not ready. You cheated, you distracted me with your jabber. Do it again." She was annoyed.

"So, the little lady wants another chance," said Traveler, sounding like a carnival barker. He held the bill between her fingers again. "Is the little lady absolutely ready now to test her skills?"

"The little lady is ready to punch you," she said.

"Well, let me know when you are really ready."

"I'm ready," she declared while keeping her eyes glued on the bill. Traveler paused just long enough, and she snapped her fingers together from the anticipation.

"The little lady just went off-sides; that would cost you five yards in football. Since we're the home team, we'll make that a practice attempt." Glenda was more than annoyed now.

*He's playing on my emotions. Deliberately trying to upset me and mess with my reflexes,* she thought. She took a deep calming breath. She held her thumb and finger apart about two inches. The bill was again resting just above the open thumb and finger.

"Is the little woman feeling lucky now?" the barker called out. Glenda did not answer, she studied his fingers for the release. The release came, and the bill sailed down again. Her fingers snapped together catching only air. "Now that's really bad luck," said Traveler.

"One more time?" asked Traveler.

"No, this time you catch it." She took the bill while Traveler put his elbow on the table. "Spread your finger a little wider."

"Two inches is the official catch and keep distance," said Traveler. Glenda measured it and reluctantly agreed.

"So, do you think we have any of last night's cake left?" Glenda posed the question as a distraction and immediately released the bill. Traveler's finger snapped on it before it had fallen half an inch. "You cheated," she declared.

"How so?" asked Traveler.

"I must have some unconscious tell that told you when I was going to release it."

"Nope, no tell, just superior reflexes."

"There has to be a tell," repeated Glenda with frustration written across her face. A slight redness was again on her cheeks; this color signified irritation not embarrassment. "You could not close that quickly, no way!"

Actually, Traveler was as surprised as Glenda. He did notice a tell from her dilating eyes, but still he had never closed that quickly in school. On a good day in high school, he was able to catch the bill about half the time by using the dilation of the dropper's eyes as the tell. Even then, he could only catch the bill on its top before it slid past his fingers, and never at the bottom.

Traveler looked at Glenda and said, "You're right, there is a tell. The holder's eyes dilate just as they release the bill. Despite your cake distraction, I knew when you were releasing, but I should not have been able to close on the bottom of the bill like that. Do me a favor, put on sunglasses and let's try again."

Glenda went to her room and returned with very dark glasses. "I can't see your pupils, so bombs away." Once again, he closed on the bill before it had barely started to fall. Now they were both fascinated in what was happening.

"Let's add another obstacle in the very off-chance I am still catching eye or body movement. I'm going to hold a newspaper in front of my face so that all I can see is your hand and nothing more."

They made another five drops while talking, laughing, and eating a bit of chocolate. Nothing changed. Traveler had a new ability: super-fast reflexes.

"Well, you have certainly gained amazing reaction times," admitted Glenda. "How will you use this talent?"

"I have no idea," said Traveler. "Maybe I'll grab the biggest muffin before you get to it."

"You did that without enhanced reflexes," retorted Glenda.

"Well, I'll show it to M over dinner," said Traveler.

"Yes, show him. It proves we are improving our bodies as well as our minds with all our study. M will be glad to know that."

Inwardly, Glenda wondered, *What's my improved skill? What can I show M? I cannot believe Big Boy has gone ahead of me. It's just not fair. Do the books somehow play favorites? Do the books favor boys over girls?*

Traveler presented his new skill before dinner. As it turned out, M had acquired the skill a very long time ago. "I won quite a few free beers in my gambling days," M declared.

Traveler was deflated. *Great, I've got a neat skill but not a unique one, and I don't even drink. Has my book given me the bargain-basement skill? I wonder what skill Glenda's books are working on? Probably something sensational, girls always get the big awards.*

More days and weeks passed, and Glenda had emerged from her "Poor me, no specials skills" funk. She immersed herself in her studies and trusted the book to develop her any way the book felt was right.

One evening Theo came to the table after dinner. M placed his hand on Theo's head, pulled his ears then said, "Theo has a message for each of you and it is very good news indeed. Theo has found you have unbreakable defenses now against any possible mind intruder. Nothing can enter your mind; however, you are now capable of entering others' minds. You can make a dog obey you without verbal commands.

"Regarding the mind intruders, turnabout is fair play, but I strongly suggest against that. If you entered one of the searching minds, it would be like placing your brain inside a beehive. The mental noise coming from the hive could burn out your individual thought paths, rather like short-circuiting your intelligence. I tried it once and only Theo's intervention saved me from becoming a zombie."

*So, this is my new big skill,* thought Glenda, *I can read these mind viruses but go zombie-stupid if I do. What a great skill.*

# 35
## Road Trip, Meet Mom

Mental staleness hit Traveler one early afternoon like a blindsiding cement truck. His big stretch and big yawn at the study table told him he was studied-out. *I need a break! You do understand that even the best efforts become non-productive at some point, right, Book?* He thought he received an agreeing reply.

A brilliant idea popped into his mind. *Road trip! Time to visit Mom. I need dinner, and this will fit perfectly into Mom's early dinner schedule. Let's find out if all this Groundhog Day stuff is real.*

Traveler headed toward the fountain area calling out, "M, need to ask you something." There was no answering response. "M, can you hear me? Where are you?" Still receiving no response, he turned to Glenda, "Can I interrupt you for a minute?"

"I believe you just did," she said, but her face made it clear that she was kidding.

"I'm totally burned out and need a break. I'm going to go back to the Drake and catch my mom for dinner. This is about the time she expects me back, assuming all this frozen time business is real. Will you tell M what I'm doing and that I'll be back later?"

"Sure," Glenda said as Traveler headed toward his room.

In his room, he put on his heavy coat and gloves and headed for the door. *I'll put on the muffs when I'm out of the alley. I don't need one of her smart remarks right now.*

As he passed Glenda, he noticed she looked gloomy and he blurted out, "Want to take a break and join me? You have to eat, and my mom is very cool."

Glenda looked up from her book, "Is this a pity invitation or do you need help finding your way back?" She immediately kicked herself. *What a stupid thing to say. He's feeling sorry for me, but I don't need to feel sorry for myself. He's the old school gentleman trying to help a lady and I put him down with a mean retort. Shame on me.*

Traveler ignored her response and smiled back. "Au contraire, study buddy, bringing you along would help me out. Mom likes me to make new friends and I'm sure she'll like you. Besides, you can do the girl talk about shopping and clothes. I'm a simple T-Shirt and jeans guy and pretty boring company for Mom."

Glenda's controlled face dropped its veil and she looked excited, "Yes, I'd really enjoy a night away from study, thanks for inviting me. I feel like I already know your mom, and she sounds great. Besides, it will be fun to get away from this boy's club. Give me a minute to get dressed." Then with a grin she added, "We modern girls move fast."

"Take your time," said Traveler. He almost added, "You can even put on your makeup before we leave," then he realized how insulting that was. *If any girl did not need makeup, it was this one.*

Glenda indeed moved fast. She came out of her room dressed for a festive Chicago Christmas winter. She was wearing an outfit a Paris runway model would enjoy showing off. Her long reddish hair was tucked up into a green ski hat with a bell on top from St. Moritz, Switzerland. Her fur-lined greatcoat promised warmth even in a Chicago winter. She had knee-length red leather boots with small Christmas bells strung across the top.

As she walked toward Traveler, the bells from top to bottom made a comforting seasonal jingle jangle sound that resonated softly in the great room. Theo lifted his head and looked her way. *Did that beast smile again?* thought Traveler. *Definitely part Cheshire cat in that DNA.*

Glenda knew exactly how she looked and said with an innocent face, "I like to jingle a little when it's Christmas time. I wore a hat all day in the orphanage with a big bell on top. I was the big elf and the younger kids loved it. Bells make a proper yuletide statement, don't you agree?"

Traveler would have agreed to anything she said in that moment, however his frog had returned. He finally muttered, "Yeah, I like the bells, quite a merry sound."

Once outside they headed up the alley. "Recommendation for a first-time alley exit," said Glenda. "Be careful when you step outside onto the normal street. This alley only appears to us. You don't want people to suddenly feel that aliens are among them."

Then she grinned, "Of course we are sort-of aliens at this point. Tally ho and away we go!" she said as she ran the remaining distance to the street. Traveler found he had to sprint to keep up.

She got to the entrance of the alley, saw the street was empty, and motioned for Traveler to follow her quickly as she ducked out. Traveler stayed close behind but was thinking, *How do I always end up following her? Guys are supposed to lead.*

Once on the street they both took deep breaths of the cold air. "It feels great to be outside again," Glenda said. "All that study makes Glenda a dull girl, and a girl's just gotta have fun."

Traveler felt energized as he walked up the street with Glenda beside him. Once on a main street filled with shoppers and businesspersons, he knew he had a stunner beside him. He felt the envious looks from the young men and the older men as they passed by. *Be careful what you wish for guys, she's a witch. And not always an agreeable one, believe me.*

"Let's pick up the pace but be careful, the streets can be slippery," said Glenda as she strode quickly forward. Wanting to reestablish his male presence Traveler offered, "I know the best way back to the hotel. Want me to lead in this Drake dance?"

"Sure thing, Mr. Bojangles, dance away; but I suggest you skip the high jumps. Because you're leading our conga line dance, could you get us quickly onto Michigan Avenue? I want to see the Christmas decorations and store windows."

"Your wish is my command," said Traveler as he thought, *Nice to know she still has a normal female shopping side to her. She and Mom will hit it off.*

The minute they were on wide, straight Michigan Avenue a heavy, snow-covered wind whipped them in the face. "Ouch!" said Glenda. "I never saw that coming. I'd muff up, big guy, if I were you."

Traveler accepted "big guy" as a compliment rather than a sarcastic poke. He immediately had his muffs on. "Hope I don't embarrass you."

"The only embarrassment would be if your ears froze and dropped off. Kids may use them as pucks to play ear hockey. That would be embarrassing."

Their sidewalk chatter stopped. There was too much cold wind off Lake Michigan for witty conversation. When they hit cross streets with red lights they both put their backs against the wind. The only thing Glenda said after walking along Michigan Avenue was, "Rats, it's too cold to look up. I'm missing the joy of window shopping." Traveler nodded in agreement.

# 36
# Mom, the Inspector General

They were overjoyed when they arrived at the front entrance to the Drake. Their faces were stiff, and Edward's earmuffs were frozen on the outside.

As they passed the doorman Traveler inquired, "Excuse me, sir, what's the time?" The doorman pulled back his heavy sleeve and affirmed it was about five o'clock, just as M had promised.

"I wondered if all this frozen time stuff was real, I guess it is." Glenda shook her head sadly like a teacher looking at the slow student in the class.

Traveler pushed the big door open before the doorman could get there. Part of him wanted to impress Glenda that male courtesy was still a good thing. He held it open and stood to the side so that Glenda could enter first. "Thank you, sir," she said.

Once inside they quickly took off their muffs and gloves. Glenda kept her winter hat on. "I'll call Mom from the house phone to alert her I'm bringing a friend. She'll probably want a few minutes to get ready."

While Traveler was dialing his mom, Glenda was enthralled by the Christmas scene. She looked at all the decorations hanging from ceiling and along the front desks.

She heard a whistle and a chugging sound from the large Christmas tree. She moved to the tree and was captivated as she watched the steam locomotive wind its way around boxes and through tunnels. *Feels like magic. I think magic is anywhere you find it.*

When Traveler returned, he saw her looking like a seven-year-old mesmerized by the moving train. "Pretty cool, huh?" She nodded. "Mom's ready but let me show you another place I think you'll like." He took her elbow and escorted her up a set of mini-steps. He noticed she did not jerk her arm away.

At the top of the mini-stairs, they were looking into an area reserved for adults. The area was set aside for the grownups to have drinks, finger foods, and conversations. In the center was a large fountain with tables positioned around it. "Remind you of anywhere?" Traveler asked and added, "What a great fountain area for conversation without the pressure to study."

Glenda agreed, "I love it."

"OK, it's show time, let's go meet The Mom."

As they rode the elevator up to the seventh floor, Traveler noticed Glenda was suddenly very quiet. She seemed subdued as they came off the elevator. Traveler sensed she was nervous about meeting his mom, but he had no idea why. He started some light patter to take her mind off meeting Mom.

"This is a great hotel. It was a landmark place in the 1930s. I think Capone stayed here for a while. They had a jazz band up by the fountain and there was a speakeasy room downstairs off the lobby.

"Our suite is great, as you'll see. We have two bedrooms, and each has its own bathroom. I can clutter everywhere and not bother Mom. Of course, nothing compares to our sanctuary, but for a hotel suite it's special."

Edward found he was portraying himself as an experienced traveler who knew his way around big city hotels. Of course, he knew his hotel experience was limited to the Omni hotel on the Downtown Mall in Charlottesville, but a little exaggeration never hurts any story. *Why am I exaggerating to impress her?* he wondered for a moment.

"We're here," he announced and knocked twice. Glenda jumped slightly at the knock. The door opened, and Virginia was standing there to welcome them in.

Traveler and Glenda both stared at Virginia, she was dressed to kill. She was in a formal evening gown. She was wearing a pearl necklace and long emerald earrings. Her dark hair rested on her shoulders with a Cleopatra cut across the front. "Looking great, Mom," Traveler said.

Traveler found he was unexpectedly nervous with Mom in the doorway and Glenda beside him. He made the introductions while still in the hallway. "Mom, this is my friend Glenda. Glenda, I guess you know this is my mom."

Virginia smiled and extended her hand to Glenda while she motioned for the two to get inside. "Please come in! You two look like you've just done the Iditarod Sled Dog Race. You really need to get out of those coats."

Glenda's mind was racing. Everyone knows when they meet somebody new that an immediate scrutiny takes place. Boys scrutinize girls, and girls scrutinize boys.

Glenda also knew that the toughest assessment came from mothers scrutinizing girls that their sons bring around. Glenda knew she was being placed on the mother's scales and being weighed. Anubis could learn a few things from a mother's sizing-up inspection.

Traveler noticed the tension vibe between Glenda and his mother. *Weird,* he thought as he went to help Glenda out of her heavy coat. What he received for his gentleman's effort was a look that said, "Back off buster." Glenda removed her coat and then handed it to Traveler. "Thanks, and would you stick my hat and scarf in there please?" said Glenda.

Virginia watched the interplay between the two over the transferring of clothing. *She is sure independent. She looks accustomed to being in charge. I like her assertive style, that may keep my son's ego in check.*

Once Glenda was out of her hat, coat, and scarf, Virginia continued to study the young girl. Glenda's red hair sparkled as it cascaded down to her shoulders. Her jeans and sweater were appropriately loose but still showed off her long legs.

*My little boy could be in very serious trouble with this one,* thought Virginia. *She's strong-willed, and an eleven on a scale of ten. Thankfully, we're heading home in five days, so she'll soon be a memory he can brag to his buddies about.*

"Please sit down and get comfortable," she motioned to the long sofa in front of the picture window. "There's a great bird's eye view of Chicago, Glenda. I love the city and we can see the heart of it from here.

"Can I order some hot chocolate for you two frozen snow birds?"

"That would be great, Mom," said Traveler.

"Yes, please. Thank you," agreed Glenda.

Virginia dialed room service and asked for a rush order. "Lots of whipped cream on both," she said then put down the phone.

Traveler and Glenda immediately took seats on opposite ends of the long couch. Virginia noticed the distance and thought, *Boy, are they making a statement. Don't know whether it's for me or between each other. Interesting.*

Virginia pulled up a cushioned chair across from them and gave Glenda another sweet smile. "What do you think of the room?" she asked.

"It's wonderful and you're right. I have never viewed my own city like this. It looks like one of those fantasy places in the glass snow globe you shake up."

Glenda knew she was still under a mother's close inspection. She felt trapped. She was beyond uncomfortable and was desperate to get the spotlight off herself. Then she had an inspiration. "Edward has talked about what great parents he has. How did you and your husband meet?"

Virginia smiled to herself. She understood Glenda was trying to get herself off the interview chair using a reflective question, but Virginia liked the question. There were positive dating messages contained in how she met Daniel that would be good for these two young people to hear.

"I'd love to tell you the story, Glenda, thanks for asking. It was one of Eddie's favorites when he was a preschooler. He hasn't heard it for many years, so it will be a walk down memory lane for him.

Traveler gave an enthusiastic nod. He remembered the story, or at least parts of it, and wanted to hear again how a young Mom and Dad fit into his own young adult experiences.

# 37
# Virginia Tells What Can Happen
# in a Library

"Let me start this tale by putting it in its proper setting," said Virginia. "As kismet would have it, we started college at Northwestern University outside Chicago at the same time. Your father was taking engineering and pre-med classes, while I was taking a double major in drama and computer science.

"My two majors were an unusual mix. I was both Beauty and the Beast. I was Beauty as the drama major, and Beast as a computer nerd.

"Early on, my college counselor was puzzled about my choosing to mix academic cats and dogs, but later she was quite supportive. She understood that if the theatre did not put food on my table, the computer degree would. Being a modern woman, I planned to take care of myself and not be dependent on a man."

Glenda gave a big nod of understanding and approval at this reflection. Traveler had a slightly puzzled look on his face, *I thought Mom always expected Dad to take care of both of us.*

"While we started at the same time, we never met. We ran in quite different social circles. I was with my artistic drama friends in my social time while your dad was a lone-wolf engineering student. He had decided to go on to med school, so his life was just study and grades. He had no social time.

"Being a drama major, my social dance card was full. I was attracted to the bigger-than-life personalities of actors, and they were attracted to me. Nowhere was there a thought regarding lone-wolf engineering nerds."

Virginia noticed that once again she had connected with the young girl. Glenda had a knowing smile that said, "I sure understand."

Traveler sensed there were two conversations going on, but he wasn't sure he was following both threads. *I remember Dad telling me that women never quite say what they mean. You have to read between the lines.*

Traveler smiled at his mom's bigger-than-life comparison and injected, "I believe Dad said that he hired one of these bigger-than-life drama guys for a commercial. The actor plays a guy who gets to mumble a few words about the efficacy of Dad's invention as he's wheeled into the OR. I recall Dad saying the actor was not going to get an Academy Award, but at least he'd have a little coffee money."

"Thank you, Eddie, for that insightful Dad comment. Anyway, we met quite by ⸻ 'e were preparing for final exams on a Saturday ⸻ late spring. We were both trying to study in the c ⸻ ⁄ and it was filled with cramming students.

"As fate would have it, we ended up sharing a two-person study table in a quiet alcove area of the library. Eddie, would you like to continue the story as you recall Dad telling it?"

Traveler perked up, he was getting a chance to join in the female conversation as a surrogate for Dad, "Sure thing, Mom. It was spring, and that means final exam stress. Even we high school students can relate. The library was packed. With finals approaching, all the grasshoppers who had spent the school year having fun were in the library cramming."

Traveler looked at Glenda and explained, "Glenda, Dad called the liberal arts students who seemed to slide through college 'grasshoppers.'"

Glenda looked him in the eye and said, "Yes, Eddie, I get it, the old 'Grasshopper and Ant' story." Virginia smiled at the mild rebuke.

Unfazed Traveler continued, "Being a hard-working ant, Dad normally spent a lot of time in the library. He had certain quiet areas where he preferred to study alone. On this particular Saturday, he had exercised early with a long run and arrived at the library later than usual. All his preferred study areas were occupied by grasshoppers.

"He was annoyed as he was forced to walk around trying to find a quiet study nook. Finally, he spotted an isolated area tucked into the furthest p--- -f *h- '--rary. He saw a table sticking out between two                    ɔticed that the table's outside chair was empty. H                 'd lucked out.

"When he got there, h                 ɪside chair was taken. Sitting in the chair w;                 ˙ course, who had her writing materials anc                 cross the table. Dad thought she was claiming the entire table, which is rude to say the least.

"Dad asked her if she minded sharing the table. He admits that his tone of voice made it sound more like an order than a request."

Again, Glenda and Virginia exchanged knowing looks. They both understood the male territorial perspective.

"He said she never looked up, just grunted and said, 'If you really need to.' Dad said that she was very dramatic in pulling her books to her side of the table."

"I'll continue the story now, Eddie. You've done a nice job describing your dad's side of our meeting."

Glenda found she was both amused and invested in this story. *Like father, like son,* she almost blurted out.

"So, this geek intruded into my space just at the time that I was on fire writing a short play. When you are in your own creative world, any interruption is a major annoyance. Still, I politely moved my materials when he asked.

"Your dad was carrying a hundred pounds of books and promptly dropped them on the table; the noise startled half the library. 'How rude is this guy?' I thought.

"Then I realized it was springtime. Many of the male students are sick of study and are looking for female entertainment. I thought y~~~ ~~~ ~~~~ probably just another lone wolf on the prowl. I ~~~ tally ignoring him he would move on to greener ~es.

"Once he settled do~ he was quiet as a gravedigger. That was I was able to fall back into my writing zone. · so passed, I became aware of his sitting there like a rock, 'Does it breathe?' I thought."

Glenda was captured by the story. She could visualize Traveler as his dad with a super-sized ego and a level of disdain for non-science students. She loved how Virginia described Daniel as a silent rock while studying. *That fits big boy to a T.*

Virginia saw that both Glenda and her son were enjoying her story. Of course, their reactions to the story were quite different. The drama major in her increased the energy she was putting into the story.

"I admit I was slightly curious about him since he had not attempted any conversation. I wondered whether he could be a silent stalker in the stacks. I began to create a short one-act play in my mind. I surreptitiously glanced at his books and confirmed my suspicions about his being a geek, they were all science books.

"Then I noticed his posture. It reminded me of a rabbit pressed against the ground to hide from a hawk. His head rested on his hands with his nose a foot from the pages; he was the living caricature of an introverted geek engineer.

"At least he won't bother me, I thought. Like all geeks, he's too shy to talk to a pretty girl. He probably struggled to pass English 101."

"Mom, can I pick it up now? I think Dad needs his time in the witness box."

"Of course, dear. I know you want to be sure your dad's side is well represented."

"After some intense study time Dad had to stretch, every runner's body tightens up after running. He said that since he could not stretch in the confined area without hitting the grasshopper girl, he had to stand."

"In standing up he naturally took a quick look at what the grasshopper was doing. He said he was mildly curious about her nonstop scribbling. What masterpiece does she think she's creating? He saw her drama books that confirmed his suspicions that she was another grasshopper killing time in college.

"As he was stretching he noticed she had a book on advanced computer system designs buried under her sea of writing paper. He thought, 'She's probably carrying it to impress technical people. Maybe it's her grasshopper trap to catch the attention of a future Bill Gates.'

"Dad said that while he was standing his eyes naturally shifted to her face. Because she was hunched over and scribbling, he only had a fast impression. I remember Dad saying that he thought she could be pretty.

"Another hour passed, and Dad was suddenly thirsty, running will do that. Since he was late getting started, he had skipped his usual hydration routine and was now quite thirsty.

"When he stood up he had to move his chair back. He said it made a long-wicked scraping noise like fingernails going down a blackboard. The grasshopper flinched as if she was hit from behind.

"Dad said he was embarrassed and immediately gave a short, 'I'm sorry' apology. He said the girl simply nodded but never looked up. Dad compared her to a queen acknowledging a lowly servant who had screwed up and dropped a dish.

"Despite being ignored, Dad felt it would be rude not to at least offer water to the queen and said, 'I'm going for some water, would you like a cup?' He said she looked up and stared at him. He saw her lips start to form a 'No thank you. Please be quiet' answer.

"Mom, this part of the story will make you feel great. Dad said that when he actually looked you in the face he was stunned. He said you were a show-stopping beauty. He admitted his legs got wobbly and he had a frog in his throat."

Glenda grinned at this mental picture of a tongue-tied Daniel. *So, frogs in throat are an inherited male trait from father to son. Now I know where Traveler gets it.*

"My story now," said Virginia. "I was really annoyed at the long scrape. It broke my focus a second time. I thought, 'What an inconsiderate dolt.' I was prepared to chastise him by pointing to the 'Quiet' sign, and then he offered water.

"I was ready to snap his head off with a fast 'No thanks! Try to be quiet.' when I looked up and saw him for the first time. He was tall, lean, and rather good-looking in a disheveled, bad boy way. My mom and dad would say he needed a shave and a haircut. His hair was dark and down to his shoulders. He could have been a drama student.

"Something amazing happened when we made that first eye contact, it still does right to this day. I felt myself blush and was at a loss for words. Modesty aside, I'm a very good writer and a natural impromptu actress; I'm never at a loss for words. 'This is very weird' was all I could think and just nodded 'OK.'

"He returned with water and the table glacier melted. We started to talk. Conversation was easy, intriguing, and fun. His water offer later turned into a beer and pizza offer. Over pizza

I thought, 'What's happening here? This is too weird.' The rest, as they say, is history.

"So, was our meeting magic or just an accident? Eddie, your dad the scientist tried to explain it as 'particle entanglement.' He said that quantum physics tells us that when two particles are entangled they affect each other regardless of the distance between them. He compared us to entangled particles that had been circling each other on campus for years."

Virginia closed with, "I prefer the 'magic' answer, Eddie. Particle physics is in the realm of magic, so I think strange forces were at work on us. The proof is that we now have a magical son."

Traveler reflected on his mom's story. *It's a funny thing about parent stories. You've heard them all many times, but each time you hear them you find something a little different and interesting. It's like rereading a good book or watching a great movie multiple times.*

"Wow," said Glenda. "What a great story! Sounds a lot like magic to me, and I can tell the magic is still there." Virginia gave a big affirmative head nod.

# 38
## Change of Plans

"Ah, Mom, what's the schedule for tonight? You're dressed to kill, and I thought this was a casual eat-in with a movie."

Virginia laughed, "That was the plan, but guess what changed?"

Traveler had a blank look on his face. "No idea, Mom. Did you run into an old college girlfriend from the theatre?"

"Nope, even a bigger coincidence. Do you remember Mr. Mert, the nice magician from the train that entertained us? We called him M. Well, he called and invited both of us to a musical tonight. He knew I was alone, well with you of course, Eddie, and thought the two of us would like a night on the town. I can call him and see if he could get another ticket for Glenda."

*Dad alert,* thought Traveler as he saw the excitement on his mom's face. Virginia read Traveler's face and smiled to herself. *I'm not as ancient as you think, son. A fit forty is the new thirty.*

Glenda was watching Edward's reaction and thought, *M, you old dog, and you are certainly a very old dog. Good for you. Squirm, young Traveler, I like to see you off balance.*

Virginia continued, "He is such an old-world gentleman. He actually called your dad before inviting us out. He made the effort to track him down in New York. He introduced himself to your dad and asked permission to invite us out. Apparently, he knows people in common with your dad and suggested he be reference checked.

"Your dad made some calls and called me back. He was quite pleased that M had offered to show us the town for our first night. 'Now don't do it unless you have the energy,' he said.

"I assured your dad that we had lots of energy. The train ride and hotel were both restful. I told him our suite was marvelous and wished he were here with us. He called M back, thanked him for his thoughtfulness, and here we are."

Virginia added, "Dad also said that while talking with M he had the strangest sense of déjà vu. 'I swear I've met him somewhere but can't put my finger on it. I've got a strong memory, so this is a bit weird.'" Traveler and Glenda exchanged looks that went way past Virginia.

"OK, Mom, that sounds like a great night for you. Since I invited Glenda for a casual burger dinner and an in-room movie, I think we'll stick with that plan."

"Of course, dear, whatever you two want to do is fine with me. If you order room service, please get whatever you want. It's a great menu and you can do better than a burger, so feel free to pick whatever sounds tempting." Traveler thought she looked a bit pleased to have the evening to herself but decided he was imagining things.

A knock at the door announced the hot cocoa had arrived. "Boy, that was fast," said Traveler as he tried to make simple conversation. He went to the door and the room service man placed the mug tray on the table between the three people. Virginia signed the bill and the server left.

"Enjoy what only hot chocolate can do on a freezing Chicago night," said Virginia.

Traveler and Glenda both took their mugs and began to stare into the whipped cream. The mugs provided a conversation safe harbor. Virginia enjoyed their nervousness. *Better she's nervous right now than being a look-at-me girl.*

"Well, how did you two meet? This is a big city, so it must be a nice story. Eddie, why don't you take the lead and let Glenda enjoy her hot chocolate?"

Glenda jumped a tad with the mention of her name. She was aware that Virginia was continuing to measure her, and she felt a slight blush come to her cheeks. Edward enjoyed her moment of discomfort then he started his story.

"We met at the museum, Mom. What a great place and what a fantastic display from ancient Syria." Traveler proceeded to tell the story, including his meeting with the curator. Naturally, he omitted how he had broken in.

"The display had just reopened, and I was the only person there when Glenda showed up. It turns out the curator was there and the three of us got into a discussion of ancient tribes and their religions. He gave us a lecture about the portal and the fears even modern city people have about it." Glenda was amused by how casually Traveler fabricated their meeting but she also sensed Traveler was omitting something important.

"Your turn now," said Traveler, "my whipped cream needs attending." Glenda picked up on Traveler's story and wove her own story into it. She used part of her story to add embellishments to Traveler's tale.

As Glenda talked, she became relaxed. The mother was clearly enjoying her tale and seemed to be accepting her as a companion for her son. *She is certainly protective of her precious son Eddie. I guess all mothers have that mother bear instinct.*

# 39
# Glenda Tells a Personal Story

"Can you tell me a little about yourself, Glenda?" asked Virginia. "You look like you have Scandinavian blood. Where did you grow up? What are your parents like? Please don't be offended, this is the usual stuff all parents ask about their children's friends." Then Virginia gave her a knowing look and added, "Yes, we mothers are also a little nosy."

Glenda was now relaxed with the mother's questions. In fact, she found she liked talking with ego boy's mom. "You are very perceptive about my heritage. Yes, I am a girl of the north. I was born in Norway and both of my parents were Norwegian. I love cold weather and snow."

Traveler thought, *I knew she was an ice princess. She has frost hanging on half her words with me.* Wanting to get into the conversation he asked, "Are you a good skier?"

Virginia laughed, and Glenda looked at him like that was the dumbest question ever. "Of course, I am. Norwegians ski before we walk. How are you as a skier, Eddie?"

Edward knew when to retreat with grace and humor, "Well, the short answer is pretty bad; I fall over when I'm on skis, I'm a serious danger to all around me. In my defense, I grew up in Virginia and our big snow may last a few days and then it's just a lot of sloppy mud. I could probably mud ski if I put my mind to it." Both Virginia and Glenda laughed at the image of a tall Traveler skiing down a steep, muddy backyard.

"What do your parents do?" asked Virginia, bringing the focus back to the young lady. Glenda looked distant for a moment and said, "They died in an auto accident when I was five years old. I was placed into an orphanage in Oslo. Then I was brought to America to live with my father's sister.

"Sadly, she died two years later, and I was raised in a Chicago orphanage for children of Scandinavia descent. We studied our native language and customs there. In many ways Chicago feels like a Norwegian city, particularly in the winter."

Traveler suddenly felt embarrassed over needling Glenda about being an ice princess. *I guess she really is a kind of ice princess, but without a kingdom. No mom and dad, that's a sad way to grow up.* Virginia gave Glenda a sympathetic look that told Glenda she felt her loss.

Virginia immediately changed the subject with an upbeat offer, "I'm off shopping tomorrow, Glenda. I would enjoy your company if you have some free time. I know Edward finds shopping painful, as does his dad. All they do is stand there, look at their watches, and twitch.

"I don't know whether my tastes are close to yours, but we'll have fun anyway. Tell Eddie if that works for you, and we'll connect tomorrow if it does."

Glenda immediately answered, "Don't need Eddie on this one. I know right now that it would be a lot of fun. Thank you for letting me tag along, I know I can really help you spend your money. Let's spend some of Eddie's college tuition, shall we?"

Virginia laughed, "A splendid idea." Traveler knew it was all a joke but again he was annoyed being the outsider in the conversation. Before he could think of some witty rejoinder, Glenda spoke.

"What time would you like me here? I'm very flexible, anytime works for me."

"Oh, let's say around eleven o'clock. I may be moving slowly tomorrow after a night on the town." Traveler frowned at this "night on the town" comment. He was reconsidering that maybe he should go along on this outing. However, it was too late for a change in plans, the room phone rang, and Virginia picked it up.

"Good evening to you too, M. Don't worry about timing, I'm a modern woman and won't keep you fashionably waiting. I'll be down in a minute."

*Are all women today born as modern women, whatever that means?* Traveler wondered.

Virginia took her formal coat out of closet. "That's my curtain call. You two enjoy the movie with room service or go for a pizza or both. Remember, Eddie, the best pizza is at Gino's East."

"Yes, Mom, I think I know that. By the way, what's the musical?"

"Oh, it's a great one called *Cats*. I actually had one of the leads a long time ago in our college production. M has seen it many times, he seems to know a lot about cats. He says he finds them magical creatures. Bet I hear a lot more about cats after the show."

Traveler and Glenda again exchanged knowing looks. "Yeah, he strikes me as a guy who probably keeps a pet cat," said Traveler with a sly smile. Glenda had the same sly look and Virginia wondered if there was a private joke in there somewhere.

*How could these two who have just met already have a relationship with private jokes? Yikes, come to think of it, I guess Daniel and I had our own insider jokes starting with beer and pizza after the library.* Then she thought, *Did I just use the word "relationship" with them? Oh, no, I hope she doesn't break Eddie's young heart. He needs to start dating when we get back, there's nothing like a new girlfriend to dim the light of the old favorite.*

# 40
# Pizza and Conversation

After Virginia left, Traveler waited a few minutes then checked the hallway. "The coast is clear," he said, "we can head back to the sanctuary now."

"Why would we do that, Eddie?" Traveler winced at her pejorative use of Eddie. "I'm hungry, and besides it's clear your mom wants us to go to Gino's. She's feeling guilty about leaving us while she's out on the town with M. She'll ask me about Gino's when I see her, and I don't want to hurt her feelings. Of course, if Eddie's too tired from all the walking let me know and we'll head back. Your call, big boy."

Traveler knew a playful challenge; besides, it sounded a little bit like an ice princess invitation. "Gino's sounds like a good plan to me. Besides, we know M will not be preparing a feast tonight. I suggest Sallyforth put on all of her coat, gloves, scarf, and ski hat and we head out."

Glenda gave him a look, "Touché, big boy."

When they got to the lobby, Traveler asked for directions to Gino's East. The doorman looked skeptically at them. "It's a good six blocks and it's freezing. Let me get you a cab."

Glenda smiled, "Thanks but we love cold weather. This is just a brisk night in Norway. I'll help my friend here into a cab if he fades on the way."

*Hoof-it challenge accepted,* thought Traveler.

They turned right out of the hotel and were quickly on Michigan Avenue, it was a deserted white wonderland. Streetlights made the sidewalks glitter and a few diehard Salvation Army Santas were still ringing in Christmas, but mostly they were trying to stay warm.

As Traveler passed the last Santa, he dropped some quarters in the kettle. The quarters sounded sad as they left a warm pocket to go into a freezing pot. "Merry Christmas," called the Santa after them as they fast-walked down the avenue.

"Nicely done," was what Traveler thought he heard from Glenda through her scarf. A compliment from the ice princess strangely warmed him up a bit.

Neither acknowledged the biting cold wind. Neither would ask how much farther to go. Then Gino's appeared as an oasis in an artic snowstorm. They were quickly inside taking off their coats when Traveler said, "Just a nice stroll in a Norwegian night, right?"

"Well, OK, maybe it was a bit more than that. And yes, I'm glad to be inside now."

Once in a booth they ordered the famous pizza. "What size do you feel like?" asked Traveler.

"Let's get a large. I'm ravenous, and I think Theo would appreciate a piece."

*The beast eats, could have fooled me,* thought Traveler. "Have you actually seen him eat?" asked Traveler.

"Of course, M prepares special meals for him. He is a quiet, polite eater. If you were not watching you would never know he eats at all. He's nothing like a noisy dog gulping down whatever is in his dish."

"I'm a dog person but I agree dogs have no pride around food. While cats seem aloof about their food, they are also aloof about a lot of other stuff, like affection. At least dogs show you their love."

"Au contraire, I know for a certainty Theo appreciates affection. If you find him standing beside you, staring at you and you wonder why, the answer is he wants his fur rubbed.

"There are the most amazing electric sparks that jump off his fur when it's rubbed. He also makes a noise like purring, but it feels more like a sonic vibration. You'll feel like 'the force is with you', it's a great feeling."

After the deep dish arrived, they both took large slices and began serious eating. Both concentrated on the pie and ate in silence. Occasionally they made slurping sounds with their sodas. Traveler launched an unintentional belch and turned a shade of red. Glenda laughed at both his embarrassment and the sonic boom of the male burp.

Finally, they both came up for air, and Traveler asked, "So are you really an orphan from Norway? Was there really an aunt here?"

"Yes, yes, and no," answered Glenda. "Yes, on Norway, and yes, my parents died when I was just five, but there was no American aunt. I was placed in an orphanage outside of Oslo after my parents died."

"How did you really get here then?"

"It started less than a year ago when I was almost sixteen. All of us in the orphanage came into Oslo for a field trip over the Christmas holidays. We were getting hot chocolate inside a Santa Village exhibit when M struck up a conversation.

"He seemed like a friendly young man, and I was with friends and teachers, so I felt quite safe. I was also a bit flattered that a rather handsome young man would start up a conversation with me." Traveler held back a grimace at the thought of "handsome M" engaging his mother with his stories and his magic.

"We were discussing the Santa Village exhibit when he changed gears. He began to describe a toy factory that he said was exactly like Santa's workshop. He claimed it produced marvelous toys that seemed magical.

"I laughed, of course, assuming he was kidding with me. I remember looking at him and saying, 'You do realize I'm sixteen and quite a few years beyond childhood fairy tales.'

"M did not seem annoyed at all by my skepticism and just smiled back. 'Well, I'll let you judge the quality of their creations. I can't really call them toys, I find them remarkable. Here's a sample, tell me what you think of it.' He handed me a book with a leather cover. I looked at the illustrated cover. The cover presented a smiling Santa elf in his sleigh in front of a charming cottage in the woods. I looked at the title and, naturally, it was *The Night Before Christmas*.

"'Of course, I know the story,' I said. 'We all grow up with it.'

"'Well, open the book and tell me if that's the story you remember.'

"I opened the book and an amazing thing happened. The drawings in the book were animated. It was much more advanced than what you have on a smartphone. It was interactive in a totally realistic way. It felt like virtual reality, but in a book, I was stunned.

"M said, 'If you think that's interesting, you are invited to visit the workshop. Here's an invitation card. I have to return the book, but if you visit I'm sure I can find a copy for you.' He then headed off into a busy part of the city.

"Of course, I was now fascinated and wanted to visit this workshop. I felt the book would be an amazing gift for our orphanage. The next day I was in downtown Oslo again with my friends. Feeling bold, I left my group and followed the map on the back of his card.

"As I followed the map, I discovered I was on less traveled streets, but I felt very safe. People in Oslo are no longer dangerous Vikings, but are very caring and polite to others.

"Then on a deserted side street I saw the map suddenly projected dots that ended before the next intersection. As I approached the intersection, an alley just seemed to appear, and the dots indicated to enter it.

"I am adventuresome by nature, but not foolhardy. I stood there and looked down the alley. It was empty except for a lamp hanging part way down the wall. I decided the lamp must mark the workshop, so I went down to it."

"Let me guess," said Traveler. "There was a heavy iron cat head knocker that opened the door after one knock."

Glenda smiled, "I think you know the rest of the story."

Traveler nodded his head and said, "This is just too strange. Can I ask you a kind of personal question?"

"Sure, fire away," said Glenda.

"How old are you in real time? Are you a hundred- or thousand-year-old time-traveler?"

Glenda laughed, "I wondered when you would ask. Do I look a hundred? Do I remind you of Yoda?"

Traveler looked embarrassed, "Well, you could be. How would I know with all this *Groundhog Day* stuff going on?"

"Relax, southern boy, I'm close to my natural seventeenth birthday, it comes right after Christmas, early February to be precise. I just arrived at M's sanctuary castle a few months ahead of you. Of course, my studies have made me a very advanced person despite my youth."

*She's really just a bit ahead of me on the study side, and she is my age.* He felt a sense of relief on both counts.

"So back at you, Traveler: how old are you in normal time?" Then she paused. "Wait. All your time so far is normal time. You haven't lived in the sanctuary very long. Anyway, how old are you?"

"My seventeenth birthday is also coming up after Christmas, February thirteenth to be exact."

Glenda looked taken aback, "That's my birthday also. This shared birthday business seems very weird. As Alice said to the Cheshire cat in Alice in Wonderland, this is curiouser and curiouser."

"I know one thing for sure," said Traveler.

"What's that?" asked Glenda.

"We're certainly not brother and sister. Whatever we have in common, besides birthdays, we're not siblings." Glenda gave him a strange look and nodded her head in agreement.

"OK, I think it's time to head back, it's going to be really cold out there," said Glenda. "Let's put on our artic gear and brave the Chicago elements."

Traveler nodded and picked up the bill, studied the amount, and then paid the waiter in cash. Glenda gave him a sweet smile and said, "A gentleman of means, thank you, sir. More to the point, thanks to your parents."

The warm dinner mood turned frosty, Traveler was clearly annoyed. "If I'm a man of means it's because I work, I always have. I cut five yards a week in the summer growing up. By the time I was fifteen, I worked sixty hours a week in the summer at a local grocery store. How's your work-life so far?"

Glenda thought, *Whoops, I stepped on a Traveler ego landmine. He's sure sensitive about his parents funding his teenage lifestyle.* "Sorry for the dumb comment," Glenda immediately said. "Too many kids today do not work. I assumed you were one of them coming from such a prosperous family.

"Let me start over, take my foot out of my mouth and say again, thank you, Traveler. The pizza was excellent, best I've ever had. The conversation and company were more than acceptable also.

"By the way, I did grow up working in the orphanage. I was never paid, but all of us had daily work responsibilities based on our ages. Early on, I cleaned the kitchen after dinner.

When I got older, I tutored the younger kids. Believe me, cleaning the dishes was easier than tutoring young kids."

Traveler knew a sincere apology when he heard one; he also knew the best response was to accept it graciously. "Sorry for the snap back. I was lucky to be able to find work. I think you had the tougher end of the work stick."

Glenda found she liked that quick dismissal of her faux pas. *He's not taking advantage of a simple slipup, good marks for big boy.*

# 41
# After Dinner Ambush

Once outside Traveler looked for a cab, saw none and said, "I know a shortcut from here. We'll go on a few side streets, walk fast, and be there before our ears freeze and drop off." Glenda nodded, it was too cold for conversation and a shortcut sounded like the ticket.

They had walked about ten minutes when Traveler stopped. "I need to get my bearings. This snow is making navigation a bit harder. Can you read that street sign on the far corner?"

While Traveler and Glenda were squinting at the sign, a raspy voice behind them asked, "Lost, children? This is our street, so we can direct you, but first there is a matter of a toll."

Traveler and Glenda turned to find a large twenty-year-old behind them. The man had thick, dark stubble on his face, close-set narrow eyes with bad teeth that made a nasty smile. *Big Bob lives in Chicago,* flashed through Traveler's mind.

Flanking the leader were two slightly smaller but equally nasty looking thugs. They wore the well-practiced smirks that are common to gang members showing off to each other and their leader.

The center man was in charge and put his hand out, "You can consider me a Chicago Robin Hood, and these are two of my Merry Men. I'll warn you though; they are really not very merry on a cold night like this. I would not rile them up; they are not a pretty pair once angered.

"From your attire it's clear you're both rich spoiled kids, so a little contribution to Robin and his men will make you feel better about yourselves." Looking at Traveler he said, "Just hand over your wallet and you can continue on your way. If your cash is light, credit cards will make up the toll. Chop chop now."

Traveler watched as the two less-than-merry men took positions to the right and left of Robin. It was clear they all had bad intentions. Traveler knew his wallet would just be the beginning of the toll. It was likely that once he handed it over, Robin would up the ante for their moving on.

"Robin, I think your better name is, 'Robbin in the Hood.' Your Merry Men look like sad high school dropouts. You all need a shave and a long shower; I can smell you through your coats. Now we're going to ignore you and continue on our way."

Robbin gave a wolfish smile back at Traveler. It reminded Traveler not so much of a smile as a flashing guillotine blade as it fell. The smile reminded Glenda of a cruising crocodile. She knew this croc certainly had nasty intentions.

The man's smile turned downward, the guillotine blade approached the victim's neck. "A smart-mouthed boy, huh? Big man on the college campus with Dad's allowance? Trying to impress the girlfriend. Very big mistake. Meet Groan and Moan," and he motioned to his crew.

On cue, both thugs closed beside him and held up their hands. Covering each hand was a steel gauntlet fashioned after fifteenth-century knight's armor. The metal gauntlets covered the fists and went half way up the forearms. They were new but fashioned after fifteenth-century knight's hand armor. One blow could be lethal if it landed solidly. Etched on one was "Groan" and on the other, "Moan."

Traveler studied the gauntlets. *Everything is available on the internet. Probably made in China. A lot of Chinese steel is poor quality, but I guess a punch will still do the job.*

"In case you need more history lessons, pretty boy, meet 'Brutus.'" With that, the leader reached into his open long coat and withdrew a gladius sword. "As a college boy you do know what Brutus did to Caesar, I assume?"

Then he motioned with the point of the gladius, "I'm getting chilled. You've taken too long to pay the piper, so the toll has just gone up. We'll start with those heavy coats you're both wearing along with the babe's purse. You should have paid the first toll, college boy. Pay now then run like hell home to Mommy and Daddy."

Glenda was breathing hard with a racing heart. She had a rush of adrenaline coursing through her body. She looked at Traveler to see what their move should be. Traveler was patiently watching the three men.

She noted he seemed relaxed then she heard him calmly say, "You three hoods are the furthest thing from brave Saxons, Romans, or knights. You're just a pack of mean-spirited street bullies. Since it's Christmas, I suggest you take your internet bought toys and leave."

The leader's face flushed, Groan and Moan were watching him, the college boy was embarrassing him. By nature, he was a thug of action. He had learned early on that actions on the street mattered, not words. He intended to affirm his toughness with his gang and place the mouthy kid in a private room at the hospital.

"Too bad the babe has to see this, but she chose to be with a smart mouth college boy. Live and learn, gorgeous."

Robbin made a classic forward lunge with the gladius. He had practiced the move many times by watching knife and fencing moves on YouTube. The gladius was aimed at Traveler's stomach with bad intentions.

What happened next was a blur to the three thugs. Traveler stepped to the side of the incoming gladius, took the man's wrist and twisted hard. The gladius fell into Traveler's hand. Holding the gladius Traveler stepped back a pace, "Brutus, here's a little payback from Caesar." He snapped the sword over a knee and threw the broken pieces across the street.

Without pausing, he stepped forward and delivered an open palm slap that stunned each thug, their eyes rolled up. The slap was instantly followed by a powerful leg sweep that had the three thugs collapsed into a mixed pile on the ground. Traveler reached down and pulled the gauntlets off the stunned Merry Men. "I'll put these toys inside my gerbil terrarium. I'll think of you three tough guys whenever my gerbil pees on them."

As Glenda and Traveler stepped around the three prone hoods Traveler looked down, "Sheriff, strongly suggest you stay out of Sherwood Forest. By the way, call me 'Little John.'"

As they headed down the street neither was breathing hard. Glenda finally laughed and said, "Wow! I am very impressed. Your super-charged reflexes made that look easy. Well done, Little John!"

While trying to appear as Mr. Cool, Traveler still had a strong adrenaline buzz going. He smiled at Glenda's compliment. "Thank you, Maid Marian. It appears there is still a need for knights, even in this modern world. But, now would be a good time to exit Sherwood and mach schnell it back before we draw a crowd. Those cowards will cry like babies and claim to be victims."

Their return required fast walking into a fierce Lake Michigan wind that seemed determined to push them backwards. Both kept their heads down and eyes focused on the sidewalk immediately ahead. It was past ten o'clock when they were back at the entrance to their alley. Once in the alley the wind stopped, and they took deep breaths. "Home sweet home," muttered Traveler as he pushed the door open.

They put away their winter gear and proceeded to the fireplace. They sat down in front of it with Theo between them. Traveler tentatively reached out his right hand and rested it on Theo's massive shoulder.

He did a small fur rub and was rewarded with a purring vibration. "Let's spoil him rotten tonight," said Glenda. She put her left hand on Theo's head and rubbed it with little tugs on his ears. The room was now vibrating a message of calm and happiness. They sat by the fire, relaxed and enjoying the shared bonding with Theo.

Traveler wanted to stay up to catch M coming home; he had many questions to ask. He was doing his best to hold off Morpheus, but he was failing miserably. Glenda saw his conflict and said, "Come on, big boy, rise and move. Your mom's just fine. Mr. M is more of a proper chaperone than anybody else I've ever met." Traveler slowly got up and followed her.

With a serious look she said, "Our study really ramps up tomorrow after a day off. We need to go into hyper-study mode or bear the wrath of our books. By the way, be sure and put the book under your pillow tonight. The book will enjoy your use of enhanced reflexes to put the thugs down." With that, she went into her room.

In his room, Traveler took off his shoes and put the book under his pillow. Morpheus greeted him immediately and he collapsed into a deep dreamless sleep.

# 42

# News Over Breakfast

Glenda woke the next morning with a rush of energy; she felt like a fully charged cell phone. She failed to consider that the energy was a carryover from the prior day's fun activities.

As she showered, she planned her day. *I feel like my book approved of the time off yesterday, but is expecting a full-steam-ahead effort today. A solid ten hours of bookwork before I head out to meet up with Virginia will do the job. After my ten hours, I'll take the shopping break with Virginia and then come back to study for another four hours. I'll keep advancing relative to big boy. There's no way he keeps up with this Nordic goddess today.*

Glenda found she was really looking forward to shopping with her newfound friend. *Virginia seems very young to be anybody's mom; maybe the better word is youthful. She exudes a lot of positive energy. I wonder what his dad is like. I hope he's held up as well as she has and isn't another potbellied businessman.*

Glenda's stomach gave her an additional wakeup call. *Wow, I'm hungry despite all that pizza. I smell M's homemade pastry and coffee, but first I want a slice of fresh pineapple, yum.*

She slipped into a simple one-piece, loose dress with a wide silver belt and admired the look in the long mirror. *I feel like wearing a blue outfit inside and maybe a Christmas green and red one when I join up with Virginia.* For a moment she was considering what shopping coat and boots to wear, but then pulled her mind back to the day's study requirements.

As she came into the hallway, she gave three loud knocks on Traveler's door. "Up and at 'em before the sun sets, big boy. Time waits for no one. Actually, time does wait here, but you get the idea."

She was Tigger bouncing her way into the main room when she passed the study alcove. "Good morning, princess. Did you dance the night away and need to sleep late for your beauty rest?" came a familiar annoying voice.

*Rats, I don't believe it. He beat me up and sounds as annoying early as he does late in the day.* "Actually, I've been up for some time and decided to study in my room, thank you."

Traveler looked at her, grinned and said, "I'm sure. By the way, early bird, you want to get the muffins before they cool off. There are assorted berries that look good. I ate the pineapple; it was so ripe I just had to finish it." He put his head back to his book and missed the glare coming from Glenda.

Glenda headed to the fountain table. She felt her early morning joy being burned away by annoying boy's consumption of the pineapple. As she sat down M joined her.

"It's nice to see you are already rubbing off on Traveler. He was here half an hour ago looking for you. Said he wanted to try to keep up with you. By the way, he said the pineapple was particularly fresh this morning and insisted I save a nice wedge for you."

Glenda felt the early morning's positive energy coming back in a wave. *So, he's only been up a little while and knows I set a hard pace. At least he has enough drive to try to stay up with the leader.*

She bit into a chunk of pineapple and the sugary morsel was a bugle call in her mouth. *Wonderful pineapple! I guess he is not quite as selfish as he first seemed,* she thought, taking another chunk of the juicy, yellow fruit.

Theo was standing beside her at the table. M motioned at Theo, "I think he wants a piece of the pineapple and maybe a morning head rub. You and Traveler spoiled him last night. I know when he's had head rubs, he was a slumped kitty when I got home."

Glenda smiled at Theo. "Does my big boy want a nice piece of pineapple and another head rub?" she said, while feeding a choice morsel into the waiting maw.

As she was scratching his head she suddenly thought, *Shame on me. Did I just call Theo big boy? For sure I'm not mixing up annoying boy with the mighty Theo.*

She poured herself a mug of the cinnamon and nutmeg scented coffee and grabbed a warm muffin. "Excuse me, M. I'd better get into studying before my book gets mad at me. I'll see if Traveler needs any help this morning."

"Help him all he needs, tutoring benefits the teacher as well as the student. I suggest you take him a muffin. He only ate two, I'm sure he wanted a third but was saving it for you. Don't let him know I told you he's already had two," M said with a grin.

"Oh, before you go, here's an interesting article from the morning *Sun-Times*."

With two muffins wrapped in a napkin and the *Times* paper, Glenda bounced to the alcove. She sat down to find Traveler immersed in his book. "M suggested you may like another muffin," she said sliding one over to Traveler.

Without looking up he said "Thanks" and kept his head down.

Glenda watched him eat the muffin without looking up either at her or the muffin. *Amazing. Maybe the ability to eat on the run was how men survived all the way from the cave days to the present. I don't think they could have appreciated what they consumed. To them it was probably just calories.*

When Traveler had finished inhaling the muffin Glenda said, "M also suggested we read a story in this morning's paper." She slid next to Traveler and they both began to read a front-page story.

"Karate Kids Clobber." The story recounted how a passing Yellow Cab driver saw multiple bodies on the sidewalk late the prior night. He immediately notified the police who arrived in minutes.

The squad car team made a cursory inspection of the injured. Even though they appeared roughed up, they were certainly fine from the officers' view. At the same time, legal prudence required they call an emergency medical van. The lead officer said to his partner, "Last thing we want is these punks suing the city for failing to get them medical treatment ASAP. What a waste of taxpayer money."

The newspaper detailed the story told to the police by the victims. They claimed a young man and woman had accosted them with guns and Tasers demanding money. When they could not pay the demanded toll, they were zapped and severely kicked while lying on the sidewalk.

The gang leader had his fifteen minutes of media fame as a victim. "They were monsters. They were copycatting the old movie, *A Clockwork Orange*. They copied what those London street thugs did and used karate kicks with steel boots. They almost killed us."

The police had their own idea of what had actually happened. At the morning precinct meeting, the sergeant summed it up for the seated patrol officers, "We know this crew of thugs, a nasty bunch. They use steel gauntlets to sucker punch. They likely ran into a tougher gang. We can hope the punks will thin the herd fighting with each other." Heads nodded in agreement as they headed out into the freezing Chicago morning.

# 43
# Sanctuary Life

The two settled into their normal, deep study trances. The only break in their routine was for bathroom breaks. Glenda was the first to stand up and thought, *Surely, he is not challenging me about who can sit the longest. Maybe I'm letting myself see challenges when there are none. He likely has the big boy bladder of an elephant.*

Once she was up, Traveler lifted his head, *Thank God, she moved. She has the bladder of an elephant.* He rose and headed for his own bathroom. They came out of their doors at the same time.

"Hope I didn't break your concentration," said Glenda.

Traveler thought of a couple of smart replies then grinned, "I had my legs crossed the last half hour. Thanks for taking the potty-break lead."

Glenda laughed and said, "Trust me, I know what you mean. Study pressure comes from a lot of sources."

When they got back to the alcove, there were sandwiches at each of the chairs with chips and a flavored iced tea drink. "I think M is giving us a little break," said Glenda. "Food is not only good for the soul, it's essential for concentration. It's funny how hungry you get by just sitting and thinking." Traveler agreed as he took a big bite of his sandwich.

As they ate, they discussed Traveler's progress. "Amazingly, I am now on page eighteen," he said. "I don't know how many pages there are since we can't look ahead, but I think my book likes me."

Glenda gave an encouraging nod. "You are making the required effort and the book appreciates and rewards that. Keep it up and you will finish that first book in the near future."

"Then what?" asked Traveler.

"Well, you'll know your study path when you finish this first book. This book is laying the foundation for all future learning. There are a lot more books but as you finish one it leads you to the appropriate next book. As M told me repeatedly, 'Trust your books' and I found that works."

"Is there an end to this study?" asked Traveler.

"I've wondered about that, honestly, I don't know. I don't think we want to go questioning in that direction. I sense what we are building in ourselves has no finish line. We are being prepared for something big, but I don't know what that is."

# 44
# Glenda and Mom Shop

The demanding study routine was their normal day. There was welcomed relief only when their books told their bodies to take a break. One of these breaks gave Glenda time to enjoy her shopping trip with Virginia.

Glenda emerged from her room bouncing in tune to a Christmas song in her head. Traveler glanced up and thought, *She's hearing Jingle Bells.* Confirming his thought, she headed to the door with jingling bells sounding on her knee-high leather boots. Passing Traveler, she pushed her hair under her ski hat, gave a shake of her head and another bell announced its presence.

"Enjoy yourselves, gentlemen, while I shop till I drop. I want Virginia to spend a big chunk of Traveler's college fund on her wardrobe," Glenda said laughingly.

Once Glenda was out, Traveler felt a moment of loneliness. He left the study alcove and decided to sit near M by the fountain. He slipped back and forth from studying into small talk with M. He found M easy to talk with and prompted M to tell fascinating stories.

He liked that M seemed to enjoy his own stories regarding sports and just day-to-day events at home. M obviously enjoyed having someone to talk with, and Traveler came to realize how lonely M was on a day-to-day basis. Theo did not seem to be much of a conversationalist.

When Glenda finally returned from her shopping spree, she was an excited, normal teenage girl. She gushed about the clothes, the stores, and the fun conversations with Virginia. She described their lunch at the Four Seasons Hotel. "It was top-shelf in every way. There was a wall of glass looking out over Chicago, and the servers doted on us. They treated us like royalty."

Traveler tried to act interested but shopping stories didn't light his fire. He was also not sure he liked his mom bonding with the ice princess. *Bet they talked about me and Mom regaled the princess with my many shortfalls.*

"Your mom started to tell me all about her dinner with M last night. I told her to hold on and tell us together, so you could enjoy hearing about her great evening."

"Yeah, I sure want to hear more about that night on the town," Traveler said in a sarcastic tone.

"I also covered for you. She noted you were not in your room in the morning. I told her that you had said you were taking an early morning long walk by the lake then were heading back to the museum. She seemed pretty relaxed about where you were."

Traveler nodded and thought, *She's relaxed because she's found a daughter to go shopping with.*

# 45
# Graduation

Traveler finished the first book in another week of normal time. M referred to that book as the basic primer for all subsequent learning. M was quite pleased with Traveler's accomplishment and gave a graduation feast upon its completion.

As they were enjoying the graduation dinner, Glenda found that she was also pleased with the speed of Traveler's progress. She had come to acknowledge that she needed an exceptional study partner to keep herself moving at the speed she knew the books demanded. *I guess putting up with wonder boy is part of the price I pay for my own progress.*

*I wonder how much Batman really needs Robin the Boy Wonder. Do any of the superheroes really need a sidekick, or is the sidekick there to highlight the strength of the hero?*

A disturbing thought shot through her mind for a moment, *I'm certainly not his sidekick, am I? No way! I'm obviously Wonder Woman, or maybe the Nordic goddess Freya, but I am certainly nobody's sidekick,* she assured herself.

As the graduating student, Traveler got to order a special dessert and he chose Baked Alaska. He had never had that, but had read about it. Baked Alaska was a blend of cake and ice cream layers with a meringue topping. Liqueur topped off the dessert. The liqueur was poured on top and then lit on fire.

When it arrived, the Alaska lit up the fountain area, it also lit up the appetites of the seated diners. "Wows" came from Glenda and Traveler at the same time.

The dessert followed a full meal, but both students suddenly found an extra pocket in their stomachs. The half-life of the cake was measured in minutes.

All three looked down at the remaining slice. "I believe the guest of honor claims that." Then all three noticed Theo had joined them. Traveler knew the right thing to do. He lifted the piece up and placed it on a wide waiting tongue.

A satisfied purr warmed the table. Traveler thought, *I don't think it's about the cake, I think he appreciates my doing the right thing. Well, maybe it is about the cake, who knows.*

As Edward rose to leave, he made a small bow to M. "My compliments to the chef for a wonderful meal. Thank you, M. The way to this student's mind is through his stomach."

# 46
# Who Has Stealth?

It was difficult for either student to tell how much time had passed inside the sanctuary's time bubble. Time was measured by their progress, not by hours, days, or weeks.

Their study paths sometimes overlapped but then would suddenly diverge into different areas of individual growth. This parallel then zigzagging course resulted in strong common skills while creating differing individual strengths. Neither student was complete without the differing skills of the other.

One skill they mastered together was being able to blend into their immediate surroundings. They referred to this skill of "hiding in plain sight" as their stealth skill. The stealth skill permitted them to enjoy ultimate camouflage far beyond anything the military could employ. They were superior in being able to totally disappear into their surroundings; they simply became part of the natural background.

Standing against a wall, they were part of the wall. If they lay down on the floor, then they appeared as part of the floor.

Of course, if they were on the floor and somebody walked on them, their presence would immediately be discovered.

To maintain their virtual invisibility required a high degree of mental focus as well as absolute stillness of body. If they dropped their concentration or moved slightly their image would appear much like an old-time, flickering movie.

They enjoyed practicing stealth together and challenging each other's invisibility skill. Their practice often took on the characteristics of hide-and-seek. With shared practice, their skills became honed to a high degree. Of course, once they mastered the skill they used it to prank each other and, on occasion, M. They wisely chose not to prank Theo.

One early morning Traveler pranked Glenda by simply sitting in her alcove chair. She had just returned from her room and she was anxious to begin her study. She never noticed her chair had been moved slightly away from the table.

She shrieked upon sitting down when she discovered the chair was already occupied. She sprang up and with a red face and declared in a heated voice, "You will pay for that funny boy, believe me you will pay." The chair laughed back at her.

One of their favorite pranks on M was to be sitting at the fountain table at mealtime while being virtually invisible. Then they would suddenly appear just as M was placing food down. He never failed to look startled and jump a bit. This reaction always brought hoots of glee from both stealth warriors.

M accepted their pranks with good nature. He was pleased that they could use humor to break the constant stress of their study.

# 47
# Museum Uphill Runs

As significant study time passes, a condition called Study Boredom invariably shows up. Every student knows this as early as kindergarten.

Students also know afternoon classes are really killers. The height of boredom happens after lunch when a teacher drones on to finish the lesson plan while food digestion makes for sleepy students. Traveler and Glenda were no exception.

It was midafternoon when Study Boredom struck both. Their heads came up from their books at the same moment. Traveler looked at Glenda, grinned and said, "Road trip?"

"Let's roll, big boy!" she fired back.

"May I suggest a destination to the Nordic princess?" asked Traveler.

"Suggest away, I'm seriously brain dead right now."

"Let's head to the museum. The Syrian portal exhibit will fascinate you. The curator gave me a personal lecture and I'd consider myself a qualified tour guide. You may want to take notes while I lecture." Her stare back made it clear what he could do with his lecture, but she gave a strong nod for the visit.

Traveler was excited about a second visit. He was the expert now and wanted to show off his knowledge to Glenda. He also wanted to inspect the portal further. "You'll love the exhibit on the portal for the Syrian temple. I told you and Mom about it, but seeing is believing."

"Sounds like fun, I like it!" said Glenda. "Maybe some pizza afterwards, my treat this time. Of course, that's only if your gentleman's ego can handle a lady paying; or we could go Dutch to ease any gentlemanly embarrassment."

"No embarrassment here. Don't forget your wallet."

They quickly retired to their rooms and suited up for another walk into the wild winds off Lake Michigan. This time Glenda was waiting at the fountain for Traveler. "Don't forget your snappy earmuffs, they're so cute," she said. Traveler just grunted but he noticed she was again decked out as if she were auditioning for Miss Chicago Winter.

M was by the fire with Theo and glanced up as they were leaving, "Have fun," was all he said. Theo yawned.

When they exited the alley onto the public street, they found it was a relatively clear winter day. There was the usual chilling wind, but it was manageable. As they walked up Michigan Avenue Glenda paused to window-shop.

"I see a store your mom would want to visit," Glenda explained. Traveler wisely adjusted to Glenda's annoyingly slow pace. *How many shopping stores are there in Chicago anyway?* he thought.

Finally, they reached the museum steps. The steps were clear, with scattered salt pellets maintaining the dryness. They entered the big lobby, purchased their tickets, and prepared for an exhibit visit. Traveler was determined to act as the tour guide.

Traveler paused for a moment by the large display stand for the portal. He noticed the pamphlet box was still nearly full. *The curator was right. People don't want to work at reading, most visitors just want to be entertained by casual viewing.* This observation made him feel superior to his fellowman.

He took out a pamphlet and gave it to Glenda. "You can read it later, but I'll give you all the important facts, follow me." He liked the sound of "follow me," it felt right.

Traveler glanced at Glenda. "Decision time. Easy elevator ride to the top floor or a girly gait up a long staircase?"

Glenda knew a Traveler challenge; they were not subtle. "Oh, let's hoof it," she said. They walked to the wide staircase and could see it was empty. Without breaking stride, Glenda hit the first step in a bound and said, "See you at the top, stop if you need to rest." With that, she was a leaping gazelle.

Traveler was caught off guard but quickly headed after her. He was confident that after a flight or two of the steep steps, he would catch her. After three levels, he found he was further behind. He was a strong cross-country runner and knew his body. He knew he had to slow slightly and take controlled breaths.

Then his male testosterone kicked in and he found the runner's extra kick. Sadly, for his ego, his kick came a little too late. Glenda was standing on the top floor looking down. "Are you OK?" she asked with a sincere look.

*Is that a smirk I see?* thought a winded Traveler. Traveler was somewhere between embarrassed, angry, and mortified. A variety of responses vied in his head, starting with, *Well, you sandbagged me with a big jump-start.* Then he started to laugh. "You destroyed me, princess, and I'm impressed. No kidding."

Glenda broke into a laugh. "I forgot to mention I was the star distance runner and sprinter at the orphanage. I learned to run at an early age in Norwegian winters and at high altitudes. The altitude running gave me bigger lungs I guess."

Now both could put their guard down and concentrate on their breathing. "I'm glad we have a long enough walk to the exhibit to get my heart and lungs under control," said Traveler. "You woke up every body part with a jolt."

"If it makes you feel better, I'm beyond happy that was the last floor. I was maybe two seconds ahead of you and heard you coming fast."

*Mutual respect is a good thing,* they thought simultaneously.

They arrived at the exhibit and found the door was locked. The curator had obviously gotten security to repair the door.

"Can we get in? How did you get in last time? Was it locked then?"

"Kind of," answered Traveler. Glenda gave him a questioning look and he added, "Follow me; I think I have an answer." He led Glenda to the curator's office.

"This is the man in charge of the museum as well as this display. Let's see if he's available."

Traveler knocked, and a voice said, "Come on in."

The curator looked up and smiled. "Edward, back so soon and with a friend. I bet you want to see the display again and give your friend the Cook's tour.

"Of course you both know that the expression comes from an English tour guide named Cook who became famous by moving people rapidly around different sites in the early part of the twentieth century." Both Traveler and Glenda nodded with thank-you smiles while neither had any idea of what the expression meant or how it had originated.

Traveler quickly introduced Glenda and she immediately extended her hand to the curator. "It's great to meet you, Eddie was captivated by your tour." The curator beamed.

"You're timing is spot-on, the crane operator and crew just arrived. We're placing the keystone in a few minutes and you can watch. Once the keystone is in place, the portal and exhibit will be complete, and we'll be open to the public. You two will be the first official visitors."

They walked back to the exhibit's entry door and the curator opened it with his master key. "We're keeping it locked until the keystone placement is completed." He glanced at Traveler and added, "No need for heavy hands this time." Glenda noticed Traveler react with a weak smile and she thought, *I wonder what that was all about.*

# 48
# The Portal

Inside the exhibit hall, teams of workers were preparing to insert the keystone. One team of four workers was standing in a circle around the keystone. Two other men were beside the crane holding the low hanging hook that hung down from the crane's boom.

The workers around the keystone had just finished attaching the support chains to lift the keystone. They appeared to be waiting for final instructions from the curator.

The curator motioned to Traveler and Glenda, "Please stay right here. Don't get any closer, this part of placing the keystone can be very dangerous. Notice that all the workers are wearing protective eye goggles, long leather coats, and heavy leather work-gloves. Once the hook is attached to lift the stone all the workers will back far away.

"The danger is real. If one of the support chains snaps and the block falls, it can easily splinter; rock shards would fly out like shrapnel from a grenade. Not only that, if a chain snaps in the wrong place it can become a long steel whip that will cut through anything in its path.

"We protect against these risks by having multiple support chains and protective clothing, but you never can be sure."

While the curator was talking, Glenda had been staring at the support columns. *I hit a home run with the princess,* thought Traveler. *She's captivated by this display.*

His mood changed when he heard Glenda say in her directing voice, "Before you do the insertion lift, I would like to take a closer look at the support columns. I think I see a couple of glyphs on the left side column that look fragile. They may get jarred loose when that keystone settles into place. All that force going down the columns will dislodge anything that's not totally secure." She then offered her most beguiling, "Pretty please, may I" smile to the curator.

For a moment the curator was ready to say "No," then he changed his mind. The smile did him in. "Well, if your eyesight is that good we can take a little time right now and make a final inspection. I've inspected those columns many times, but I may have missed what you see, please lead on."

Glenda replied, "Thank you, sir," and headed to the left column. The curator walked alongside her, and Traveler trailed after them. *What is she doing to slow down the parade?* Traveler thought. He was excited to see the keystone put in place and he was annoyed with Glenda for getting in the way.

Traveler joined them as they stood by the column. Wanting to show off his knowledge of early Egyptian glyphs, he said, "Amazing hieroglyphs, huh."

Glenda ignored him and said to the curator, "These glyphs predate Egyptian hieroglyphs." As the curator agreed with her, Traveler felt himself shrink down. *Who's the slow student in the room? Guess it's me.*

Glenda was staring at the cuneiform appearing designs with the same intensity Traveler saw when she was immersed in her studying. She stood transfixed for several minutes then she passed her fingers very lightly over a few of the slightly eroded glyphs. "These must be the ones the Germans tried to remove, I detect chisel marks," she said aloud.

The curator knew he shouldn't let her touch the ancient stone but held his correction, he had seen other professionals get the same focused look that she now had. "What's going on?" Traveler finally asked in a hesitant voice. "Don't tell me you can read that stuff."

Glenda ignored his question and quietly answered, "Pick a symbol and stare at it. Do not move your focus from that symbol, tell me what you see." Traveler was ready to make a joke but the look on Glenda's face stopped him.

"Any particular symbol?" he asked.

"Just pick one and focus on it," was her tense reply. The curator was already following her lead.

Traveler picked one that was at eye level. He went into his study mode and let him mind and eyes focus on it. Once in his study mode, his mind took over and he was oblivious to everything except the symbol.

He suddenly jumped, the symbol was moving. *Impossible,* he thought. *My mind is making it move for some reason.* He changed his focus to another symbol nearby. This time the second symbol moved as soon as he had it clearly in his eye and his mind. He felt a bad premonition and broke contact with the glyphs.

Glenda was studying him and had seen his jerk reaction. "What did you see?" she asked.

"Call me crazy, but as I looked at my first symbol and then a second one, they both moved. That's impossible, of course. I also have a very bad feeling. There is a vibration here that reminds me of Theo's purring, but this is a different vibration and not good. What do you see?" asked Traveler.

"A lot more," said Glenda, "The keystone cannot be put in place."

The curator had focused also, but saw nothing. At the same time, he had a sense that both these two young people had indeed seen something. He had experience with autistic students. He had seen some of them recognize patterns that others could not see. He was skeptical about whatever these two thought they saw, but to his credit, he did not automatically dismiss them.

Glenda turned and faced the curator. "This keystone cannot be put in place. Not ever." Her tone of voice, words, and bearing made chills go down the curator's back. She sounded much older.

The curator took a deep breath and regained his composure. He gave her a fatherly smile. The smile said, "Trust the adults, my dear, we know what we're doing." He did not go so far as to pat her on the head, but his smile conveyed that same message.

"Thank you for your concern, Glenda. I did look at the glyphs that you were looking at, and I am comfortable they are well-attached. Thanks for making me triple check. Now we need to proceed with the insertion. The men are anxious to finish this project; they have worked late hours here for over a month. Christmas is coming, and they get paid as soon the keystone is in place."

Glenda repeated, "Please listen to me! This is critical." Traveler knew that voice and his mind changed gears. He was now listening to her.

The curator heard a voice that was commanding but coming from a teenage girl. He was throw off balance, annoyed but curious. He looked at her. "Yes? Is there something else bothering you?"

He was now regretting his invitation to the students to watch the final step in the display. He recalled the old adage, "No good deed ever goes unpunished."

"You cannot place this keystone. This portal cannot be permitted to have its loop completed. There is a danger here beyond anything you can imagine." The curator stared at the girl. She was tense, dead serious, and obviously unbalanced.

"Glenda, I do understand the risk of cracking the keystone, but I have taken many precautions to safeguard it. I understand your concern over it being broken but trust me we have many years of experience working with ancient artifacts."

"The problem is not that you break it, but that it stays intact and gets put in place. Better you break it on the floor right now than put it in place. Even without the keystone, this display should be dismantled. Separate the arch from the support columns. Send the separate pieces to different parts of the country. Keep them far apart."

The curator was studying the girl closely. What he decided was that her boyfriend had told her about the superstitious belief of the Syrian mountain people. She had decided the tale was factual and was now reacting to it.

She was probably a young person with a strong religious upbringing combined with an out of control imagination. Part of him felt sorry for her, but the rest of him had a job to do.

"I appreciate that old artifacts are often imagined having some type of ancient curses associated with them," he said smiling. "Please remember we are a museum and displaying ancient symbols of religious beliefs is part of our stock in trade.

"Trust me, no god has ever shown up here to complain about an exhibit or a display. If an ancient deity did show up, we would welcome it, but we would also insist it buy a ticket to enter," he chuckled, trying to break the mood.

Glenda did not respond to his humor. "There is much more to this universe than our science has even started to dream of. I know you think I'm bonkers but what if I prove something to you right now. Would your scientific mind accept a demonstration of the impossible?"

The curator was torn between letting the girl down easy with her fantasies and having Security remove her. He had a young daughter and thought of how he would like some other adult to handle her in a similar situation.

*I'll let her down easy without breaking her spirit,* he decided. In addition, her boyfriend was an exceptional young academic. It was likely that the girl picked up some half-truths from him. "OK, you have my attention, what do you want to show me?"

# 49
## Glenda Translates

Glenda said, "Permit me to translate the column for you."

The curator smiled, "I wish you could, my dear. Believe me, we have had the best linguist of ancient symbols working on that for six months. Our problem is that we do not have a Rosetta Stone to help us. There is no parallel written language we can use to decipher these symbols or runes or whatever they are."

"Au contraire," said Glenda, "you have me. I am a living Rosetta Stone. The inscribed language predates Sanskrit and hieroglyphs. Those ancient languages were based in part from the symbols on the pillars. You need to project Sanskrit and Egyptian hieroglyphs backwards in time to read the column's symbols."

"Really? And are you also an expert in Sanskrit and hieroglyphs?" asked the curator.

"Absolutely! Would you like to test me?"

The curator thought, *She's laid her own trap. I'll close it on her, but do it gently.* "Fair enough, follow me. Let's see how well you translate some of the writings we've already deciphered."

The curator led them back to the room where Anubis was holding court. The curator walked over to a large sarcophagus with an intact mummy inside. The lid was upright beside the open coffin. "Care to read the lid's inscription?"

Glenda skimmed the upright lid, "Well it's just the usual propaganda about how deserving this guy was. He was a rich businessman trying to bribe his way into the afterlife. The inscription literally reads as…," and she proceeded to translate the whole message while explaining her reading one glyph at a time. The curator nodded his head while following her reading.

Her interpretation matched the official transcript very closely. He was stunned. "I am very impressed, Glenda, seriously impressed. Your reading is very close. You only have a couple of minor technical errors."

"Please point them out."

As the curator went to specific translations, Glenda corrected him at each point. She said, "You have made a close but inaccurate translation. Our businessman was trying to sneak a lie past Anubis.

"He did contribute a large amount to charity as he states in this highlighted central hieroglyph, but this side bar hieroglyph indicates a much smaller contribution actually made it to the charity. There were significant expense deductions even back then. The deductions cycled back to the man's own business. This was a small lie, but one that would never get past Anubis."

The curator was silent. He was now studying the two referenced hieroglyph areas. She certainly made a case for her reading. "Let's try another one," and he led her to a parchment enclosed inside a glass vacuum case.

Glenda said, "This is a very old message. It goes back to the third or fourth pharaoh. This is the time period when the priests were establishing pharaoh as a god.

"This is a simple narrative that presents the bravery of the pharaoh as he killed a hippo." She then read the hieroglyph narrative one character at a time. "What you have missed is that the hippo bit off his lower leg. The pharaoh survived the loss of the leg, but he was disfigured. That could not happen to pharaoh the god.

"The scribe needed to report this leg loss to maintain the truthfulness of the story to Anubis, so he used these hieroglyphs as a metaphor for the lost leg being regenerated by pharaoh the god. In fact, there was an artificial limb created by the priests so that the pharaoh appeared to his subjects as having fully recovered from the hippo battle.

"The scribe was very clever; he told about the pharaoh's bravery to the Egyptian people while confirming that pharaoh was a god by regenerating his missing limb. The subtle difference is that the leg was manmade, not regenerated by the pharaoh. The scribe stayed honest with Anubis."

The curator was stunned. This young lady had demonstrated a facility with hieroglyphics that he had never seen before. "Is your family involved in Egyptology?" asked the curator.

"Not exactly. Language is just one tool for trying to understand the universe; mathematics is another tool, but both are primitive at best," answered Glenda.

The curator gave Glenda a respectful look that he only gave the most eminent of his peers. "Yes, you have certainly confirmed your incredible translation skills and rather blown me away in the process. Let's go back to the portal and I'll listen to your translation."

As they walked back, the curator paused at the entry door, "I can say unequivocally that I will take seriously whatever your translation says. I'm not committing to accepting an old curse, but I do want to know what you translate.

"We will pass your translation on to other experts. If they agree, we will include your translation as an important part of this exhibit. You will receive credit for this translation breakthrough. Believe me, top graduate schools will fight to throw scholarships at you."

Glenda accepted his comments and replied, "I can only ask you to be prepared for the warning, and it is not as simple as a curse. The portal is more of an energy map for the beings it references. Please keep an open mind and tread slowly around placing the keystone."

Traveler trailed along behind both. Once again, Glenda was leading, and he was following. He felt he was way out of his league right now and was adding no value.

He had to ask himself whether Glenda's studies had taken her that far ahead of him or was she a natural language savant born with a genius that the books amplified. *Do I have some hidden genius? And when will it show up?* he wondered.

They came through the open exhibit door to find the workers were relaxed, eating their lunches and laughing. It certainly did not feel like an end of the world atmosphere. The workers all stood up when the curator entered but he motioned for them to continue their break.

Glenda stood back about ten feet from the columns and the resting keystone and began to focus on the hieroglyphs. She suddenly found her heart was racing, her skin was perspiring, and she was unbalanced with a sense of vertigo. The message did not want to be read. By attempting to translate the inscriptions she felt like she was opening a door that had a killer waiting on the other side.

She fought her primal fear, took a controlling breath, and calmed herself before reading the message. She stood facing the arch for several minutes before she realized she had to start now or she would never start. Like a skydiver standing by the open exit door, she had to either leap out or return to her seat. She knew she had to leap, sitting was not an option.

She focused all her energy, took a deep controlled breath, and said to herself, *Time to roll the dice, here we go.* Once she began speaking, she felt her control return. Whatever was trying to control her had lost its hold. She was again Wonder Woman or the Norse goddess Freya and was ready to face the threat head on.

"You read the symbols from the left side column starting at the bottom. You read the inscription on the base before moving up the column. You continue reading across the arch until you reach the end of the arch where the keystone will rest. You read the keystone, then move down the right-hand column and finish with the base.

"The symbols are a language, including mathematical expressions but much more. The symbols connect with each other in a manner that permits them to reorganize themselves as necessary to make the portal fully functional.

"They work together somewhat like neurons in a brain. Once the keystone is in place the arch completes all the circuits. With the keystone in place, the portal's brain is complete and turns itself on."

"Are you telling me this stone artifact has intelligence?" asked the curator.

"I guess that depends on your definition of intelligence. It is intelligent to the extent that it serves to provide a flexible conduit platform. The best I can tell is that it may be for transferring energy. The energy may come outside of our four-dimensional, space-time world. Think of it as a self-aware and self-adjusting Einstein-Rosen bridge.

"In layman's terms, you can consider it a 'wormhole.' However, this wormhole is much more flexible than what Einstein and Rosen imagined. Actually, with their limited understandings, this portal could never exist, but here it is.

"I can't read further. I think once the keystone is back in place my reading may become irrelevant as it redesigns itself. The risk to placing the keystone in place is that we activate something far beyond our understanding.

"We could be the Aztecs lighting bonfires to help the Spanish conquistadors find their land. We know how that turned out for the Aztecs. I would add that my intuitive reaction to this portal is pure fear."

# 50
# A Heavy Load: Proceed with Caution

*Well that's enough,* thought the curator. *She sees moving symbols on a rock surface, knows more math than Einstein, and thinks there is a wormhole in front of us.*

*None of this is possible, even if she is an extraordinary linguist. She has almost pulled me into her fantasy world. I can see that she is genuinely scared, but that goes back to the tale Edward told her. Edward joked with me about the mountain people's superstition, but she took his story at face value.*

*She may be a true language savant, but is unstable as a person. Many savants are. I'll explore her translation talents once this display is finished. I'll look into setting up a trust fund to advance her language genius, but right now I need to move ahead with the exhibit.*

The curator had determined his course and now looked at Traveler and Glenda. "All right my prize students, I respect both of you a lot. However, we need to get on with finishing the exhibit. Please move back to the safe zone so we can lift the keystone."

Glenda looked at Traveler and said, "This is going to happen, and we cannot stop it. We need to warn M and Theo."

"What exactly are we going to warn them about?" asked Traveler. He trusted Glenda, and yes, the symbols seemed to move a bit, but all he could see was an old stone arch ready to receive a big carved keystone.

Traveler looked again at Glenda and realized how disturbed she was. He had never seen her scared, or panicked, or distraught. She was all three now. He felt like he had to be the knight who would assure the princess about the dragon and calm her down.

"Let's try this," Traveler said. "Let's carefully watch what happens once the stone is in place. If there is something supernormal, we will catch it even if these people don't. Then we'll know what to report, assuming we need to report anything."

Glenda gave him a sad smile and said, "We have no choice." Then she tried to put on a brave face and added, "I hope, Sir Knight, you're good at fighting dragons."

The curator walked to the keystone and inspected the binding chains a final time. Multiple chains crisscrossed each of the four sides. As an additional protection, the curator had wrapped the keystone with a strong, thick, covering robe.

The robe would contain flying splinters if the stone disintegrated under lifting stress. If the stone cracked while being lifted, the binding cover and the chains would keep it intact while the crane lowered it back to the floor.

If it cracked, the museum could use specialty glue designed to repair ancient stone. Once repaired, the stone would be stronger than in its current state. The curator had anticipated all possible outcomes.

Satisfied, the curator backed far enough away to protect himself. He gave a hand signal to Mike the crane operator to begin slowly applying lifting pressure. All chains became fully taut. Mike and the curator saw the chains were uniformly taut on all sides, confirming they were properly placed.

They gave each other the thumbs up signal. All systems were a go and Mike added to the lifting force. The stone did not move.

Mike slowly increased the lifting force. He reached a force level that could easily lift a larger block of solid steel. This stone was just rock, and, despite its size, it could not be close to the density of steel. Mike motioned to the curator to get on his cell phone and waited until they were connected.

"I am at a lift force that should be easily moving it right now; actually, I'm well above that force level. What do you want me to do?"

The curator studied the chains. His concern was if a chain broke free. "Are you comfortable with the chains holding?" asked the curator.

"Yeah, they're hardened titanium," answered Mike. "You could lift the Statue of Liberty with them."

"Are your leg struts doing OK?" asked the curator.

"Yeah, they're the same titanium as the chains, but they're stronger."

"How close to your max lift power are you?" asked the curator.

"I have some lift left in this baby. In addition, I have an auxiliary hydraulic pump that can act as a supercharger if we need it. I've never needed it."

Before proceeding, Mike studied all his power and pressure gauges again. "Let me ask you a question, Doc. Any risk of my punching a hole in this floor? I don't want to disappear into the floor below and become 'Mike the fallen-crane-operator exhibit.'"

"Not a chance, Mike," said the curator. "The floor is three feet thick of solid cement with reinforced rebar. It could support the Statue of Liberty if you could get her here."

"OK, Doc, let's see what's holding this chunk of stone down. My irresistible force ultimately beats the immovable object, at least that's been my experience."

"Proceed, Mike."

With that go ahead, Mike added additional force in small increments. Fortunately, the boom was close to vertical, so the increased force was at an angle that did not multiply the leveraged weight of the stone by much.

*Basic physics,* thought Mike. *If we were at forty-five degrees I'm not so sure, but at seventy-five degrees, I own this rock.* This had become a contest between a determined man with his machine and an equally determined rock.

Mike was an experienced professional and rarely got emotionally involved in any project. When he was at ninety-five percent of his normal maximum force, he discovered, much to his own surprise, that he was emotionally engaged. The rock was trying to beat him down and Mike would not be subdued.

Without further thought, Mike turned the supercharger on. The supercharger multiplied the hydraulic lift power by a factor of two. Since the power was already at near maximum, there was a surge of enormous unexpected power.

The rock yielded, and the stone was suddenly free swinging. Mike found that once off the ground, the stone seemed compliant. He quickly backed down the supercharger and resumed using the normal power settings.

He discovered that now he only needed fifteen percent of his normal power and reflected, *That's all I thought it would take. Why did we need to go to the DEFCON 1 power level? Maybe I should have punched up the power faster. It's as if that stone adjusted its weight somehow to match my smaller power increases. Could it be a thinking rock?* and he laughed to himself. *I'm getting rocks in my head now. In any case, this was one very strange lift and one for the record books. Certainly, one for beer talks with the crew. Now for the insertion, and we're done.*

With the stone hanging about four feet off the floor, the workers approached and removed the thick cover. The chains were across the front and backside and would be released from the hook once the stone was in place.

Both the arch and the stone appeared ready for their marriage ceremony. Mike was the priest who would do the honors. He slowly raised the keystone until it was five feet above the open space in the arch, then proceeded to slowly lower it down.

*What could go wrong now?* the curator thought. *I feel like I'm a native in the Syrian mountain watching the Germans working on the arch. Yikes, that girl seems to have put a bit of her superstition into me.*

Both Glenda and Traveler were mesmerized as they watched the stone slowly descend. Glenda's earlier trepidation had infected Traveler. They were both barely breathing and hoping nothing would explode out of the portal when the circuit was complete.

When the bottom of the keystone was less than three feet above the opening in the arch, the stone gently twisted to a side angle with the opening. Because the sides of the arch were not parallel to the sides of the keystone, Mike decided to take it up and start over.

Once the keystone was raised to about four feet above the arch, the twist in the holding chains seemed to vanish and the sides again lined up. Mike lowered it a second time and the twist again appeared.

This up and down process went for another half a dozen tries. Everything was in line at four feet above the opening and then the twist happened between two and three feet. *This makes no sense,* thought Mike. There was not a twist in the chains. The stone was absolutely still until it was almost less than three feet away. He called the curator on his cellphone.

"We have another weird situation here, Doc," Mike said. "It is all systems go until we're less than three feet away, then it's suddenly twist-and-shout time. It reminds me of watching racehorses being led into their starting gates. Most walk right in, but others balk at the last minute. I know horses can get spooked, but what would spook a rock?" he asked rhetorically. "What do you want me to do, Doc?"

Glenda and Traveler were watching the drama play out. "Something is trying to keep that keystone from going into the opening," said Glenda.

"Maybe a Syrian medicine man put a jinx on it to protect the mountain people," Traveler said trying to lighten the mood. Makes me wonder how that keystone ever got removed in the first place."

"Yeah, I've been wondering the same thing," said Glenda.

The curator was conflicted. He was very close to finalizing this display. So much time, effort, and money had gone into getting to this point. Now a little twist in the chains was denying him the finish.

He thought of the old adage from Ben Franklin, "For the want of a nail the shoe was lost. For the want of a shoe the horse was lost..." Eventually the battle, then the kingdom was lost. Because of a little twist in the titanium chains, his display exhibit could be lost. Everything was hanging by a thread. Literally, a titanium-chain thread.

"Mike, I think it's time to be bold," the curator said. "Take it down to just below three feet. Hold there and wait to see if a twist starts. If there is no twist, lower it until the twist appears. Then raise it up a few inches at a time. Find the closest spot before twisting starts and call it out to me."

"Will do, Doc." Mike skillfully raised and lowered the keystone. He made multiple up and down maneuvers. With each set of attempts, he closed in on the target distance. When he was approximately two feet and six inches and holding steady, he gave a thumbs-up signal from the cab. He spoke into his cab's phone and said, "Doc, this is the sweet spot, want me to release it?"

"Yes," answered the curator.

"Bombs away and hold onto your seat belts!" said Mike as he pulled the release lever.

The stone dropped without twisting. The arch seemed to embrace the keystone with affection. All sides were snuggly together. The marriage of arch and keystone had taken place and the bride and groom seemed content. The portal and the display were complete.

# 51
# A Dangerous Marriage

The marriage party started immediately. An iHome speaker blared out the hard rock song, "We Are the Champions". Bottles of iced champagne were popped open and corks shot across the floor. The champagne was very well chilled due to it being kept chilled for hours longer than expected, but nobody ever complains that champagne is too cold.

The toasts began. The curator and the workers first toasted Mike. His effort not only required a great deal of skill, it also required bravery. He was on the front line in winning the battle with the stone. If the chains had snapped, they could have whipped into the cab and Mike.

Next, the curator toasted the workers. They had also displayed bravery as they had worked around the hanging arch and finally around the swinging stone.

Finally, all toasted the curator. He modestly accepted the praise, and then he delivered a surprise to each man. It was an envelope with a significant and unexpected bonus. The resulting cheers reverberated inside the domed room.

While the cheering and toasting was happening, Glenda turned to Traveler. "You stay here, and I'll get back to M and Theo. We have a situation here and I know they'll want to get here immediately. I already sense a vibration coming from the portal; I don't know what it means, but probably nothing good."

Traveler nodded in agreement. "I can feel it also. I'll put on my best stealth suit and fade into the background. I'll be the invisible fly on the wall. Mach schnell!" he added.

Glenda accepted the charge with a smile. "Take care, Sir Knight, and hold the castle." Traveler moved to the back wall, sat down and became part of the wall.

Traveler picked a spot facing the portal with an unobstructed view. The crane was to his right. With his viewing angle, he could see everything in the room. He looked up at the glass ceiling and saw that the sun was starting its descent. The room was gradually losing its natural lighting.

*It's winter, so naturally it's going to be dark in here fairly soon. I wonder if the lights will be left on when the party ends.* He settled back, took slow deep breaths and fell into a restful state. He distanced himself from the emotional turmoil of placing the keystone. He chose not to think about Glenda's premonitions.

Glenda was out the door with fire in her walk. She had a very bad feeling about leaving Traveler alone in that space. She ran to the staircase and went down as fast as she could. She literally ran through the museum, slowing only in the congested places.

The portal party was closing down. The workers were all feeling a nice buzz from the champagne as well as their bonus checks. Then it was like a quitting time whistle sounded. The workers shook hands a final time, picked up their personal effects, and left the museum.

When the room was totally empty, the curator looked around, and found himself coming down from the emotions of completing the exhibit. He noticed the boy and girl had left while the celebration was going on. *I guess the show ended with a whimper not the end of the world bang that the girl expected.*

*She did have me going for a while. I'll put her Cassandra-like warning to rest. I appreciate that the young Trojan girl, Cassandra, was right when she warned the Trojans about bringing the large Greek horse into Troy, however there are no hidden demons ready to invade my museum from the portal. Curses are nonsense.*

Traveler felt uncomfortable watching the curator without the curator's knowledge. It felt like spying and that never felt right to Traveler. He knew some people enjoyed looking into the privacy of others, but he did not. He would never read someone else's diary, even if it were easy to do. *What's their business should remain their business.*

He watched the curator stand beside the left side column. He bent down and appeared to be studying the bottom symbols. Then he walked to the right-side column and did the same thing. Finally, he backed away and took in the entire structure. He shook his head, came to the door and turned out the lights. Traveler heard the door lock as the curator left.

A momentary shiver ran down his spine. *Museums are creepy places without people. It's so quiet I feel like I'm trapped inside an Egyptian burial tomb.* His sense of being in a tomb was amplified as the receding light from the overhead windows provided a simple hazy glow to the room with declining illumination.

Seeking light sources, Traveler found two red exit lights. They projected a comforting glow into the darkening space of the room. One exit light was by the main entry door and was close to where Traveler was sitting. The other was on the back wall to the left of the portal and it cast a red light across the closest column.

Traveler appreciated both lights; modern civilization was still present and working. In addition to giving a little illumination, they also provided a sense of direction should he need to bolt from the room. *Now why would I need to bolt?* he thought, and quickly dismissed any answer.

With the faint exit lights softening the darkness, his mind slid back to Halloween nights a long time ago. He always kept his nightstand reading light turned on.

He recalled reading one of his favorite cartoon books, *Calvin and Hobbes*. He became Calvin, the young boy, lying in bed with eyes like saucers. Calvin was gripping the sheet to his chin as he asked in a trembling voice, "Are there any monsters under the bed?"

"Nobody here," a voice called back from under Calvin's bed.

"Shut up, stupid," came another monster voice from under the bed.

Traveler yanked himself away from Calvin. He was well aware of how we play mind games with ourselves. *Man, I'm reverting to being the scared five-year-old, alone in my room. I remember always being sure my closet door was closed before turning out my light. Right now, I need to be the "big boy" Glenda is always poking fun at.*

With a calmed mind, Traveler began to focus on his training for stealth mode. Controlling his breathing also slowed his heart rate. He understood how breathing is critical to controlling your heart's pulse rate. As a distance runner in competitions, he would focus on controlling his breathing. If breathing got out of control, the distance runner was doomed.

Edward's doctor had explained that one measure of how good your body conditioning is, is to time how long it takes an elevated pulse to return to normal. The shorter the recovery time, the better the body's conditioning.

With these reflections, Traveler had become relaxed. He had established his body-mind connection. He took slow, even breaths and dropped his pulse rate well below forty. He was leaning back against the wall in a relaxed sitting position with his legs tucked underneath him. *I am Sitting Bull, the mighty Sioux Indian chief. I defeated the yellow-haired General Custer and all his troops at Little Big Horn. I fear nothing.*

# 52
# Creatures from the Portal

His reverie was shattered. He felt a low-level vibration coming out of the wall and the floor, this vibration was what Glenda had first noticed. Then came the impossible; a flicker of light appeared at the deepest part of the interior display. Traveler was suddenly at DEFCON 1 alert. His head came up and pressed against the wall. His eyes glued to the light's movement inside the portal's temple.

The initial light source now advanced and appeared as a flickering flame. The flame was moving from the back of the temple display toward the portal's opening. The flame's forward movement appeared to Traveler as a cautious advance, much like a deer eyeing a feeding spot during hunting season.

Traveler struggled to keep his breathing and pulse under control. *Must maintain stealth control.* This realization made it even harder to control his mind and his body. He redoubled his efforts to stay focused in stealth mode. He visualized how he and Glenda had kept stealth control to prank M. He used that mental image to help him focus.

*What in the world is that thing? It looks like a huge, reddish amoeba moving around inside a petri dish. The size of this amoeba would require a Titan's petri dish to contain it.* A second and then a third flame appeared behind the portal by the temple. These newcomers moved slowly forward toward the first being.

As they got closer to the portal's opening, their shapes became more clearly defined. Traveler observed that they did not have a rigid, skeletal-based shape but rather a shape that was in constant motion. The shape was deciding how to adapt to the current environment. As each being came closer to the opening, multiple appendages appeared out of their central masses. As the mass moved, the appendages altered their lengths and thicknesses.

Despite the fact that appendages had been created out of the central mass, the mass itself did not reduce in size. New mass seemed to be created out of the very air. Their coloration was also changing; it was morphing from a reddish pink to a deeper red.

The three creatures reached the portal's opening and stopped at the threshold. They remained stationary for several minutes. The middle creature slowly extended an appendage through the opening and into the room. Traveler felt an increase in the floor and wall vibrations as the arm entered the room's common space.

The extended arm suddenly withdrew and flowed back to its central mass. Then the two flanking beings moved to join the central being. Their own masses and appendages melted into the central body's mass.

In a matter of seconds, the three beings became a single being. This new being had a pulsating glow that resembled a burning flame. Its coloration constantly shifted across a spectrum of deepening reds.

Finally, the merged flame shifted into a semi-rigid shape. It was a simian shape but where there should be a head there was only a denser central mass. There were a series of shifting geometric shapes within the body. Some of these shapes suggested interior eyes. The being was a nightmare cross between a monkey and a spider.

As Traveler stared at the multiple-armed fire-being, he thought of the Indian god, Shiva. Shiva was the Indian god of destruction, the destroyer of worlds. Traveler knew that he was looking at the threat to Theo and our world.

Traveler was close to panicking. A big part of him wanted to bolt for the nearby door. The calm part of him realized that to move would be a swift death sentence. This being was not simply hostile; it was evil in a cold, impersonal form. It was a serial killer without conscience.

Traveler accepted he had no option except to maintain his stealth camouflage. He could not permit himself to think of M and Theo arriving to rescue him. When you are running a long-distance race, you cannot permit yourself to think of the finish line. Anticipating the finish line was the surest way to self-destruct in any race.

Forcing a slow calming breath, he shifted his eyes away from the fire-being and focused on the rear exit sign. Once his focus was secure on the exit, he closed his eyes.

Now he was visually separated from the being's presence. This was truly a case of out of sight out of mind. Sometimes to regroup you need to become an ostrich with your head in the sand.

As he felt his body calming, he let his mind recall the lessons from his book. The book became his mental and emotional ground zero; it sent him a reassuring message of encouragement. "You can control your body and your mind. Continue to do that right now," was the message he received.

With his back pressed against the wall and eyes closed, he was back in control; it had only taken him a few long seconds. He slowly opened his eyes and had them remain focused on the rear exit glow. Once focused he let his peripheral vision expand to include the fire-beings. He was aware of their presence without directly staring at them.

His approach to observing the beings was similar to entering a cold swimming pool. Ease in slowly, splash water on yourself, and let yourself adjust to minimize the shock. He gradually permitted himself to look more directly at the beings.

Traveler saw there were again three beings, the single being appeared to have separated back into the original three. The separate creatures were independently examining the contents of the room. One being climbed the crane's boom. From the top of the boom, it extended an arm to the louvered windows and opened the glass.

Another being was in the cab. Multiple arms with varying sets of finger-like appendages moved across the control panel. The being was clearly absorbing how the machine operated.

The third being was beside the electrical motor and the hydraulic lift pumps. It was examining the various conduit cables and the magnetic armatures.

The creature from the top of the boom had descended back to the floor and was roaming near the portal. It leapt up to the far exit light and stared into it. It projected a single finger into the covering glass and explored the bulb without breaking it. Then it dropped to the floor. It understood the reddish exit light and recognized it as a simple light source without intelligence.

It proceeded from the rear of the room to the front near Traveler. Its movement was a smooth float rather than the jerky animal movements that result from legs. Traveler sensed its mass did not touch the floor, but he could not verify without moving. Again, it reminded Traveler of an amoeba floating in a petri dish.

The fire-being reached the entry door and put an arm against the door. Traveler heard a click as the locking mechanism opened; it had easily opened the door without using any apparent force.

Traveler watched as the being examined the room from its new position. He noted the eye-like internal shapes seemed to move to take in a complete view of the room. It reminded him of a stationary photographer using a video camera to scan a scene.

It concluded its scan and focused on the table close to Traveler. It floated across the floor and elevated itself to rest on top of the table. Mike had left the operator's manual on the table while enjoying the champagne; obviously he had forgotten to take it with him.

Traveler could see movement within the flame. Traveler again thought of an amoeba in biology class and how the internal working could be seen using a microscope. Unlike the amoeba, these internal movements appeared more like brain synapses firing; there was a kaleidoscope of complex signals traveling around inside the central mass.

The fire-being extended an appendage to touch the manual. Traveler thought he saw an array of internal eyes absorbing the manual. The being had apparently understood the written manual without ruffling individual pages. The review of the complex manual was over in seconds.

The being floated off the table and headed toward the crane. Halfway there, it turned and stared at the wall where Traveler was resting. Traveler held his breath; the being with the internal sets of eyes seemed to be looking straight at him.

Traveler immediately shut his own eyes and pulled the book into his mind. He pictured its first page with its image of intertwined galaxies. He held the image in his mind and focused on individual stars within one of the galaxies.

When he focused on a single star, the book brought that star and its satellite system of planets and moons into an amplified image. The viewer could focus and then magnify as much as desired of a single planet or moon.

Thinking about the book magnified his control over his stealth skill. Traveler felt his stealth camouflage strengthen. When Traveler finally squinted he saw the being had turned and floated back to join the other two by the crane.

All beings came together a second time and folded into each other. The resulting flame being was larger and seemed to vibrate with a pulse. As it pulsed, its colors varied to some internal rhythm.

Traveler realized that the single being was absorbing all the recently acquired information. The pulsating colors resulted from the digestion of information happening simultaneously for each of the component beings.

The time it took for this entire process of digestion was a matter of a few seconds. Apparently, the complexity of the various studied subjects was easily understood, no serious thought was required.

Traveler watched as the single being separated back into the individual entities. *This thing can multitask and share at the same time. The speed with which it had understood the operator's manual, electrical systems, and mechanical systems was astounding.*

Traveler wondered how much of this absorption of information could be done with more advanced concepts. *Could the beings also absorb abstract concepts such as the math that supported theoretical physics? How much of this digestion process is just memorization instead of genuine comprehension?*

*Maybe these beings are no more than an advanced form of a mobile video camera. They may be the equivalent of a Mars rover roaming around the surface taking pictures and soil samples. Maybe all they do is just record and transmit information back to a lab for analysis. If that's the case, where's the lab and who operates it?*

As Traveler watched the beings he thought, *No, these are definitely sentient creatures, they are self-directed. They are more like aggressive explorers. They strike me as similar to the Vikings and Spanish conquistadors. Explore, subdue any opposition, then send the wealth home, wherever home is for these creatures. I think Montezuma would recognize these bad boys. I bet Theo and M know them.*

Suddenly the beings stopped their movement. For a moment, Traveler was scared that he had dropped his camouflage due to his change in focus. Then Traveler heard a rattling of keys outside the door and realized the curator was coming in.

# 53
# Fight or Flight?

The curator put in his key to open the door and discovered the lock was already open. *I know I locked this door behind me. Could that boy and girl have broken in again? I hope not for their sakes. I'll have to report the entry to Security.*

Inside, Traveler continued watching the beings. The three beings immediately divided into nine beings. The nine approached the door. After the division, their mass still appeared unchanged. As the nine beings closed around the door Traveler realized they were forming into an ambush deployment.

There was a creature on each side of the door with the remaining seven curving into a fronting semicircle. Traveler immediately understood their strategy. They intend to block his escape once he is inside, and then they'll absorb him. With his knowledge, he's a walking library.

Traveler felt himself torn between self-preservation and saving the life of the curator. He had to extend his mental control to manage the "fight-or-flight" adrenaline rush. He could not permit his stealth camouflage to drop.

In this case, it was "fight or keep hiding"; there was no option to flee. *Will I be General Custer, bravely but stupidly charging into the Sioux warriors? We know how that ended.*

Is there another fighting option for being outnumbered and out-gunned? His mind jumped to Hannibal facing a large Roman army at Cannae.

*Hannibal was outnumbered, but he prevailed. He tricked the Romans by having his front-line soldiers, who were facing the advancing Roman Legions, begin a clear retreat. Smelling victory, the Romans broke discipline and broke ranks. They charged forward as individuals.*

*Then Hannibal released his elite Numidian cavalry. They swept along the Roman flanks and came up behind them. Hannibal then ordered his foot soldiers to reverse direction and create a shield wall to block the advancing but disorganized Romans.*

*The Romans could neither advance nor retreat. Hannibal tightened the noose. The Romans in the center literally had no space to move, much less fight. That noose hung forty-five thousand trained Roman soldiers. As Ben Franklin would have said, "By their individual actions in breaking ranks they ended up hanging together."*

*I don't have any elite cavalry to save me. I'm a Roman foot soldier trapped in the center and these fire-beings are closing the noose on the curator and possibly me. I know I'll lose my concentration when the curator becomes information food for these beings. I like the man!*

Traveler's mind raced. *What if I'm absorbed? They'll gain all my study knowledge. They'll know all about the books, and Glenda, and M, and Theo. They'll know the location of our sanctuary.*

There are times in life to either act or keep pondering; Traveler's instinct took over. He clenched his fists and found himself shaking with anger. He had a deep visceral reaction against these beings. They were predators against the helpless and all living earth beings, including people, would be helpless against them. Traveler's respect for King Arthur's courage and willingness to confront marauders took over. It was time to act.

The curator had just opened the door and was stepping in when Traveler charged off the wall. Traveler roared his fighting challenge at the beings.

He stood in front of the curator in a braced defensive position: his knees bent, and his arms cocked. His fists were tightly closed and pointing outward at the beings. It was the classic Bruce Lee fighting stance. He was a valiant knight of the round table ready to fight the fire dragons.

As he stood braced, with an overload of adrenaline, he felt power surge through his body. He knew his body could deliver a terrific knockout strike. Big Bob would never have a chance against him. Part of him wanted to test his power against the beings.

The beings were startled; the challenger had appeared from nowhere. The beings had carefully confirmed the room was empty and contained no threat. They immediately understood this challenger had abilities well beyond the human man behind him. They assessed this threat.

The challenger chose not to attack them, and that suggested he was a limited threat. At the same time, they could sense that he had a power source that was outside of the evolutionary development of this species.

In their long existence they rarely faced a true threat, but caution was always appropriate. First assess any threat, then attack. Always attack. The nature of their attack relied on the nature of their assessment, caution was appropriate in this case.

The nine beings flowed together into three enhanced beings. By merging, they expanded both their offensive as well as defensive power. The number of mergers is determined based on their threat assessment and they always erred on the side of overkill.

They felt comfortable that no further merger was necessary in this case. This challenger was unexpected but easily confronted and absorbed with their merged power.

Once merged, the three creatures were positioned for their attack. The center being was directly in front of Traveler about fifteen feet back. The other two beings flanked Traveler. The three formed a small semi-circle facing the entry door.

The curator was frozen in place; he was totally focused on Traveler. The boy had leaped out from the sidewall straight at him. "What are you doing in here?" the curator shouted at Traveler. "You know you cannot be here!" The curator stayed focused on Traveler and had not yet noticed the flame beings.

# 54
# The Cavalry Arrives

"Permission to enter?" came a calm voice behind Traveler and the curator. Traveler was startled at the voice and jerked to an upright position. The curator was beyond startled. The museum had been closed for an hour, and suddenly it was tourist season.

"What's going on here?" asked the curator to nobody in particular. He viscerally knew some "game was afoot," as Sherlock Homes famously declared, but like Watson, he had no idea what the game was. *Could this be the beginning of a robbery?* he thought. *Were the two brilliant young students simply ploys to gain his confidence and bypass normal security?*

M and Theo moved past the curator and Traveler. Now M and Theo were facing the flame-beings. Glenda tucked herself in beside Traveler and gave him a small hug with her right arm. "The cavalry is here," was all she said.

The beings performed an immediate threat assessment and fled. They floated quickly to the crane. Using the far side of the crane's cab for protection, they broke back into nine beings. Two of them disappeared through the portal, while the remaining seven raced up the boom and out through the open glass louvers.

As the fire-beings fled, the curator broke out of his trance and turned on the lights. The room was suddenly illuminated, and he had to squint while his eyes adjusted to the bright light.

The curator saw moving red flames close to the crane. His immediate reaction was a concern for a museum fire. *Could an electrical spark from the crane motor somehow have ignited oil drippings?*

While he was pondering, he saw a movement of fire behind the cab of the crane. Rats, he thought. *There's a fire that's started from the crane. Mike had too much champagne; he must have left some switches on in the cab that caused an electrical short.*

Next, he saw smaller flames moving from behind the crane in two directions. Several flames went through the portal toward the temple. Others went up the boom and disappeared. *This could be a flash fire,* he thought. *The sprinkler system should be turning on.* He waited, but none of the sprinklers activated.

He ignored the people standing in the entrance and headed toward the portal. He was not concerned about the portal itself burning, it was stone, but the temple was constructed of semi-flammable material and it could burn. He walked quickly through the portal to see if the fire had jumped to the temple.

He carefully looked around and saw no signs of beginning fires. He noticed the air was clean without a smell of burning oil, wood, or fabric. Satisfied the temple was secure, he came back out into the center of the room.

He looked up and saw the dome louvers were open. The louvers were never opened except for cleaning. He considered the possibility that his museum had just experienced an unlikely intrusion through the open windows.

His instincts told him that whatever had happened, it was a threat, but he had no idea of what the nature of the threat was. Maybe a well-planned theft was going to start with thieves coming in through the domed windows. *None of this makes sense,* he thought.

*Somehow, today's strange events seem to involve these two young people, but I don't see a connection yet. The tall man by the door can answer either to Security or to me.* He turned and walked to join the group standing by the entry door.

As the curator walked back toward the group, he had his hand on his cell phone. He shot M a look that said, "You're going to explain to me why you're here, or you can explain to Security. Who are you? And what are you doing in my museum at this hour?" M read the look and was ready for it.

# 55
# M Explains

Before the curator could begin his questioning, M took the initiative. "Doctor Smith, please permit me to introduce myself. My name is Mert, sometimes I'm called Merlyn, but basically everybody calls me M. Then he laughed and added, "Let's skip the humorous references about King Arthur and James Bond, I've heard them all since the first grade."

"You've already met my niece, Glenda, and my nephew Edward. I'm also Glenda's legal guardian. Finally, this big tabby is my faithful companion, Theo."

The curator focused on Theo for the first time. His body tensed and his eyes dilated. His breath caught in his throat. *Scary animal,* went through the curator's mind.

M anticipated his next question, "Theo is a domesticated mixed feline breed. They are doing the same DNA crossbreeding with cats that they are doing between dogs and wolves. Theo is the best mix of domesticated house cat and panther.

"He is an affectionate, highly intelligent companion, and a guardian in our house. One look and no burglar would ever want to mess with him. We all sleep very well at night."

The curator relaxed. He was comfortable that neither M nor his feline companion were threats. He knew about the crossbreeding of dogs, and accepted the likelihood of the crossbreeding of felines. He admired the cat's imposing body with its wide shoulders, large head, and slanted ears. *Majestic,* he thought.

Then he looked into the cat's eyes and did a double take. The cat was quietly inspecting him. *Good kitty,* flashed through his mind while a small shiver passed through his body.

For a moment, he saw a striking resemblance with the Egyptian cat god, Bast. A giant statue of Bast was in the mummy room close to the statue of Anubis. He thought, *This crossbreed cat beast looks like it could have sat for Egyptian sculptors four thousand years ago.*

M smiled at the curator as he saw the curator's reaction and recognition of Bast, and then he continued, "When my two young friends were late for dinner I thought they may have come here and then overstayed their welcome. They have watches but forget to use them when they're focused."

The curator nodded at this comment, he knew they were both exceptional students and he had seen the semi-trance state that Glenda had gone into when inspecting the portal.

M continued, "Edward regaled us earlier with his stories of the portal as well as your terrific brochure and lectures on the subject. I could see that Glenda was intrigued with his tale and a bit jealous that she had missed the visit with you.

"They are quite competitive with each other and I knew she would want to have a firsthand examination of the artifact.

"As I said, I am her uncle and naturally like to brag about her. She is a true language savant. She has an avid interest in ancient Middle Eastern artifacts including their written symbolic language. Of course, she is justifiably proud of her talents and can be a bit of a showoff. She enjoys challenging other language experts on obscure translations."

Glenda gave a frown at M's "showoff" comment, but she bit her tongue. If Traveler had used that description on her, it would be another story.

The curator's head was nodding. *Now I understand. She just wanted a chance to show off to me and used the keystone insertion as an excuse. Like any teenager, she just wanted a little time in the spotlight.*

"Of course, the museum was closed when I got here, but I explained to the front guard that I thought Glenda and Edward were still here viewing the portal exhibit.

"The guard did his job checking me out, so please no reprimands. He checked all my IDs and confirmed I am a reputable person as well as being a very good friend of the museum.

"Actually, I have a special pass from the museum's Board of Directors. The pass permits me to enter when I please in off hours; however, this is the first time I've actually used it." With that explanation, M handed his special access credential to the curator.

"Of course, this access pass only comes after a significant donation. I am a longtime patron of the museum, but I doubt you know me. I prefer to contribute on an anonymous basis. I believe the truest gifts are ones that only help the receiver and not serve the ego of the giver.

"Because I'm a bit of a recluse, I don't attend benefactor dinners and other such high society events. I usually give a generous donation at Christmas time. Since the holiday season is underway, may I hand deliver this year's donation?" M presented the curator with a closed envelope decorated with Christmas scenes.

On the front of the envelope was a message written with hieroglyphics that declared, "Continued discoveries in the new year, James Smith, my favorite curator." The message ended with a large handwritten "M" signed in fancy calligraphy style.

The curator was stunned. He was aware of the few special passes that were granted to exceptional donors. He knew each of these donors personally, except one. That one was in front of him right now.

He took the envelope and warmly shook M's hand. "Sir, you have more than made my day. You and the portal will make our coming year very special. Thank you so very much."

# 56
## Theo Asserts Himself

"Well, since we're conveniently here, may I possibly have a sneak preview of the portal exhibit?" asked M.

"It would be my pleasure and I would enjoy giving you any background about it, although I bet you've heard my lecture already from Edward."

M and Theo advanced to the portal. They stood looking at the columns and the arch, and then they walked up to the columns. M bent down and studied the base of the left side column while Theo pressed against the other column.

They studied the inscriptions and then the newly placed keystone. For a moment, the curator was going to ask M if he could keep his pet cat from leaning against the column then decided to let it happen. *What harm can he do?* thought the curator.

Glenda knew M and Theo had a mission to perform around the portal and that the curator needed to be distracted. She positioned herself, so the curator needed to face her and the door and asked, "Have you seen the movie, *Night at the Museum?*"

"Of course, I have, Glenda. Every curator worth his salt has seen it. It's a fun movie and one of my daughter's favorites. We've watched it together half a dozen times. I half expect Teddy Roosevelt to ride by when I'm here alone at night."

"Which movie was your favorite, the first or the second about Egypt?" asked Glenda, keeping the curator's attention.

Once the curator had his back turned away from the portal to talk with Glenda, Theo moved directly under the keystone. He stood on his hind legs and stretched upward. As Theo stretched, his body began to elongate and swell.

He continued to grow until his head was even with the keystone. Now he was the size of the Bast statue in the mummy room and he was tall enough to look Anubis directly in the eyes. If the curator had turned around at that moment, he would have fainted.

Traveler and Glenda glanced at Theo's progress while keeping the curator occupied with more questions about the movies and how accurate they were. The curator was pleased at their interest in his movie opinions and remained oblivious to the events behind him.

Theo placed two massive paws on each side of the keystone. There was a surge of energy between his paws. For a moment, the keystone was wrapped in a green glow. The glow proceeded to stretch across the arch on both sides and down each column into their support bases. The glyphs glowed with the green force, and then faded into their original appearance. The glyphs had been short-circuited.

While standing, his back was over fourteen feet above the floor. His fur, or what passed as fur on him, bristled like any angry cat's back. Then he descended into a tiger's crouch and landed with four large paws squarely on the floor. His tail remained vertical during his decent like a stabilizer fin on a plane.

Once on all fours, his tail fell flat against his back and curled completely around his tiger-sized body. He rapidly returned to his normal size. When the curator turned around, M and Theo were walking casually toward him.

"Thanks for the up-close-and-personal look at the portal," said M. "It is indeed an object of beauty from ancient craftsmen." The curator beamed at the compliment from the newly met benefactor.

As they were walking back to the main lobby the curator whispered to M, "I must tell you that Glenda became very emotional when she saw the portal. She translated the symbols and viewed them as an ancient curse. Anyway, it shook her up a lot; she was very disturbed.

"I tried to explain that messages to the ancient gods, including curses, were inscribed everywhere in the ancient world. I told her not to worry, that curses are the standard bill of fare when exploring the distant past. I suggest you reinforce that message tonight, so she sleeps well. She really does not need to worry about ancient gods messing with us modern humans."

The curator smiled and added, "With her looks and brains I think her only worries should be young men and how to use a smartphone and Instagram wisely."

M returned an understanding nod that said, "Message understood." He added, "I will absolutely do that. Teenagers have great imaginations and curiosities. That's generally a good combination, but as you noted, it does need to be monitored and channeled properly.

"Coming back to Glenda's portal translation," M said, "I have a few ideas. I'll let her know I translated the portal, and that I believe it is not a bad curse but a blessing curse on those of goodwill who pass through into the temple. After all, curses do come in a variety of intentions and interpretations. One man's curse is another man's blessing, rather like teenagers," he added with a chuckle.

"Of course, I run the risk of correcting her. Like all teenagers, she hates to be corrected. I'll expect some serious pouting over dinner tonight as well as arguments over the correct translation."

The curator laughed saying, "Very nice spin, M, well done. My own teenage daughter frequently debates my statements; we live in a world of teenage lawyers."

Traveler and Glenda had watched Theo in action and they heard the exchange between M and the curator. They understood that M was confirming Glenda's reading of the script, and that M's spin was for the curator.

Despite knowing M agreed with her, Glenda found she was mildly annoyed. She resented being publicly labeled as a teenager with self-control problems. "M did not need to add that comment about me pouting," she said to Traveler. "I am very mature and accepting of corrections when they are deserved."

Traveler looked at her and made a sympathetic face, "I know that, but M simply needed to tell the curator something he could accept." He reflected, *M is always right on target.*

As they walked the curator looked at M. "Please help me out, M. Was it my imagination or did you see small fires jumping around the room?"

"No, you were not imaging things. I saw them and believe I can explain. What we saw was most likely some residual St. Elmo's fire. As you know, St. Elmo's fire is an electrical discharge that occasionally happens around magnetic fields or during thunderstorms. It's the big brother to static electricity."

The curator nodded, "That explains it. The museum has lightning rods on the roof to avoid strikes; however, with the crane's metal boom so close to the rooftop it would be an alternative grounding point for electricity."

"Excellent observation, James. I would definitely say we were all very lucky tonight." The curator beamed at M's compliment.

# 57

# A Mutual Admiration Society

Glenda and Traveler gradually dropped back until they were walking about ten feet behind M and the curator. They were wired over the events and needed to talk to each other. Traveler had gathered his thoughts and his emotions, and he began, "I know for sure how lucky I am the cavalry showed up when it did. I owe you my life. If you had not shown up when you did, my scalp would have been hanging inside one of those fire-beings. I know you used your amazing foot speed to save my behind."

Traveler was even more right than he could imagine. Glenda had run as fast as she could out of the museum front doors. She had almost fallen as she bounded down the museum steps. She hit Michigan Avenue in full stride at a sprinter's pace.

She sprinted down a snow-covered Michigan Avenue. She leapt around slow-moving shoppers and stationary Santas. The bells on her boots sang out a merry jingle. The Santas rang their bells faster and louder as she passed. She appeared as a

Christmas spirit bringing joyful energy down the Chicago streets.

She maintained her all-out sprint effort even on the slippery side streets. She finally fell hard when turning the last corner to the alley street, but she sprang up and kept running. She came into the sanctuary a blazing comet with cries for help. M and Theo responded immediately.

Glenda never felt the hip pain from the hard fall until walking now with Traveler. Her body knew the crisis was over and sharp aches were permitted to flood her injured hip and leg. *Boy, am I going to be sore tomorrow. I'll have a major black and blue "tat" tomorrow, but not one I'll show off at the boy's club.*

As Traveler was expressing his sincerest thanks for her effort, Glenda thought, *Wow, he's focused on my efforts not his own actions.* She felt a warm glow and a blush coming; welcomed endorphins arrived to ease her aches.

Glenda looked over at Traveler, "You were the real hero today. I was a messenger while you were Horatio at the bridge. You were the Roman soldier that stood on the bridge and blocked the invader's passage. You stood up to the dragons!

"You denied those beings their kill of the curator. It took enormous courage to face that threat. I don't know if I have that kind of courage. You truly were a brave knight and I'm very proud of what you did."

Both were now floating on a cloud of mutual praise. Their feet seemed to barely touch the museum floor as they walked. It was an ego high and felt wonderful.

M glanced back and knew they were reliving this shared life-threatening experience. He noticed Theo was walking beside them and thought, *Theo knows they more than met their first shared challenge and he's proud of them.*

When they arrived at the museum's main doors, they all paused for a moment. The curator asked M, "Would you consider lending me these two as student researchers? Glenda is obviously a language savant and Edward has a talent for understanding history."

The curator smiled and added, "You are already a significant benefactor, and here I am asking for another big contribution. Hope I'm not pushing my luck right now."

Both Glenda and Traveler beamed at the praise. They were pleased that M was getting a good report card about them from the accomplished curator.

M smiled back, "You're certainly not pushing your luck, James. To the contrary, I'm very proud that you see each of their skills. I'll let them determine how they can help you. I believe in letting them take direct control over their own decisions. That's the best way for them to develop their potential."

The curator turned to both Glenda and Traveler. "Does that sound interesting to each of you? Do you think you can give me a few hours a week? More if you have the time. Of course, you'll be paid."

"Frankly, I want to keep both of you as our museum's secret talent as long as I can. I get selfish around my museum. Right now, the New York museum is doing a bit of strutting and needs a little friendly competition."

Glenda was now floating on another praise cloud. *How much praise can a girl handle in one day?* she thought. *Oh, lots and lots.* She smiled at the curator. "I would love to help you, count me on board."

Traveler was equally excited as he basked in the curator's praise. He did his best to control himself and replied, "Me too, count me in!"

The curator and M were both all smiles at the outcome. "Outstanding resolves! This is a twofer; I get two stars for the museum. I love it. Look out New York, there is a strong Chicago wind blowing your way."

# 58
# Back to the Sanctuary

The three waved goodnight to the curator as they left the museum. Once on the steps they noticed it was snowing harder; they carefully watched their footing as they descended to the street level.

Once on Michigan Avenue, M pulled up his coat collar. "Theo and I are warm weather beings, while you two seem to enjoy this Arctic Circle climate. Enjoy the walk back; we'll see you there." With that, he and Theo were gone in a blink.

They walked a few blocks when Traveler said, "OK, I'll admit I'm a wuss. I'm a southern boy and too much of this cold wind and white stuff gets bothersome fast. The only good thing about snow in Virginia is that an inch of it closes the schools down."

Glenda was smiling as she walked beside him. "None of you would last in Norway. You'd whine out loud, and that's a signal to the roaming wolf packs. Wolves smell the weak and invite them for dinner back in their lairs. Naturally, the guests are the dinner."

"When you're right, you're right," said Traveler. "Speaking of dinner, I'm hungry. Actually, I'm famished. Let's muff up and double-time it back. No, I've got a better idea, let's cab it back."

For a moment, Glenda was going to playfully challenge Traveler. Then her sore leg spoke up and cast its vote for a cab. "When you're right, you're right, big guy. Do your cab hailing thing." Traveler waved his right hand in the air, and on command a yellow cab stopped beside them. "You're definitely the cab man," Glenda said appreciatively.

Fortunately, it was a good time to cab through the city. Traffic was light, and the signal lights helped by staying green. The cab dropped them off within a block of their destination in less than ten minutes. After the cab left, they fast walked up the street to their alley entrance. Once inside the sanctuary, they let the warmth and calmness sweep over them.

"Welcome back," M announced. "Drop your coats close to the fire and join me for hot food and hot drink. I think tonight will be a hearty soup with just-baked bread and hot cider. How does that sound?"

"Perfect," said Traveler, "especially if there was hot cider sooner rather than later."

In a matter of a minute M returned and presented steaming mugs to both. "These mugs are my own design. You will find they have the ability to keep the content's temperature at just the right level for your personal preference, just hot enough, but not too hot."

"Goldilocks would love you," said Glenda with a bright smile as she sipped the cider.

"I'll brag a bit and say this is my own hot cider recipe. You'll detect the usual blend of spices, including cinnamon and nutmeg; however, I've added a secret spice that makes it unique."

"Thank you, M," they said in unison as they took tentative draws from their steaming mugs. The cider sent a surge of warmth and energy through them. Both took much deeper intakes and their faces lit up, "Truly fabulous, M," said Glenda.

"Now I can feel my nose," said a grinning Traveler. Traveler took another big mouthful, then another. Finally, he came up for air and said, "My mom and dad would love this. I mean they would really love it."

M smiled, "Of course they would. Sadly, even if I shared my recipe they would never find the secret ingredient: it's the spoon that stirs this drink."

Traveler put his empty mug down, and looked concerned. "I need to get out of these clothes. Do I have time for a hot shower before we eat?" He had a beseeching look on his face.

M understood Traveler's request. Traveler's body, like all conditioned athletes, was a perspiration machine. The machine cooled the body but gave out a distinct odor of sweat. M noticed that Glenda was also keeping a discrete distance from both him and Traveler. He was amused as he thought, *She thinks she's the odor-producer and is embarrassed.*

"Of course, you both can," said M. "It is my experience that hot showers soothe the soul as well as the body. I highly recommend one, particularly after this day." Glenda and Traveler looked relieved and immediately headed for their respective rooms.

Once inside his room, Traveler headed straight for the bathroom. He quickly peeled off his clothing, took a little whiff, flinched, and threw the clothes into the hamper thinking, *Nothing smells worse than the smell of sweat, particularly sweat produced by fear. Maybe when those Norwegian wolves smell it, it's like hearing their dinner bell ringing.*

He moved quickly under his shower and felt the hot water work its magic on his body. He increased the heat level as far as he could stand. Soap could come later, right now he just wanted the cascading water to wash away stress as well as the scent of fear and sweat.

By the time he applied the soap, he was relaxed and back to his old confident self. He did a little out-loud boast toast, "Home again, home again, jiggity jog. Now I'm clean and don't smell like a hog." He laughed at his own wit. "Just another day in the fox hole. To quote a recent President, 'Mission accomplished.'" He felt a shiver pass through him and quickly added, "I'll take that brag back, we definitely don't need any more of these fire beast confrontations."

Glenda moved as fast as Traveler. Once in the bathroom she also took a sniff of her clothes, wrinkled her nose, and quickly threw the garments into the hamper. "Man, they smell like I've been in gym class for five hours. I never realized girls could sweat this much, thank goodness for showers and sweet-smelling soaps."

She began increasing the temperature. *It's like the kids' game of hot and cold. Right now, I want hot, hotter, and almost scalding. I've got to wash away the smell of sweat. Even my hair stinks.* She placed her head fully under the waterfall. She stayed there and let her body and mind relax. M was right about the power of a hot shower.

Next came multiple hard scrubs, alternating soaps and lotions. Once she felt sparkling clean, she made the water go cold, colder, freezing. "Great for the blood flow. If it doesn't kill you, it makes you stronger. I'm part Brunhilda, a Viking Valkyrie, and part polar bear," she said to her washcloth.

She decided to skip the time-consuming process of hair drying. She was ravenous. She dried her damp hair with a fluffy towel. Her hair fell in thick waves down her face and neck, its natural russet color was sparkling after the shower and shampoo.

She inspected herself in the mirror and nodded at her image. She was quite pleased with the look. "Prom Queen, if I do say so," she said aloud. The face in the mirror looked like it absolutely agreed and would vote for her.

Because Glenda had skipped the long hair drying ritual, she and Traveler emerged from their respective showers at the same time. Both walked into their bedrooms and discovered new outfits on their beds. Both outfits served as part pajama and part lounging wear.

Glenda studied her evening wear and nodded in approval. *It's casual me,* she thought. She stepped into a single piece, loose fitting dark blue dress. A wide black leather belt tucked the dress around her waist.

The dress presented big gold buttons down the front. On the buttons were inscribed unicorn heads. She studied their faces for a moment. The unicorns looked back at her with serious expressions. *What do these guys know that I don't?*

Once dressed, she looked at the full-on Glenda. Her hair made a strong color contrast with the blue cloth and gold unicorns. She grinned, "Enjoy boys, the Prom Queen is here."

Traveler looked at his outfit and had an immediate reaction of "Oh yeah, this is so me." He put on a traditional two-piece black warrior outfit. There were trousers and a top jacket. Both were loose fitting to ensure unencumbered high kicks and hand strikes. The only color was a single gold bar over his heart.

The traditional warrior belt was long and wrapped around his waist twice. It took Traveler three tries to make it perfectly centered and cinched.

Before leaving his room, he admired his warrior look in the mirror. He nodded his approval. The warrior seemed to nod back. He said out loud, "Yep, I am one tough guy and I am dressed to kill. Literally, kill. Come on back, you cowardly flame-beasts." Then he quickly added, "But not tonight, definitely not tonight."

When Traveler stepped into the hallway, he was suddenly facing Glenda head on. He found Mr. Frog was back in residence in his throat. He felt embarrassed and thought, *This is ridiculous.* He blurted out, "No time for your hair, princess?" *Smooth,* he thought, and mentally kicked himself.

Glenda smiled back and shook her loose locks at him. She thought, *Prom Queen Cat got your tongue, big boy?* She casually retorted, "Leave your sword outside the door, there are no weapons permitted at the dinner table in Norway; too many Viking cousins died fighting after too much beer."

Once at the fountain table they settled into an amiable truce. Both slyly looked at the other. Glenda thought, *Cleans up nicely. Pretty cool outfit, fits his warrior persona.* Just as they were awkwardly trying to make conversation, M appeared with the promised dinner.

# 59
## Feasting and Explanations

M placed a covered pot on top of a thick protective cloth. "It's very hot so permit me to do the serving honors." He removed the top and a cloud of steam came out. The aroma suggested many good things in the stew and their mouths automatically watered. "Let's let it cool while I go and get more good stuff."

M returned shortly with a large loaf of steaming bread. He sliced thick slabs and left them to cool also. He used a ladle to generously fill each bowl. "For our beverage, I've done the same cider but it's chilled. The chilling creates quite a different taste. I hope you both like it. We need something cold to offset the hot stew. Bon appétit."

Glenda and Traveler bent to the task of eating. They were starved. There was a long silence at the table while the food was consumed. Finally, their heads rose from their bowls, each with an embarrassed smile. "Please excuse me, but I'm not sure I breathed while eating," said Traveler with a laugh. "This is all so good, and I was so hungry."

Glenda grinned back, "My only concern was not getting my hair in my bowl. I was so bent over eating I thought I was Petunia Pig eating directly from the trough. Oink, oink."

M placed his utensils on the table, took a deep sip from his mug, and began to talk. "Please continue to enjoy your food while I talk. Round two of a feast should be taken in more slowly and savored. To start, let me share observations about today's travails.

"The most compelling event was the unexpected challenge from the fire-beings. Neither Theo nor I had any idea that was going to happen. For Theo to be blindsided is almost impossible, I've never seen it happen before today.

"Glenda, you were absolutely correct in your translation and warnings. Today's events happened because the museum activated the portal.

"The portal was closed by Theo following the killing of the Germans. He placed safeguards against it ever being reactivated. He removed the keystone and placed a gravitational force on it that prevented it being lifted.

"If somehow it was lifted, it would not permit itself to fit into the arch's opening. Theo created a force similar to that between poles of a magnet. The keystone and the arch were like magnets of the same polarity and repelled each other.

"His lifting precaution broke down when the crane operator used the hydraulic auxiliary and created a sudden unexpected power surge. This large power surge overrode the lifting resistance. The polarity protection broke down when the curator took an unexpected risk and dropped the stone into the slot. Both breaks in Theo's protections were the result of unexpected human actions.

"Once the keystone was in place, the portal was activated. The activated portal sent a message via a wormhole dimension. The fire-being host body had scouts waiting, and they immediately entered our time-space dimension.

"Because the portal is now intact, it is formidable. Theo has again closed it, but it may only be a temporary closing. The portal has the necessary intelligence to rebuild itself. Theo has placed a counterforce on the portal to slow its rebuilding process, but cannot stop it.

"The fire-being host is now aware of Theo's presence. They have been searching for Theo for millenniums. The host will transmit energy to increase the power of the portal. The increased power will help the portal repair itself as well as defend itself against further attacks, even from Theo.

"Further complicating our lives is that a few scout beings are now in our world. They present a significant challenge due to their power and knowledge. They have the knowledge and power to move freely in our world in both space and time. They will plan their attacks when we are most vulnerable.

"When we face them again, we must do so on our terms. We will need surprise; even so, the outcome is not assured.

"Theo understands the unpredictable nature of the universe and the quantum probabilities that rule it. He uses his understanding of probability outcomes to create our strategies for defense and offense. However, even for Theo, the universe generates many unpredictable outcomes.

"Some outcomes occur when mathematical predictions say they should not. Case in point, a large hedge fund, Long-Term Capital, was founded in 1994. Some of the smartest economists and statisticians, including Nobel Prize winners, managed it.

"Their fund used a highly sophisticated predictive model to make their investment decisions. The Fund combined brilliant minds, mathematics, and state-of-the-art computer programming. What could go wrong?"

M answered his own question. "What went wrong was that actual events that statistically should not happen, did happen. As investment outcomes went against them, the Fund stayed the course in backing its model. Outcomes continued to go against the model's predictions and the Fund collapsed under a mountain of bad bets. It was bankrupt just four years after inception. The true reason for its collapse was human hubris. We're not nearly as smart as we believe."

M leaned back, "Notwithstanding the unlikeliness of today happening, the fact is that it did happen. Equally improbably, from the fire-beast's perspective, was that they were thwarted in their expected easy arrival. The universe humbles all who believe themselves superior in their knowledge.

"Now permit me to give well deserved praise to each of you. Glenda, you set an Olympic running record to get here and alert Theo and me. I am aware you took a very nasty fall and did serious damage to your hip. Yet you immediately got up and ran on while others would have stayed down or hobbled at best. You saved Traveler's life by your painful, courageous effort.

"In case you are wondering, your dress tonight is modeled after the Roman goddess Diana. Diana is Goddess of the Hunt. She was worshipped by the early Romans, but she goes back much further in time. She can race through the woods without pausing. Nothing can confront her when she is on the wild run of the hunt. You were Diana personified this afternoon."

Traveler was stunned at this news. He fully appreciated that Glenda had forced a running pace that he could not have maintained himself; however, he had no idea she had suffered a heavy fall yet continued the race.

He looked at Glenda and saw that her face, while partially covered by her hair, was now quite red. *I love it, Miss Chill is embarrassed. Could this blushing possibly be about me?*

M now turned to Traveler. "Traveler you displayed the highest level of courage, you did it twice. First, when the beings appeared you were alone in the dark. You were naturally shocked and scared. You had to control your body and mind under the most stressful of conditions.

"These beings exude a vibration which causes deep fear in all living beings. This instilled fear allows them to locate hidden adversaries immediately. They are almost impossible to surprise.

"Our advantage is the vibration can also work against them. Theo can detect it. The hunter can, on occasion, become the hunted.

"The second test of your courage was when you chose to confront the beings to save the life of the curator. This courage came in the face of the greatest of urges to stay in hiding and save yourself. The curator was oblivious to the beings and unaware of how close his death was."

Glenda was staring at Traveler. Traveler felt her eyes on him and he looked down at the table. Glenda had seen part of his action confronting the beings, but M painted a much more vivid picture. *Wow, he is a true warrior hero,* she thought.

She noticed that Traveler had developed a touch of red in his cheeks as she looked at him. *I do believe warrior boy is blushing. I do believe I am affecting his Mr. Cool persona.*

"You were both unexpected heroes today. The universe works in strange and unpredictable ways, a humbling lesson for all of us who believe we are superior in our knowledge and powers.

"Now, enough with the praise, I have a special treat. It is a cake of my own creation; actually, I just created it tonight. I have named it the 'G&T Hero Cake.' I expect you two will appreciate a cake dedicated to both of you. By the way it is absolutely delicious!"

M rose, went into the kitchen and returned with a high cake. He put out three plates then sliced the cake open. The cake had many layers. Each layer had its own distinct look. Between the layers were frostings that complemented each of the touching layer sides.

"Tell me what you think. By the way, milk is the correct drink to accompany it. The taste of milk is just the right complement to the various tastes inside the cake." M proceeded to pour milk from a canister into new mugs.

Unlike the hot cider and the hot stew, the cake was fair game for immediate consumption. Forks went to work. Once again, there was silence at the table. Milk washed down the dessert, but drinking did not seem to slow the cake's disappearance. M was delighted.

"Room for another slice?" asked M.

"Yes, please," said Traveler, "I have no pride right now."

Glenda nodded a "Yes," but felt compelled to add, "not a big one, though."

M inwardly smiled at Glenda and gave them both a second slice just as large as the first. He enjoyed watching Glenda take care of business with her second piece just as fast as Traveler.

Between bites, Glenda snuck another look at Traveler. *Well, I do need a prom escort king. If he walks a few feet behind holding my robe, he may be a candidate.*

As M was finished with his cake he made his closing remarks, "While neither of you needs a reminder, I'll remind both of you anyway. Please tuck your books under your pillows tonight.

"There is a fascinating thing about these books; they are similar to Anubis in always seeing the truth, judging it, and respecting it. You may rightly consider them to be alive. Like all living companions, while they share with you, you are also sharing with them.

"They learn from you while you learn from them, it's a symbiotic relationship. They receive nourishment from new experiences, and today's experiences will be well received by the books. On this happy note, we can all call it a day."

# 60
# Glenda's New Skill

It was the beginning of a new study day and they had just sat down in the alcove.

"Rats," said Glenda, putting down her unopened book. "I need to go to my room for a minute."

Glenda had not yet pulled her chair under the table, so she stood straight up with her usual Tigger spring. Rather than simply standing, she was elevated three to four feet above the floor, and then she slowly descended. Her eyes opened wide as if she was coming down from a roller coaster ride. "Oh!" she exclaimed. Traveler was staring at her.

"What was that about?" asked Traveler.

"I have no idea," said Glenda. "I just stood up in a hurry and kept going up."

Traveler was studying her and said, "Step away from the table and give a little jump." Glenda nodded, she bent her knees and straightened them up quickly with a small hop. This time she rose over six feet above the ground. "Amazing," was all Traveler could say. Glenda was still shocked at the levitation event and was unsure of what was happening.

"I think you are the proud possessor of a levitation skill. Yes, I am impressed and envious. Try a real vertical leap now," said Traveler. "Imagine you are going to dunk a basketball." Glenda looked straight up and confirmed there was a high ceiling over her head. She made a Michael Jordan effort and soared nearly ten feet off the ground.

While she went up fast, she came back down on a slow descent. Somehow, gravity seemed to obey her will and protect her descent. She landed softly.

She looked down at Traveler and gave him a huge Cheshire cat grin. Traveler was grinning back at her, "I remember Glinda the white witch in the Oz movie also controlled her flight, your name sure fits you. We need to show this to M."

She headed into the great room but carefully slowed her walking. Her normal Tigger bouncing stride could create a lot of mischief. She found that when she walked normally, gravity was normal, and her pace presented no unexpected explosions of height.

She and Traveler entered the great room to find M talking with Theo. The two literally had their heads together by the fireplace. Glenda said, "What is it about fires, cats, and wizards? They seem made for each other."

Then she corrected herself, "Of course, Theo is hardly a cat in any sense of the word, but he does exhibit certain catlike qualities. I'd hate to be the mouse, or actually anything, he pounces on."

"True on both counts," agreed Traveler.

Glenda came up to M and Theo while Traveler stayed a distance behind her. Traveler understood this was Glenda's showoff moment. "M, excuse me, but I have to show you something. This is so weird; please tell me what's going on."

Traveler added, "M, you're not going to believe this."

Glenda made her MJ move and soared up ten feet. She stayed there for a moment then began a slow descent.

M immediately laughed, clapped, and said, "Well done, Glenda! You will make a future hall of fame basketball player. Word of caution though, whatever you do, don't try jumping rope," and he gave another belly laugh.

Traveler knew a good straight line and added, "You will be the hero for every kangaroo out there. Jump, Glenda, jump!"

M looked at Glenda and saw the disappointment on her face. "Excuse my totally inappropriate humor. Indeed, that leap was quite spectacular. I particularly liked your controlled descent; it reminded me of Mary Poppins as she floated down using her umbrella."

"Better yet," said Traveler, "she's Glinda, the white witch in Oz, floating down. Oh no, Glenda, don't land on little Toto! Big splat!" Unable to help themselves, both M and Traveler began laughing again over the image of Glenda descending to land on sweet little Toto.

Then they saw what could be the beginning of tears. They were both instantly embarrassed and feeling guilty. "Shame on me again for joking around," said M. "Kidding aside, I truly appreciate that you have a terrific new skill. Your book has clearly rewarded your strong study efforts. I suggest you thank the book when you go to sleep tonight.

"Let me share a bit more about this skill. It is a higher-level skill. You have acquired both an understanding of gravity as well as how to bend it to your will. This is a very big deal. Understanding gravity has eluded the best minds in physics from Aristotle, Galileo, Sir Isaac Newton, and Einstein.

"Einstein created a model to explain how gravity bends space but not how to control it. Physicists all over the world would die to have your understanding and skills."

Glenda saw Traveler was quietly applauding and nodding his head in appreciation of her skill. Glenda felt a wave of happiness sweep over her, she had her "feel good" groove back.

M continued his short lecture on physics and gravity. "Einstein was never able to mathematically connect the force of gravity with the other three recognized forces in the universe. Gravity is the puzzling force that seems to operate independent of the other three forces. Einstein spent all his life trying to connect all four forces. He failed and nobody since has yet been able to do that."

"Well, if gravity stumped Einstein, I'm sure I have no idea how it works," said Glenda. "I never studied high school physics in depth at the orphanage. I was pretty good in Algebra II but that's about my limit."

"Actually, you do have the knowledge now. You've just demonstrated that fact. You acquired this understanding from the books. They have developed a part of your mind that now permits you to manage a basic force of the universe.

"Of course, there is a practical limit to this power. You cannot leap over the Sears Tower, but you can go high enough to wash second story windows."

Glenda had a pensive look on her face; she seemed unsettled with her newfound power. "M, what do I do with this ability? I'm no basketball player and we have elevators for going up. I have no desire to become a window washer. How do I know what I should do with my control over gravity?"

"Those are excellent questions, Glenda, sadly there are no simple answers. All new powers need to be carefully investigated. The first step in managing the power is to relax. Don't worry that you'll jump out of your skin."

M grinned, "A rather poor pun perhaps, but all in the spirit of keeping a proper perspective on this new skill. Humor is a very good tool for managing lots of challenging situations.

"My suggestion is to start by having fun with it, humanize it. Try making directional jumps of varying lengths. Imagine you are a giant frog and you can beat a running Traveler by using long forward jumps."

Traveler interjected, "I hate to admit it, but she's already faster than me. She doesn't need longer jumps." Glenda beamed as she accepted Traveler's compliment.

Then Traveler just had to add, "Now that you mention it M, I can see her playing leapfrog. A natural fit for her skills. I think she's already turning a nice shade of green." Glenda took the kidding in good stride. She laughed at the image of herself as a leaping giant green frog and felt her concerns melt away with the joking.

"I understand your concerns and that's natural. Both of you are changing physically as well as mentally. I lived through the same learning experiences and had the same reaction to my new skills. I knew I was different and I had to learn how to use those differences.

"You are just starting to develop your capabilities; these are not the only skills you will acquire. Theo and the books select skills that are appropriate based on your inherent strengths and your personalities. Trust the books, but trust Theo even more."

Glenda asked, "Did Theo train you also?"

"Yes, he did. You could say he made me the man I am today."

"Tell us about Theo, how you came together, and how you became a student," said Traveler.

"Yes, please," echoed Glenda.

"Well, I'll admit to enjoying a good story and my story is a grand one. However, this is not the time to go into my history with Theo. Let's remain focused on each of you."

# 61
# Assessing M

Once they returned to the alcove Glenda opened her book but then paused. She looked at Traveler who had his book open but was fidgeting in his chair. For a moment, she wanted to tell him to settle down but to say it in a playful way. She looked at his face and saw he was clearly bothered. "What are you thinking?"

Lost in thought, Traveler jumped at the question. "I'm thinking about the missing parts of M's explanation. I think we are only hearing a small part of what's going on here. M is keeping a lot from us and I'm not sure why. Do you agree?"

Glenda considered what Traveler said. She would not have said it herself, but now it was on the table. "You're right. There is a lot more going on with our studies than just these new skills."

Traveler said, "I am thinking of an animal. Which one is it?" He drew on the note pad in front of him. Glenda was ready to give him a joking response then she realized he was very serious. She let her mind float free with his question.

She suddenly had a mental image. She took her note pad and drew on it. She tried to add some levity before sharing with Traveler, "You show me yours and I'll show you mine."

Traveler ignored Glenda's middle school boy humor; normally he would have been all over it, but not now. He put his note page face up in front of Glenda. She stared at it then immediately placed her own page in front of him.

Both had drawn identical animals. They were looking at each other's drawing of a rodent. They were silent for several minutes. "OK, Glenda, what's going on here?"

Glenda hesitated; she knew his calling her "Glenda" instead of a sarcastic name like "princess" was not a good sign. He was way too serious. Glenda tried again to lighten his mood. "Well, for starters, mine looks like a cute guinea pig while yours looks like a street rat. I saw him in *Ratatouille,* is he the good rat or the evil rat?"

Despite himself Traveler laughed, "Well said, princess. Of course, that is indeed the question. I smell a rat and I am concerned for both of us. Good rat or bad rat? I don't care, I don't like any rat."

*Whew,* thought Glenda, *At least we are back to normal with names like "princess." Now we can start to analyze without being uptight.*

"I also think there is a lot more going on than what we see. My instincts and experiences tell me M and Theo are definitely the good guys, no question, but they are engaged in some terrible conflict. We know Theo is in danger, but I think it's more than that. They don't want to scare us while we are in early development and break our progress."

"If yesterday was some testing or training experience," said Traveler, "you and I are in way over our heads. If M and Theo had not arrived I would be a flame-being's lunch."

Glenda nodded, "For sure yesterday was the real deal, certainly not a training exercise. I think what happened stunned both M and Theo, and those two are never caught off guard. I think you and I are entry-level players in some cosmic chess game. We started our training here as simple pawns. We had virtually no power moves on this battle board. We are being developed by Theo and the books to increase our playing value."

"If this is chess, yesterday was checkmate for me without M and Theo."

Glenda nodded, "Agreed, but as go you, so go I. I think we will be checkmated together if the game goes against either of us. What do you think we should do next?"

Traveler was pleased that Glenda was asking his opinion. *Boy have I come a long way since I showed up as an unwelcomed stray dog at the door.*

"I've been thinking about that. My first instinct was to confront M about these fire-beasts. Who are they? Where do they come from? What do they intend? Why are they destructive? These are basic questions that we deserve answers to.

"On further reflection, I thought that if M wanted to give us complete answers he would have done that yesterday. He knew we were looking for him to explain what happened and he chose not to. I think it's possible that our commitment is being tested. Maybe our trust is being tested, who knows. My other thought is that Theo probably calls the shots regarding what M can tell us.

"So, with all that going through my head, my conclusion is to stay on our current study program and leave the questions for later. Maybe the answers will become obvious as we continue to develop."

Glenda nodded, "I think you are absolutely right on all counts. That's exactly the same conclusion I reached."

With that exchange, the two immersed themselves back into their studies. After a number of hours passed, M appeared with a tray of sandwiches. "I think you'll enjoy this midday pickup fare. It should hold you over until tonight's celebration feast. Anything you want to ask me before you get back to studying?"

"Nope, I'm good," said Traveler.

"Me too, and thanks for the sandwiches. They're just what we need right now. I never get over how hungry all of this studying makes me."

Traveler and Glenda devoured their sandwiches and continued reading while they chewed. Both were immersed in their study worlds. They had no awareness of time passing until they both realized their bodies needed a break. "Time for a stretch and bathroom break," declared Traveler. As they were both standing, they heard M call down, "Dinner is about ready."

"Time for a quick shower and change of clothes?" called back Traveler.

"Of course," replied M.

As Traveler peeled off his clothes in his room he thought, *How can I stink when I haven't done anything all day except sit? I guess yesterday's stress is still hanging around and has a longer shelf life than one night's sleep can fix. Still, my stink factor is improving, yesterday was "dead skunk on the road", today it's just "end of a cross country race."*

He stepped under his waterfall and muttered, "Stress and stink be gone! I command you." The cascading hot water promised to help out, at least for the rest of the evening. He stayed under until his skin resembled a prune in the sun.

Glenda threw her clothes in the hamper and thought, *So much better than last night.* Once under her shower, Glenda's thoughts turned to the evening wear, *I wonder what tonight's attire will be. If a celebration is in store, I expect the dress code would be in keeping with the event.*

She enjoyed the shower but cut it short. She wanted plenty of time to examine her evening wear and make a grand entrance. *Prom queen or princess, which shall I be?*

# 62
# An Elegant Affair on Land and Sea

As promised, M had prepared a feast. Setting the mood for the feast were decorations surrounding the fountain area. The decorations were simple, but charming. Crepe paper stretched across the lofty open spaces, and Japanese lanterns hung down from overhead beams. The lanterns provided soft lighting and the fountain produced a soothing background sound.

Traveler was first out of his room. He felt a bit awkward in his attire but accepted that it was in line with the evening's dinner. *Guess I can't wear jeans every day and at night. Well, not every night anyway.*

He sat at the table and relaxed with the fountain's music. *I still don't get how falling water produces music but it sure works. I can almost hear "Stardust" in there or maybe "Moonlight Serenade."* His mind turned to his stomach, *Wonder what's holding up the princess, I'm hungry. Sandwiches only go so far.*

"Am I fashionably late?" a voice called across the room. Glenda approached the table, but with more of a glide than her usual stride. She was wrapped in a soft green evening gown.

Her long russet hair fell straight down around the gown's lace top. She never wore jewelry but tonight she had on a pearl necklace that she found on the bed beside the dress.

She knew how to make a grand entrance and was very aware of how elegant she looked. She grinned at Traveler as she got closer, "I didn't know you could fit into a tux, big boy. It actually looks good on you. Do your jeans feel a bit abandoned and lonely back in the room?"

Traveler found Mr. Frog had again taken up residence in his throat. Instead of an embarrassing "Chug a Rum", he simply rose up, bowed, and elegantly pulled out Glenda's chair.

Despite her modern woman philosophy, Glenda discovered she actually liked this old school courtesy; there was a genuine charm to it as well as a statement of "I respect you."

Before any exchange could start, M came in from the kitchen. He was also in a tuxedo. "I am a guest as well as a server," he said with a smile to each of them.

Glenda looked at both M and Traveler and said, "Looks like all the men in my court are in formal wear this evening. Well done, gentlemen! As a reigning princess I expect to be royally entertained."

M proceeded to place a large soup tureen in the center of the table. "We'll start the entertainment with a nice tomato bisque. The tomatoes are from my own garden and are perfectly ripe. I added the usual spice suspects plus another mystery spice from my garden. You'll find the tomatoes will sing on your palate."

M ladled out a portion into the three-china bowls. He sat and said, "Bon appétit." As Traveler lifted his first spoonful to his mouth all he could think was, *Please don't let me splash tomato soup. My white tux shirt will scream out "Clumsy dolt!"*

Glenda carefully lifted her spoon and thought, *I just know he's waiting for me to get some red on my green dress.*

They ate in silence during the soup course. M enjoyed watching Traveler and Glenda go to great pains not to get soup on their formalwear. *These two are afraid to talk with the risk of dribbling soup. I forget how self-conscious teenagers are, and these two are still teenagers despite all their advanced skills.*

M broke the conversation ice with, "This table of elegant people reminds me of dining at the Captain's table on the Queen Mary. There were so many diamonds being flashed around the table, I thought I needed sunglasses.

"The seas were a bit choppy, but the Queen behaved herself and our champagne glasses stayed secure. We left New York and set a crossing-time record. She was the fastest ship afloat. We arrived at the Southampton port to British bands playing and Scottish pipers wailing."

"That's so cool," said Traveler. "You've sailed on the Queen Mary. What's it like? I've read it's over three football fields long. My parents want to take a Transatlantic crossing as soon as my dad can get away from business. Mom has a desk full of brochures. She's planning on a new wardrobe for the trip. I think they see it as a second honeymoon. I'm the third wheel or maybe a man overboard and I am definitely not invited."

M listened and then said, "Actually, there are two Queen Marys. I sailed on the original one on her maiden voyage. By the way, we always refer to a ship as a 'she.' That reference captures their grace and power." Glenda suspected this factoid was praise directed at her and she felt a touch of red beginning on her cheeks.

"The maiden crossing was in May 1936. The Queen Mary was a stunning achievement. She offered the height of elegance in her many restaurants, bars, and common rooms. The passenger suites set new standards for cruise ships at sea. She was also an engineering marvel. Her speed and size were the best in the world.

"The Queen served her country and America during World War II. She transported over eight hundred thousand troops. Transporting troops was a hazardous occupation. The German U-boats waited in wolf packs in the Atlantic for her. However, the wolves never caught her. Her captain steered an erratic zigzag pattern. U-boats could never get a straight shot at her, and she could easily outrun the wolf pack.

"She was a very fast and nimble lady, rather like our Glenda." Glenda felt increasing red in her cheeks.

"She retired in 1967 and is a floating hotel and museum today. She rests in her own dock in Long Beach, California. If you ever visit her I highly recommend the ghost tour."

"Ghosts? Really?" asked Glenda.

"Indeed. Many people swear there are phantoms onboard. Passengers have described waking up at night to find bodies beside them in bed and talking to them. Maids have made up rooms, stepped outside for towels, and returned to find the beds unmade again. A young girl has been seen repeatedly at the indoor swimming pool and then she disappears.

"Over the years quite a few passengers and staff have walked off the ship in fear and refused to return."

"M, do you actually believe there could be ghosts?" asked a skeptical Traveler.

"You tell me, Traveler. After what you have studied and experienced, do you think the existence of ghosts is really that impossible?"

Glenda and Traveler simultaneously nodded, "Possible." At this point in their lives, anything and everything seemed possible in this universe they were learning about.

"I'll be back shortly with the main course, hold down the fort please." As M carried the soup tureen and bowls back, he glanced over his shoulder. Traveler and Glenda were now talking and laughing.

*Well done, Mert,* M thought. *Those two need some normalcy in their lives. It's a heavy task to stay sane with one foot in the predictable known world and the other foot slipping around in the unpredictable cosmos.*

M returned with a large, loaded tray. It was a sampler offering fish, fowl, and red meat.

Traveler, of course, immediately took a large slice of the roast beef. His fast reaction time gave him a definite advantage at the dinner table. Glenda had a significant helping of the salmon.

M put a bit of everything on his fork, smiled and commented, "I have found mixing the tastes makes for an enjoyable dining experience. Experiment a bit and see how it works."

Glenda immediately tried M's suggestion and nodded in agreement. Traveler chose to experiment by putting multiple slices of the beef on his fork; some were very rare, while others were well done. "This combination works really well for me, thank you for the tip, M."

M inwardly chuckled. *One out of two guests was pretty good.*

Over dessert M leaned back in his chair and asked, "Do either of you have any questions for me, any question at all? Tonight is fair game for questions."

Glenda and Traveler looked at each other and said together, "No, we're good."

M began to clap, "That was the answer I was hoping for. It showed that you have a strong faith in Theo and me. I am well aware you must have a long list of questions after yesterday's travails, but you elected to keep your own counsel.

"I prompted you first at lunch today for questions and again right now. You have clearly decided to stay the course based on trust in Theo and me. We value your trust more than you can imagine.

"Your own experiences will provide many of the answers you seek. Learning by experience is referred to by educators and psychologists as Experiential Learning or sometimes as Organic Learning. It is very powerful. What we learn in books can be quickly forgotten if not applied. Students in school listen to a teacher talk, but if there is no follow up in homework or in the lab students quickly forget what the teacher said.

"For all students, personal problem-solving is the most powerful learning technique there is. When you force your own mind to focus and think, you upgrade your brain's capabilities. Solve one problem yourself and the next one becomes easier.

"Your books are upgrading your minds and bodies, but you also need to have experiential learning. Experiences will take the books' teachings and elevate your understanding of their messages. Books and experiences fit together as one powerful developer of both your bodies and your minds. Neither is enough by itself.

"Of course, in the world you are entering there are serious dangers associated with some of these experiences. Our confrontation yesterday was unexpected and certainly unwanted. At the same time, both of you gained significant development from that challenge, unpleasant as it was.

"Finally, for what it's worth, I do not have all the answers I know you are looking for. Theo has shared a great deal with me over many years but far from everything. I too am a developing student and must continue with my own studies and experiences.

"On that congratulatory note I wish you both a good night." M rose, cleared the table and retired to his library.

# 63
# After Dinner Entertainment

"I'm still awake," said Glenda, "Are you OK, big boy, or do you need your beauty sleep?"

"I'm totally awake, princess. Would you care for a little game of chance?"

"Sure. What do you have in mind?"

"Have you ever played poker?"

Glenda gave a small shake of her head, "Of course I've heard of it. I know aces are high and deuces are low. A pair is good but a royal flush always lets you win. Is that about it?"

Traveler gave a sly smile. "You know the basics. I think some game playing experiences will fill in your book knowledge. Let's start with a simple game called five-card draw; it's the beginner's game. I'll coach you after each hand is played and explain how you should have played it. Glenda gave him a sincere "thank you, coach" look. Traveler puffed up and graciously accepted her recognition of his superior skill.

"I'll give each of us a nice stack of chips. When one of us is out of chips, the other person is the winner. The winner takes the last piece of dessert."

"That sounds like a fair and fun game. Tell me again what beats a pair?" Glenda asked with a serious student look on her face.

One hour of play later, Traveler looked at the table in front of him. His chip pile was now stacked in front of Glenda. He watched Glenda as she was eating the cake and he began to laugh, "You nailed me. Like the poker saying goes, 'When you don't know who the fish at the table is, assume it's you.'"

Glenda pushed the remaining cake toward Traveler saying, "A consolation prize. Of course, if you have too much pride for leftovers, don't force it down."

"Woof, woof," said Traveler as he dug into the remaining piece. With a mouth full of cake, he said, "Now do that one-handed ruffle shuffle again. I'm a pretty good close-up magician, and that's a tough shuffle to do. By the way, who taught you how to play like a shark?"

Glenda held the deck in her right hand and proceeded to do a one-handed ruffle and shuffle. The cards danced between her fingers. Traveler noticed how long her fingers were. *Never really noticed that before.*

"You cannot survive in an orphanage without learning poker. We played for cookies after dinner. If you liked cookies you learned fast." Then she did a rainbow fan of the cards from her right hand into her left hand, which was three feet away. "And I'm out of here, sir!" *Always leave them wanting more,* she thought.

# 64
# And the Study Beat Goes On

The study days continued without a break, days rolled into weeks. Traveler and Glenda discovered they were occasionally reading a few of the other's books. "The books are doing some cross pollination," Traveler quipped, as he finished one of Glenda's early readings.

A week later Traveler was late for breakfast and ran toward the fountain. He suddenly found his normal stride of three feet was seven feet without any additional effort. He excitedly told M and Glenda "I'm now in the Glenda Roo Kangaroo Club. I can leap, just not as high, but good for a beginner."

Glenda smiled at him as she said, "Do you want that piece of bacon on your plate Mr. Kanga?"

Traveler said, "Just try and take it." Before he could move, Glenda's hand shot out like a striking mongoose. She chewed the strip while Traveler still had his mouth open.

"I have Traveler's superfast boarding house reach. Guard your dessert well tonight."

While they found that they had certain skills in common, other skills were unique to each of them. Traveler had a power strike that could stop an elephant. He could stop Big Bob with a casual slap.

Glenda had increased her running speed to a point that would have set an astonishing world record. "Who would know The Flash was actually a woman," she said. "Certainly not DC Comics."

Traveler grinned and quipped, "I would suggest you not flash anybody, you are a princess after all."

"Very funny," was all Glenda could manage. *What happened to my eighth-grade boy retorts? Wait, I never had any, and don't want any.*

While they used light banter to break up the study time, they had no awareness of time passing. Their awareness of time was similar to a serious DOTA game player. Once immersed in a tough game, time seemed to stand still.

However, even the best gamers recognize when they need a break. That need hit Traveler after an intense morning study effort.

# 65
# Mom's Night Out

"I need a break and I miss Mom. You had her for an all day shopping spree and now I want some attention. Besides, I guess I have a duty to listen about her great night on the town with Mr. Magic. Have you seen enough of Mom or do you want to join me?"

"Wouldn't miss it for the world; I want to hear all the details she was starting to tell over our shopping lunch. I want the inside story about M out on the town with a beautiful woman. Does he get a frog in his throat, or does he stay Mr. Cool?"

Traveler recognized, of course, that he was the frog guy and was receiving some good natured jabs, but said nothing.

"While your mom thinks she's out with a much younger man, little does she know," added Glenda with a laugh.

Traveler was not sure he needed that image of his mom out on the town. *Do I have a Dad alert to worry about? I don't think so, but Glenda will certainly pry out every detail. Women are masters of getting all the gossip, it's a skill built into their DNA.*

The two bundled up and headed up the alley. The alley was unusually dark, and Traveler felt an uneasy shiver pass through him. *I'm still jumpy being out of the sanctuary and away from M and Theo.* He glanced over at Glenda, *She looks like a happy camper, so it's just me that's nervous.*

They cautiously entered the side street from the alley. It was now well past sundown; the weather had dropped below freezing. The north wind arrived off Lake Michigan and was determined to freeze anybody in its path. Earmuffs were on and collars turned up. Glenda had her ski hat on as well as her long scarf. *I really need to get a hat,* thought Traveler. *I don't care if I look goofy.*

When they arrived at the Drake, it was approaching six o'clock. The doorman was inside, saw them coming to the door, and stepped out to open it. "Miserable night," he said. "Typical winter night in Chicago." He looked at Glenda then Traveler. "May I suggest the gentleman wear a winter hat? Muffs work on ears, but hats are better, we lose almost ten percent of body heat off our head. There are suitable choices to fit every taste in the Water Tower shops."

*Great,* thought Traveler, *my doorman is a mother hen.* "Thanks for the tip. I'll do that tomorrow after I thaw out." Glenda wisely said nothing but winked at the doorman.

Once inside they did another pass around the Christmas decorations in the lobby. The large Christmas tree warmed the festive lobby. The steam engine was still weaving its way around obstacles. They stepped up to the fountain area and saw that well over half of the tables were filled.

Guests were in high holiday spirits, both in their moods and in their cocktail glasses. There was a wide display of glasses to fit each type of libation, long stemmed champagne glasses, conical shaped Manhattan glasses and round sturdy Old Fashioned glasses.

"Looks like a lot of Christmas cheer is well under way," commented Traveler. "I hope their holiday fun lasts all the way to the New Year. Of course, night time libation is one of the few activities possible in Chicago in the winter."

They proceeded to an empty elevator car and rode it to the seventh floor. Christmas music was being piped into the car. "Sure, beats Muzak," Traveler said, and Glenda nodded in agreement.

Once out, they strode down the long empty hallway. They both knew they would love to take a few giant steps but held back. Fun though it would be, they didn't want to accidentally scare a maid to death.

In front of the locked door, Traveler made a rap using his knuckles. When there was no reply, he eased the door open, "Anybody home?" he called out. There was no answer. "All clear," he said to Glenda and they entered.

They went through the cumbersome process of ditching winter clothing and then collapsed on the large couch. "I love cold weather, but this is a bit extreme even for me," Glenda said.

"Wonder where Mom is? Thought she would be here waiting for me to eat. Boy, out of sight then out of mind."

As if reading his mind, the door opened, and Virginia entered. She was wearing a spiffy exercise outfit and had clearly done a serious workout. "I'm so happy you two caught up and are safely inside now. It feels like a blizzard is coming. How did you meet in this miserable weather?"

Glenda immediately pulled out her cell phone, "Technology solves all." Virginia nodded and laughed. *Mystery solved.*

"I had to get rid of some of our lunch calories, Glenda. You don't need to worry about a pound or two, but we older mortals need to keep an eye on the scales. Eddie, you must try the club; it's great with many treadmills and lots of weight machines.

"I'll order you two some hot chocolate with lots of whipped cream, then I'm taking a nice long hot shower."

With Virginia gone, the two sat looking out the window in an awkward silence. Time seemed to drag its feet. There were no books to study, nor an M offering conversation and food. When there finally was a knock on the door, Traveler jumped up, relieved to have a distraction. Naturally, it was the room service man.

Traveler had him place the tray on the table in front of the couch and added a tip to the bill. Traveler viewed the server as conversation filler and started to talk about the Bulls basketball team when Virginia appeared in the doorway. Traveler felt immediate relief seeing his mother and being off the Glenda conversation hook.

"I feel so much better. Nothing like a serious workout and hot shower to energize body and soul."

She walked to the window and looked out, then said, "I think it was close to a blizzard last night. I was so impressed with M and his arrangements to keep us warm. To start the evening, he had a stretch limo right outside the front door."

Traveler's spider senses were on full alert. "That's really great of him, Mom. Was Dad able to reach you by phone? I think he was trying."

"Strange you should ask, Eddie, indeed he did. The limo has special reception equipment, so his call came through so clear it was like he was beside me."

*Too bad he wasn't,* thought Traveler.

Glenda changed the mood away from Traveler's Spanish Inquisition inquiries to a light holiday tone. "Tell us about the play, Virginia," she prompted, as though the answer meant a lot to her. "Was it as good as you hoped?"

Virginia was relaxing in the big chair across from the couch. "Even better. The actress who played Grizabella, the glamour cat, was marvelous. When she sang 'Memory', it was hypnotic. The audience cheered so long at the final curtain call that she sang it again. I wanted to sing with her, and I believe M was singing under his breath."

"That's nice, Mom," said Traveler, "glad you had a great time." Traveler's face contradicted his words; all he needed was black inquisitor robes.

Glenda pressed on with easy questions to contain Traveler's dour mood. "Where did you eat?"

"It was a stunning little French restaurant off State Street. It was very French chic with all French-speaking waiters. Of course, M turned out to be fluent in French. They treated us like royalty. We had a corner booth near the singer. The singer was almost as good as the lead in *Cats*.

"There were lots of romantic songs as only French cabaret singers can charm with. Naturally the romantic songs were mixed with rousing songs such as 'La Marseillaise.'" Traveler had a puzzled look and Virginia clarified, "It's the French national anthem. When it started, the waiters all stopped serving and joined the singer in a rousing salute to France. M and I, as well as many other customers, stood and joined in. I had shivers run down my back as we sang their version of 'The Star-Spangled Banner.' Of course, M is a historian," said Virginia.

*Sure, he was probably there,* thought Traveler sarcastically.

"He told me how the song was created to rally French troops against an invading Austrian army in 1792. M said that France was in the middle of its internal revolution; it was their Civil War. The guillotine was busy chopping off French heads and Austria's nobility were concerned.

"The Austrian leaders worried that the ideas of the French Revolution could move into their own peasant population. They sent an army to invade France to stop the Revolution. Their intention was to send a strong message to their own people not to think of a revolt.

"M said that France drove back the Austrian army, no doubt helped by the new song. He said that Napoleon came to power shortly thereafter. Once Napoleon was in charge, France became the aggressor nation across Europe. Of course, Austria was a target, a bit of payback.

"Austria remained a long-standing adversary and opposed Napoleon over many years. M's observation was that wars always start with some declared reason or justification, but once the dogs of war are released, events rarely go the way the initiators expected.

"The rest of the dinner was wonderful. Naturally, M knew which wines to select. Do you remember his wine on the train, Eddie?" Traveler reluctantly nodded an affirmation. He was way beyond tired of hearing his mom praise M.

Glenda was watching Virginia with a look that said, "I am just fascinated with this dinner story," and Virginia knew she had an appreciative audience in Glenda. She also noted that her son was less than fascinated. Virginia thought, *Boys just eat and run, while young ladies understand the whole social dining and conversation experience.*

"We both had truffles to start then a soup followed by smoked trout. The meal went on for many courses over nearly three hours. Even you would have been stuffed, Eddie," she said with a grin. Annoyingly, Glenda supported her observation with an agreeing smile and nod.

"M said that the French often have cheese for dessert, but that sounded too heavy for us, so we went with crepes covered with fresh raspberries and thick cream. I was stuffed and wondered if I could move. Fortunately, our car was waiting outside so I didn't need to move my full belly very far in the cold weather."

Glenda continued to keep Virginia engaged and upbeat. She didn't want Traveler to leave his mom with a negative vibe regarding her nice night out. "Traveler told me that you and your husband are planning a trip on the Queen Mary. That sounds so exciting; do you know the details yet?"

Virginia became even more enthusiastic. She described the ship and all the choices they had. "One big decision we have to make," she said, "is the type of room we want. We have narrowed it down to a standard size cabin with a balcony or a suite.

"There are two levels of suites: Princess and Queen. I would skip the most expensive suite, the Queen Suite, Queens are simply priced over the top. My choice is a Princess Suite, but even so it's twice the cost of the standard balcony room." When Virginia identified the high cost of a Princess, Traveler shot Glenda a grin. Glenda ignored him.

"What do you get for double the cost?" asked Glenda. Her questions to Virginia were like feeding ice cream to a baby.

Virginia beamed as she extolled the virtues of the Princess Suites. "To start, the room size is much larger, more than double. It has a much larger common area for sitting and walking around as well as a larger balcony.

"It has a walk-in closet and I'll need a lot of closet space; clothing is terribly important for the ladies. The formal dinners require formal wear. The men only need a single tuxedo to be formal. However, women know we are on stage every evening, so a change of dresses each night is well received. Of course, we want our husbands to be proud showing us off," and she laughed.

"And there's more. The bathroom has both a shower and a soaking tub. Daniel can shower while I soak. There is a fully stocked complimentary bar. We can sip champagne on the balcony if we want privacy." Traveler thought, *Dad better order a Princess Suite right now.*

As Virginia talked excitedly about the voyage and all the fun things she and Daniel would do, Traveler felt his mood lift. *Dad's still the man,* he thought.

Glenda had started asking questions to make Virginia feel that she and Traveler were sincerely interested in Virginia's big trip. The more Virginia talked, the more Glenda developed a wistful look on her face. She could envision herself in that suite. She saw herself making a grand entrance down the staircase to the dining room.

She wanted a sophisticated wardrobe to show off. She imagined the witty conversations she would participate in. *I want to be Cinderella at the ball instead of fighting fire monsters.*

Virginia looked at Glenda and realized that Glenda was envious of her upcoming trip. *If you want to lead my life, dear, you need to put in years of hard work in college. Then have a job, marry an outstanding husband and manage a household on a budget. Then come the kids, but you're expected to stay in the same shape you were in college. You don't begin to know the effort and challenges that are required to make a marriage work. Neither does my son.*

Now it was Virginia's turn to ask the easy questions to perk up Glenda. "Glenda, how was your dinner? Was Gino's as good as I claimed?"

Glenda felt her downer mood break. "Absolutely, it was great! It was the best pizza I've ever had. Of course, nobody sang a national anthem, all the diners had their mouths full," she said laughing. "And my gallant escort graciously picked up the bill. Your M was not the only gentleman in town last night," she said smiling at Traveler.

Virginia was looking at Glenda then at her son. She saw how Eddie responded to praise from Glenda. Virginia the mother bear felt troubled. *He may be smitten, and he's only been with her less than two days. She certainly seems nice, but I really don't know her. I had better get my boy into a lot of casual dating when we get home.*

As Glenda and Virginia talked, Traveler was planning the return to the sanctuary. It was now past nine o'clock and he knew his mom was going to skip a late dinner to maintain her college shape. Her workout was part of her fitness routine. Now she was clearly ready for lights out.

"Mom, it's getting late. I'll take Glenda down to the lobby and be sure she gets a cab home. With this nasty weather, it may take a little time. I'll be right up then, but go ahead and hit the hay, I know that you're bushed."

Virginia turned her head away from Glenda and looked at her son. She started to say, "That's fine, dear," but instead her mind skipped a beat. Her son was somehow different from yesterday. There was a look in his eyes and a change in his carriage. He rose with a power and grace she had never noticed before.

*Goodness, could this girl have changed him in this short a time? Impossible,* she assured herself, *I'm just sleepy. He's still my little Eddie at least for another couple of years. I'll let go of him once he leaves for college. Until then his dad and I will remain the gatekeepers in his social life. We'll screen any college girlfriends he brings home. My mom-radar will never get turned off.*

Glenda and Traveler were both putting on their winter wear when Virginia looked at her son. "Are you going out again, dear? I thought you were just getting a cab for Glenda."

"Relax, Mom, I'm not leaving. The doorman was going off duty when we came in; I think he has a cold. I'll have to go outside to flag down a cab. You get your beauty rest."

At the door, Virginia gave Glenda a hug and said, "We need to shop again, maybe tomorrow if you can handle another day. I'm counting on you to help me dazzle on the Queen."

"Absolutely, we'll shop till we drop. Is it still eleven for anchors away?"

"Maybe earlier tomorrow, I'll have a great night's sleep. Let's say ten o'clock."

"I think we should also look for spring attire. You'll have a prom coming up and it's never too early to start shopping for that big night. None of my business, but is there a short list for prom escorts that you have your eye on?"

Glenda internally grinned; she knew what this question was really about. "Absolutely. I have three contenders on my dance card. I intend to screen them like the Bachelorette does on the reality show. One of them is slightly older, but not too old. One is exactly my age, which frankly is a tad young in a guy. The last is a great dancer with the smooth moves of a cat."

Glenda was amused when she saw the relief flash behind Virginia's nod and smile. "I know you'll pick a winner for that big dance night, he'll be a lucky young man.

"So tomorrow will be a shopping outing for both of us. Eddie can spend another day exploring Chicago. I think he's anxious to visit the aquarium and the museum again. He'll amuse himself and have a great time," *and be away from you, beautiful.*

"Eddie, tell the cabbie to drive safely in this snow. Goodnight to both of you, and sweet dreams, I'll be sleeping in minutes."

# 66
# A Double Ambush

Traveler nodded at his mother, held the door open for Glenda and followed her out. Once outside the room they walked to the elevator and pressed the down button. They began talking about Virginia's trip. Traveler said, "No question Mom wants that Princess Suite. I bet Dad has already booked it. I bet it's going to be a big Christmas present."

"Your dad sounds like a really terrific guy. Your mom got lucky."

Traveler thought for a minute and said, "Well, Mom was quite the catch. She could have had a serious career either in the theatre or in science. She runs the house like an efficient business. I think Dad may have gotten the better end of the bargain. I know my evil-minded friends all think she's a babe."

Glenda thought, *It's nice that he appreciates his mom as much as he appreciates his dad.*

"What's with this elevator?" asked Traveler rhetorically and hit the down button again. It was after nine so most of the guests were settled in and elevators should be readily available. After a few more minutes Traveler said, "Do you want to walk down? It's seven floors and we can walk, not race. I'm tired of losing."

"That's fine with me."

After three flights going down Traveler said, "The trick with walking down a long circular staircase is not to look down. The constant turning will create a sense of vertigo unless you look away from the steps in front of you. Going up is OK, but down can make you seasick."

"Good tip," said Glenda who was starting to feel a little dizzy.

They entered the lobby and proceeded to the door. The doorman was, as expected, missing. Glenda smiled at Traveler, "You are indeed prescient, Sir Knight. I'll wait here for my carriage." Traveler nodded and went out to search for a cab.

As Traveler started up the snow-covered street, a pair of headlights lit up the sidewalk in front of him. A lone cab was prowling the streets. Traveler's hand shot into the air and began waving like a windmill in a tornado. The cabbie saw a young man waving and for a moment hesitated. *Would this guy be a fare-dodger?*

An occupational hazard for cabbies is people who jump out of the cab at their destination and run away. Few cabbies ever chase them. Most of the young cabbies who give chase return empty-handed only to find Chicago's finest had given them a ticket for illegal parking. Paying a fine that's bigger than the missed fare is a bad business proposition.

The cabbie assessed the young man and considered the fact there were no other customers around. *I'll take a chance,* he thought, *all I'm doing tonight is cruising around anyway.*

The cabbie stopped and looked at Traveler. Traveler came to the door and said, "Please wait a minute, my friend's inside, I'll go get her."

When Traveler said "her," the cabbie relaxed. Guys with girlfriends were safe bets to pay the fare. Sometimes they tipped big to impress the girl, but that depended on the girl. How long they had dated also mattered, longer the dating time, smaller the tip.

Glenda came to the cab with Traveler behind her. Traveler opened the door, so she could climb in first. The cabbie looked at her and immediately thought, *I see a big tip coming. She's an easy ten and he's holding the door open to impress her.*

Once inside Traveler gave an address that was at the beginning of the alley's street and the cabbie flipped on the meter. "My mom said to drive safely," Traveler said laughing, and added, "If she asks, and she won't, I want to tell her I said that. Feel free now to drive as you want."

The cabbie thought, *Nice young guy and he listens to his mom, I should have him teach manners to my kids.*

When they got to their destination, the cabbie looked around. "Are you sure this is this where you want to get out? There's nothing open on this street. Are you sure you've got the right address?"

"This is the street, I'm sure of it." Traveler paid the cabbie leaving a very nice tip.

The cabbie thought, *I knew he wanted to impress the babe. If I were twenty years younger, I'd try to impress her. Oh well, both time and money fly too fast.*

Traveler opened the door and slid out. Glenda came out right behind him. The cabbie waited until they were walking down the street then he slowly drove past them. On a whim, he opened his window and shouted out "Still time to get back in." Traveler smiled and waved him on.

The cabbie moved up the street slowly. He glanced in his rear-view mirror and thought, *Where are those kids going? This street is closed everywhere.* He drove another few seconds and glanced back again.

The boy was walking beside the girl, but they were not holding hands. The cabbie thought, *The kid needs an older brother to give him dating hints. In this weather, the girl would expect the guy to hold her hand just to keep from slipping, plus share a little heat. Boys don't know nothin' unless they're told.*

The cabbie kept a crawling pace with looks back every few seconds. They were still walking slowly up the street. There was something strange about the two, but he couldn't put his finger on it. As a lifelong cabbie, he took pride in figuring people out very quickly. You had to read people or lose fares and possibly even worse.

These two seemed one thing on the outside, but his intuition said there was more to them than meets the eye. He looked back, and his mouth opened. The street was completely empty. The two young people were gone. *Not possible,* he said to himself. *Something must have happened to them.* Concerned, he pulled to the curb.

He turned the cab's flashing lights on and got out. He stepped in ankle height snow but ignored it. He began to walk back down the street. He looked at the ground as he walked. He continued until he found their fresh footprints. He saw they continued forward on the sidewalk, and then they just stopped.

The cabbie felt a shiver run up his back. He crossed himself, vowed to go to church the next day, took one last look at the prints and the empty snow in front and began a fast walk back to his cab.

He ended up running as fast as he could without falling. He got in his cab, checked the back seat, locked the doors, and sped away. *Nobody back at the garage will believe this. This is one I keep to myself.*

Glenda and Traveler stood in the alley looking out at the cabbie. They saw him study their footprints. Traveler laughed. "He's going to dream of UFO abductions tonight."

Glenda was also laughing. "This is kind of fun. It must be how police feel watching through a one-way mirror. We see you, but you don't see us." They laughed together, turned and headed for the warm glow of the gas light.

As they walked quietly toward their door's beacon they were both lost in thought. There were so many extraordinary events happening in their lives, by contrast the visit with Traveler's mom was an oasis of calmness and normalcy.

"I really like your mother—" Glenda's sentence was cut off. Three of the fire-beasts appeared in front of them. They froze in mid-step, their hearts raced, and their minds raced. They could barely breathe. Both of their bodies vibrated with fear.

"Back up slowly," said Traveler.

Glenda began to move backwards then stopped. "We can't go back." Traveler looked over his shoulder. An additional three of the beings were behind them.

"Stand your ground," said Traveler. "They're not sure about us. Stay controlled. Imagine you're playing poker right now. Your hand is weak, but your opponent isn't sure. Play it strong like you're the winner."

Part of Traveler's talking was to keep himself under control. He also wanted to show his brave warrior side to Glenda.

"I think they have assessed us and found us interesting but not a real threat," said Glenda. The fire-beasts in front extended their appendages and formed a semi-circle. Glenda looked over her shoulder and saw the beasts behind them had also formed a semi-circle.

"Traveler, they are going to create a circle around us then close it with us inside. What can we do?"

Traveler's mind again brought up the image of Hannibal surrounding forty-five thousand Roman legionnaires at Cannae. Traveler knew they faced the same fate unless he was smarter than those Roman commanders were.

"Glenda, right now, grab my left hand and then press against me!" Glenda immediately took Traveler's hand then stepped closer. The beasts stopped their advance. "They strengthen themselves by combining themselves. They think that's what we're doing," said Traveler. Glenda could only nod slightly. Her legs felt very weak.

There was a long pause as each side reexamined the other's battle plan. Now the fire-beasts finished their assessment. The entities at each end of the two semicircles extended themselves; the semicircles became a single seamless circle. The circle slowly began to close again. The ambush was complete; the Romans were trapped.

"OK, new formation. Let go of my hand, turn and press your back against my back. Keep both of your hands tight against your body. Make the palms of your hands into rigid, flat surfaces. Keep the thumbs tightly pressed against the first finger. We're creating a single being with two heads facing in opposite directions.

"When I say 'strike' quickly raise your arms up and immediately throw rapid arm punches from your shoulders. Our single being will appear like a 360-degree striking warrior."

Glenda whispered, "OK."

The fire circle now had a five-foot radius, which was closing toward the center. When the circle was three feet away, Traveler shouted "Strike!" Both began a rapid arm movement of air strikes. The beasts sensed the power of the strikes and momentarily expanded the circle away from the strikes. They stabilized at six feet, reassessed the threat, and began closing in again.

When the circle was close to the striking distance of their extended palms Traveler commanded, "Right now, Glenda, turn in my direction, grab both my hands, and leap forward with all you've got."

Glenda's survival instincts took over. She whirled around, grabbed Traveler's hands and together they leaped. It was an Olympic record leap. Michael Jordan would have been astonished to see it. The circle closed just as the bottom of their feet cleared above it.

The two of them landed fifteen feet away. They immediately adjusted their bodies upon landing to sprint to the sanctuary's door. "Theo!" they heard M call out from behind them. They spun around and saw Theo descending into the center of the nearly closed circle.

Theo was on his hind feet. He was already over ten feet high and growing. Startled, the fire beasts could not check their commitment to close. The circle's momentum closed on the center of Theo's body. Theo made the second ambush.

The fire-beasts became small suns circling a growing dark cloud. The cloud transformed into a swirling black hole and the suns found themselves being inexorably drawn toward the hole's vortex.

There was a moment when the fire-beings and Theo were merged into one entity. The beings pulsed, and energy flowed around their circle. Theo stood upright and expanded his height and mass. He was absorbing the fire creatures' energy.

Neither side could disengage, nor could the fire-beasts combine into a single entity. Their flowing energy went to a blue level of intensity then began to gradually advance through the color spectrum. It reached a bright red color then faded to a softer pink.

Theo continued to grow. He was an irresistible black hole that was pulling the fire-beings ever closer. The weakened beings were now shrinking and fading. As they faded, Theo's darkness became the blackness of empty space between the stars.

The beings finally broke their linkage and became separate beings. They tried again to escape the darkness but there was no escaping the power of the black hole.

Traveler and Glenda were still pressed together with locked hands. As the beings disappeared into Theo, vibrations of anguish came from them; these were their death throes.

Traveler and Glenda found their clasped hands amplified their awareness of the death throes. Their linked hands seemed to become antennae that captured the vibrations. They shared the absorption experience of the fire-beings with a single shared mind. They felt Theo's resolve as he removed the beings from existence.

Then the moment passed, they dropped their hands to their sides and stepped back. M came up to them and put a hand on each of their shoulders. "I think it's time to go inside."

Theo was now the size of a large tiger but continuing to recede in size. By the time the three of them entered the door, Theo was again simply a large panther. He passed through the door with ease.

# 67
# M Explains

Traveler and Glenda were beyond unsettled. They were both close to melting down. Survival emotions swept over them in waves starting with their own near-death experience followed by the battle between Theo and the beasts and the death calls of the creatures.

M looked at them and softly said, "This is not a time for words. I suggest you both retire to long, hot soaks in your tubs. When you are ready, come out and we'll discuss the last hour's events."

"You are so right, M," said Glenda. "I feel like cooked spaghetti. I need to go to a safe place and recover my soul as well as my strength." Traveler nodded and headed for his room.

Both turned on the faucets to their tubs. They headed for their hampers and peeled out of their garments. They both wrinkled their noses. *I know this smell too well,* thought Traveler. *It's the smell of fear and I'm sick of it.*

Once out of their clothes, they returned to the soaking tubs. When they entered the steaming tubs, they were lost to the world. Each of them forced their minds to relax.

Glenda sank down to her chin in the tub. Once immersed, she increased the hotness of the water. She added a soap that bubbled and scented her skin. Her nose wrinkled again, *I hate that sweaty smell, but I really hate the scent of fear.*

Once relaxed, her mind reflected on their narrow escape. *If Traveler had not been with me, I could not have survived. Somehow, he kept his head and gave us tricks to buy time and slow those beasts down. Seconds mattered, and he never lost his composure. After we talk with M, I'll figure out what I've gotten myself into and whether I'm up to the challenge. I don't want to drag Traveler down.*

Traveler sank down in his tub and cranked up the heat. He put a hot towel on top of his head and reflected on the events and their escape.

*If Glenda had not been there to supercharge our jump, those beasts would have caught my foot. Without her added power, I was a goner. I would be inside a beast and lost forever. She kept her cool and did what she needed to do. She's saved me twice now.*

Traveler came out of his room first. He was in his standard uniform of jeans and long-sleeved black cotton shirt. He looked across the room at a sleeping Theo. *Let me go rest on the big guy, I'll risk getting cat hairs on my shirt.*

He went to the fire and settled down against Theo. Theo simply gave a long sigh and kept doing whatever it is he does when sleeping. *I bet he's digesting those fire-beasts and having sweet dreams.*

A few minutes later Glenda came into the room. She spotted Traveler, walked over and said, "Is there room for me on the cat pillow?"

Traveler grinned, "Be my guest, but don't blame me if you get cat hair on your sweater."

"I think I can live with all the hair this cat sends my way," she said.

The two of them were laying on their backs, resting on a comforting Theo-pillow when M came out of the kitchen. M looked at the three amigos and said, "Rise and shine. If you fall asleep now, you'll never sleep later."

Traveler and Glenda slowly rose up. "I feel like I've been hit by a cement truck," said Traveler.

M nodded and said, "Very understandable. We should discuss this now. I know you are both deeply troubled over the attack."

"Who wouldn't be?" asked Glenda. M could only nod in agreement.

The three of them sat down by the fountain. M had prepared a tray of large ice cream sodas. "It's been my experience that all troubling events are best managed by starting with fun food. It lifts the spirit."

Both Traveler and Glenda took long draws on their straws followed by spoonfuls of the rich vanilla ice cream. Traveler took another deep sip and a second large spoonful of ice cream and said, "I'll admit this is a good start to winding down. Now can you tell us what happened?"

Glenda put her spoon down. "Please tell us how these beasts knew where we were? How did they get inside the alley to our sanctuary? How did Theo appear at just the right time?"

"Yes, all good questions. Let me answer them one at a time. In terms of what happened, you were ambushed. Permit me to say that both of you made the books, Theo, and me proud. Very proud!

"Despite the ambush, you kept your heads. You could see that that the fire-beasts were confused regarding your threat level. You fooled them when you appeared to blend together. That blending caused them to hesitate, and I can tell you they very rarely hesitate.

"As their circle was closing, you used your reflex skills to keep them at bay. They sensed your power and they had to reassess. Finally, you saved yourselves with your leaping skills at exactly the right moment."

"We know what happened, M," Glenda said. "We were there. Would you please answer the questions?"

"Of course," said M. "The beasts knew where you were since they can detect your vibrations. Vibrations are like fingerprints, they are unique for each person. Unlike fingerprints, however, they emanate from our mental being. Think of them as radio waves, and the fire-beasts have receivers that can track the source's location."

"That's great," said Traveler. "We have a body beacon that says, 'Here we are, find us and kill us,' and we can't turn it off."

"Well, that's not all there is to it. There is a limit to their detection range. As you advance in your studies, you will be able to reduce the range of your vibration. At some point it will remain entirely within you, just like your fingerprints stay on your hands.

"In addition, water interferes with their reception, it scrambles the vibration signal. As to how they entered our protected alley, they are beings capable of movement in more dimensions than our four. Our sanctuary uses five dimensions to protect itself and avoid discovery; consequently, it's not detectable to our normal four-dimensional world. Unfortunately, the fire-beasts can move through this higher dimension and ambush four-dimensional beings."

Glenda's frown was across her whole face, "So we send out identifying signals to beings that want to absorb us and that can ambush us at will. Is that what we have to look forward to?"

M smiled softly, "No, Glenda, it's not all gloom and doom. First, Theo has destroyed the only fire-beings that were here except the single one that never showed up. That one will be very cautious and will try to remain hidden from our detection.

"Next, Theo has placed blocking forces on the portal. There will be no further beings coming for quite some time.

"Finally, and most importantly, both of you are advancing in your own powers and skills. The books will equip you with strong offensive and defensive capabilities. Continue your studies and enjoy Chicago. There are no current threats, and Theo is comfortable with your safety."

"I guess I feel a bit better about our future prospects," said Glenda. "But, final question: how did you and Theo arrive at the absolute right moment?"

M seemed a bit hesitant with this question and he shifted in his chair. "The honest answer is usually the best, but not always the easiest to accept," said M. "You see the fire-beings also send out their own vibration signals which Theo can detect.

"Theo has been monitoring them since the museum. They moved about the city in groups and individually. They are assessing all aspects of this time period. Theo needed to find them when they were all together. He needed to be sure they could not escape him when he launched his attack.

"Theo is the alpha hunter, and the beings are very wary of him. Imagine them as antelopes on the plains of Africa; free to roam about, but always alert to the presence of the lion."

Traveler pushed back on this answer, "This sounds more like tiger hunting in India than lions stalking antelopes in Africa. In India, goats are tied to a post while the hunter waits safely on a platform in a nearby tree. The cautious tiger smells a meal. Being a smart tiger, he circles the goats before closing in. If the goats are very lucky, the hunter kills the tiger just before the tiger kills the goats. How long were Glenda and I playing the goats for Theo?"

M looked sad at Traveler's goat analogy. "You are very far from being goats. You are closer to being Theo's and my children. Theo knew that to protect you he needed to kill your fire-beast tigers. As long as the beasts were moving about you were at risk. Every time you left the sanctuary, Theo and I have been close by."

Glenda and Traveler looked at M. They saw how upset he was about the risk they had been forced to take. Glenda's face softened and she said, "I understand now, M. Thanks to you and Theo for being our guardians, as well as our study guides. I know the books are amazing, but you and Theo are even more amazing."

Traveler was listening, and he nodded in agreement with Glenda's reaction. "I'm with her. One last question, M, exactly how close did we come to being the tiger's dinner?"

M looked both Glenda and Traveler in the eye then answered, "Truthfully, far too close. There was a critical timing issue. Theo needed the fire-beasts to complete their circle so that they were bonded together before he attacked them.

"Theo could have easily broken up the circle earlier, but if he moved too quickly a number of the beasts would have escaped and been far more difficult to trap.

"He chose to wait until the circle was almost closed to catch them all. It was a difficult judgment call. He was actually ready to move in just as you two became kung fu artists and forced the creatures to withdraw a bit."

"You two confused the fire-beasts with your moves, but you also surprised Theo. He expected the circle to close at a predictable rate. However, the universe is not predictable. When you two threw the back-to-back strikes, the circle unexpectedly expanded away, forcing Theo to pause.

"Then the circle was suddenly closing much quicker then he anticipated. He only had a moment to act and he trusted in your training. He believed that you two would instinctively use your leaping skills to escape, and he was correct."

Traveler thought about asking the obvious follow-up question about what would have happened to them if they had not leaped. He decided against it because the answer was clear: they would have been tiger food.

"So, we did some good things, and some bad things, all mixed together," concluded Traveler.

M shook his head, "Au contraire, Traveler. Nothing you two did was bad. In fact, it was well beyond what we expected based on your training to date. You both exceeded our expectations and that gives us great hope for both of you.

"Theo and I need to recalibrate the speed with which your development is happening. Trust me, that's very good news.

"Now on this happy ending to a very difficult and challenging day, I bid you both adieux. Sleep well, and trust the books to keep your dreams happy ones.

"By the way, your ice cream sodas are still full and fresh; another cornucopia container of my own creation."

# 68
# Cabbie Redux

M retired to his private place and Glenda and Traveler looked at each other. Traveler said, "This will sound crazy, but I want to go outside right now, walk out of our alley and into the normal world. I don't want to go to bed feeling unsettled and needing the book to comfort me like I'm a scared five-year-old."

"I absolutely feel the same way. Let's suit up and go for a stroll in the normal world," said Glenda.

Once outside they stood at the door a moment and looked all around. It felt secure and serene. They walked slowly up the alley. When they got to the entry point onto the normal street, they looked down the alley. "Are you still nervous?" asked Glenda.

"I'd be lying if I said I'm close to being over all of this. I'm on adrenaline and information overload. Let's walk down to the end of the block and take in a little of the real, four-dimensional Chicago night air."

Once out of the alley they felt the freezing wind hit their faces. They found they liked it; it was reassuring to be back in their natural world. As they slowly walked, Glenda began to sing "Jingle Bells" and Traveler joined in. It was Christmas time and the Christmas magic was back in the air.

They walked to the far end of the street and turned to come back. When "Jingle Bells" was over, Glenda began with "Silent Night." As they sang together, small tears formed in both of their eyes.

Ironically, the same cabbie was cruising back down the street when he noticed the two young people. Something about their walking cadence alerted him. "Not possible," he said aloud. He slowed as he came closer and could hear them singing. He recognized Glenda's long reddish hair tumbling out of her hat. They appeared as two normal young people singing Christmas carols as they leisurely walked up the street. The cabbie noticed that this time they were holding hands.

He continued slowly past them and again did his rearview mirror vigilance. His eyes darted from the street in front of his cab to immediately behind him using his mirror. He made sure he did not blink as he watched the two.

He glanced ahead for a mini-second at the street in front, then instantly back to the rearview mirror. They had disappeared again. *Ghosts,* he thought. *Real, honest-to-god ghosts!*

He swung his cab onto a street heading west. *I'm going to St. Monica's right now. I need help from a higher authority than the Yellow Cab Company!*

www.ingramcontent.com/pod-product-compliance
Lightning Source LLC
Chambersburg PA
CBHW021132260626
47169CB00005B/1575